LINDA
MACKENZIE'S
MOUNTAIN
HOWARD

MIRA®

ISBN 1-55166-574-3

MACKENZIE'S MOUNTAIN

Copyright © 1989 by Linda Howington.

Visit us at www.mirabooks.com

Printed in U.S.A.

To the Fayrene Principle,
otherwise known as
the effect of water dripping on stone:
the stone loses.

Chapter One

He needed a woman. Bad.

Wolf Mackenzie spent a restless night, with the bright full moon throwing its silver light on the empty pillow beside him. His body ached with need, the sexual need of a healthy man, and the passing hours only intensified his frustration. Finally he got out of bed and walked naked to the window, his big body moving with fluid power. The wooden floor was icy beneath his bare feet but he welcomed the discomfort, for it cooled the undirected desire that heated his blood.

The colorless moonlight starkly etched the angles and planes of his face, living testimony to his heritage. Even more than the thick black hair worn long to touch his shoulders, even more than the heavy-lidded black eyes, his face proclaimed him Indian. It was in his high, prominent cheekbones and broad forehead, his thin lips and high-bridged nose. Less obvious, but just as fierce, was the Celtic heritage from his father, only one generation removed from the Scottish Highlands. It had refined the Indian features inherited from his mother into a face like a blade, as clean and sharply cut as it was strong. In his veins ran the blood of two of the most warlike peoples in the history of the world, Comanche and Celt. He had been a natural warrior, a fact soon discovered by the military when he had enlisted.

He was also a sensualist. He knew his own nature well, and though he controlled it, there were times when he needed a woman. He usually visited Julie Oakes at those times. She was a divorced woman, several years older, who lived in a small town fifty miles distant. Their arrangement had lasted five years; neither Wolf nor Julie was interested in marriage, but both had needs, and they liked each other. Wolf tried not to visit Julie too often, and he took care that he was never seen entering her house; he accepted the fact, unemotionally, that her neighbors would be outraged if they knew she slept with an Indian. And not just any Indian; a rape charge stuck to a man forever.

The next day was a Saturday. There would be the normal chores, and he had to pick up a load of fencing materials in Ruth, the small town just at the base of his mountain, but Saturday nights were traditionally for howling. He wouldn't howl, but he'd visit Julie and burn off his sexual tension in her bed.

The night was turning colder, and low heavy clouds were moving in. He watched until they obscured the moon, knowing they meant new snow. He didn't want to return to his empty bed. His face was impassive, but his loins ached. He needed a woman.

Mary Elizabeth Potter had numerous small chores to occupy her time that Saturday morning, but her conscience wouldn't let her rest until she had talked to Joe Mackenzie. The boy had dropped out of school two months before, a month before she had arrived to take the place of a teacher who had abruptly quit. No one had mentioned the boy to Mary, but she'd run across his school record, and curiosity had led her to read it. In the small town of Ruth, Wyoming, there weren't that many students in school, and she had thought she'd met them all. In fact, there were less than sixty students, but the graduation rate was almost one hundred percent, so any dropout was unusual. When she had read Joe Mackenzie's record, she'd been stunned. The boy had been at the *top* of his class, with straight A's in all subjects. Students who did poorly would get discouraged and drop out, but every teaching instinct she had was outraged that such an outstanding student would just quit. She had to talk to him, try to make him understand how important it was to his future that he continue his education. Sixteen was so young to make a mistake that would haunt him the rest of his life. She wouldn't be able to sleep at night until she had done her best to talk him into returning.

It had snowed again during the night and had turned bitterly cold. The cat meowed plaintively as it wound around her ankles, as if complaining about the weather. "I know, Woodrow," she consoled the animal. "The floor must be cold to your feet." She could sympathize. She didn't think her feet had been warm since she had moved to Wyoming.

Before another winter came, she promised herself, she would own a pair of warm, sturdy boots, fur-lined and waterproof, and she would stomp about in the snow as if she'd been doing it all her life, like a native. Actually she needed the boots now, but the expenses of moving had wiped out her cash reserves, and the teachings of her thrifty aunt prevented her from buying the boots on credit.

Woodrow meowed again as she put on the warmest, most sensible shoes she owned, the ones she privately called her "old maid schoolteacher shoes." Mary paused to scratch behind his ears, and his back arched in ecstasy. She had inherited him with the house, which the school board had arranged for her to live in; the cat, like the house, wasn't much. She had no idea how old Woodrow was, but both he and the house looked a little run-down. Mary had always resisted owning a cat—it seemed the crowning touch to an old maid's life—but finally her fate had caught up with her.

She *was* an old maid. Now she owned a cat. And wore old maid shoes. The picture was complete.

"Water seeks its own level," she told the cat, who looked back at her with his unconcerned Egyptian gaze. "But what do you care? It doesn't hurt *you* that my personal water level seems to stop at sensible shoes and cats."

But as she looked in the mirror to make certain her hair was tidy, she sighed. Sensible shoes and cats were just her style, along with being pale, slight and nondescript. "Mousy" was a good word. Mary Elizabeth Potter had been born to be an old maid.

She was dressed as warmly as she could manage, unless she put on socks to wear with her sensible shoes, but she drew the line at that. Dainty white anklets with long ruffled skirts were one thing, but knee socks with a wool dress were something else entirely. She was willing to be dowdy for the sake of warmth; she was not willing to be tacky.

Well, there was no point in putting it off; it wasn't going to get any warmer until spring. Mary braced herself for the shock of cold air on a system that still expected the warmth of Savannah. She had left her tidy little nest in Georgia for the challenge of a tiny school in Wyoming, for the excitement of a different way of life; she even admitted to a small yearning for adventure, though of course she never allowed it to surface. But somehow, she hadn't taken the weather into account. She had been prepared for the snow, but not the bitter temperatures. No wonder there were so few students, she thought as she opened the door and gasped as the wind whipped at her. It was too cold for the adults to undress enough to do anything that might result in children!

She got snow in her sensible shoes when she walked to her car, a sensible two-door, midsize Chevrolet sedan, on which she had sensibly put a new set of snow tires when she had moved to Wyoming. According to the weather report on the radio that morning, the high would be seven degrees below zero. Mary sighed again for the weather she had left behind in Savannah; it was March now, and spring would be in full swing, with flowers blooming in a riot of colors.

But Wyoming was beautiful, in a wild, majestic way. The soaring mountains dwarfed the puny man-made dwellings, and she had been told that, come spring, the meadows would be carpeted in wildflowers, and the crystal-clear creeks would sing their own special song. Wyoming was a different world from Savannah, and she was just a transplanted magnolia who was having trouble getting acclimated.

She had gotten instructions on how to get to the Mackenzie residence, though the information had been reluctantly given. It puzzled her that no one seemed interested in the boy, because the people in the little town had been friendly and helpful to her. The most direct comment she had gotten had been from Mr. Hearst, the grocery-store owner, who had muttered that "the Mackenzies aren't worth your trouble." But Mary considered any child worth her trouble. She was a teacher, and she meant to teach.

As she got into her sensible car, she could see the mountain called Mackenzie's Mountain, as well as the narrow road that wound up its side like a ribbon, and she quailed inside. New snow tires notwithstanding, she wasn't a confident driver in this strange environment. Snow was…well, snow was *alien*, not that she'd let it stop her from doing what she had set her mind on doing.

She was already shivering so hard that she could barely fit the key into the ignition. It was so cold! It actually hurt her nose and lungs to inhale. Perhaps she should wait for better weather before attempting the drive. She looked at the mountain again. Maybe in June all of the snow would have melted...but Joe Mackenzie had already been out of school for two months. Maybe in June the gap would seem insurmountable to him, and he wouldn't make the effort. It might already be too late. She had to try, and she didn't dare let even another week go by.

It was her habit to give herself pep talks whenever she was pushing herself to do something she found difficult, so she muttered under her breath as she began the drive. "It won't seem so steep once I'm actually on the road. All uphill roads look vertical from a distance. It's a perfectly negotiable road, otherwise the Mackenzies wouldn't be able to get up and down, and if they can do it, I can do it." Well, perhaps she could do it. Driving on snow was an acquired skill, one she hadn't as yet mastered.

Determination kept her going. When she finally reached the mountain and the road tilted upward, her hands clenched on the steering wheel as she deliberately refrained from looking over the side at the increasing distance to the valley floor. Knowing how far it was possible for her to fall if she drove off the edge wouldn't help her at all; in Mary's opinion, that would be in the category of useless knowledge, of which she already had quite enough.

"I won't slide," she muttered. "I won't go fast enough to lose control. This is like the Ferris wheel. I was certain I was going to fall out, but I didn't." She had ridden the Ferris wheel once, when she'd been nine years old, and no one had ever been able to talk her into trying it again. Carousels were more her style.

"The Mackenzies won't mind if I talk to Joe," she reassured herself in an attempt to get her mind off the drive. "Maybe he had trouble with a girlfriend, and that's why he doesn't want to go to school. At his age, it's probably all blown over by now."

Actually the drive wasn't as bad as she'd feared. She

began to breathe a little easier. The incline was more gradual than it had appeared, and she didn't think she had too much farther to go. The mountain wasn't as enormous as it had looked from the valley.

She was so intent on her driving that she didn't notice the red light appear on the dash. She had no warning of overheating until steam suddenly erupted from beneath the hood, the frigid air instantly converting the mist into ice crystals on the windshield. Mary instinctively hit the brakes, then uttered a discreet oath when the wheels began sliding. Quickly she lifted her foot from the brake pedal, and the tires found traction again, but she couldn't see. Closing her eyes, she prayed that she was still going in the right direction and let the car's weight slow it to a stop.

The engine was hissing and bellowing like a dragon. Shaking in reaction, she turned off the ignition and got out of the car, gasping as the wind lashed her like an icy whip. The hood release mechanism was stiff from the bitter cold, but finally yielded, and she raised the hood to see what had happened, on the grounds that it would be nice to know what was wrong with the car even if she couldn't fix it. It didn't take a mechanic to see the problem: one of the water hoses had split, and hot water was spitting fitfully from the break.

Instantly she recognized the precariousness of her position. She couldn't stay in the car, because she couldn't let the motor run to keep her warm. The road was a private one, and the Mackenzies might not leave their ranch at all that day, or that entire weekend. It was too far, and too cold, for her to walk back to her own house. Her only option was to walk to the Mackenzie ranch and pray it wasn't very far. Her feet were already numb.

She didn't let herself dwell on the thought that she might not make it to the Mackenzie ranch, either. Instead she began to walk steadily up the road and tried to ignore the snow that got inside her shoes with each step.

She rounded a curve and lost sight of her car, but when she looked ahead there was still no sign of a house, or even a barn. She felt alone, as if she had been dropped into the middle of a wilderness. There was only the mountain and the snow, the vast sky and herself. The silence was absolute. It hurt to walk, and she found that she was sliding her feet instead of picking them up. She had gone fewer than two hundred yards.

Her lips trembled as she hugged herself in an effort to retain her body's heat. Painful or not, she would just have to keep walking.

Then she heard the low growl of a powerful engine, and she stopped, relief welling in her so painfully that tears burned her eyes. She had a horror of crying in public and blinked them back. There was no sense in crying; she had been walking less than fifteen minutes and hadn't been in any real danger at all. It was just her overactive imagination, as usual. She shuffled through the snow to the side of the road, to get out of the way, and waited for the approaching vehicle.

It came into view, a big black pickup with enormous tires. She could feel the driver's eyes lock on her, and in spite of herself she ducked her head in embarrassment. Old maid schoolteachers weren't accustomed to being the center of attention, and on top of that she felt a perfect fool. It must look as if she had gone for a stroll in the snow.

The truck slowed to a stop opposite her, and a man got out. He was big, and she instinctively disliked that. She disliked the way big men looked down at her, and she disliked being forced by sheer physical size to look up at them. Well, big or not, he was her rescuer. She wound her gloved fingers together and wondered what she should say. How did a person ask to be rescued? She had never hitched a ride before; it didn't seem proper for a settled, respectable schoolteacher.

Wolf stared at the woman, astounded that anyone would be out in the cold while dressed so stupidly. What in hell was she doing on his mountain, anyway? How had she gotten here?

Suddenly he knew who she was; he'd overheard talk in the feed store about the new schoolteacher from someplace down South. He'd never seen anyone who looked more like a schoolteacher than this woman, and she was definitely dressed wrong for a Wyoming winter. Her blue dress and brown coat were so frumpy that she was almost a cliché; he could see wisps of light brown hair straggling out from under her scarf, and oversize horn-rimmed glasses dwarfed her small face. No makeup, not even lip gloss to protect her lips.

And no boots. Snow was caked almost to her knees.

He had surveyed her completely in two seconds and didn't wait to hear what explanation she had for being on his mountain, if she intended to say anything at all. So far she hadn't uttered a word, but continued to stare at him with a faintly outraged look on her face. He wondered if she considered it beneath her to speak to an Indian, even to ask for help. Mentally he shrugged. What the hell, he couldn't leave her out here.

Since she hadn't spoken, he didn't, either. He simply bent down and passed one arm behind her knees and the other behind her back, and lifted her as he would a child, ignoring her gasp. As he carried her to the truck, he reflected that she didn't weigh much more than a child. He saw a flash of startled blue eyes behind the lenses of her glasses; then her arm passed around his neck and she was holding him in a convulsive grip, as if she were afraid he'd drop her.

He shifted her weight so he could open the passenger door and deposited her on the seat, then briskly wiped the snow from her feet and legs as well as he could. He heard her gasp again, but didn't look up. When he had finished, he dusted the snow from his gloves and went around to climb behind the wheel.

"How long have you been walking?" he muttered reluctantly.

Mary started. She hadn't expected his voice to be so deep that it almost reverberated. Her glasses had fogged from the truck's heat, and she snatched them off, feeling her cold cheeks prickle as blood rushed to them. "I...not long," she stammered. "About fifteen minutes. I blew a water hose. That is, my car did."

Wolf glanced at her in time to see her hastily lower her eyes again and noticed her pinkened cheeks. Good, she was getting warm. She was flustered; he could see it in the way she kept twisting her fingers together. Did she think he was going to throw her down on the seat and rape her? After all, he was a renegade Indian, and capable of anything. Then again, the way she looked, maybe this was the most excitement she'd ever had.

They hadn't been far from the ranch house and reached it in a few minutes. Wolf parked close to the kitchen door and got out; he circled the truck and reached the passenger door just as she opened it and began to slid down. "Forget it," he said, and lifted her again. Her sliding motion had made her skirt ride halfway up her thighs. She hastily pushed the fabric down, but not before his black eyes had examined her slim legs, and the color deepened in her cheeks.

The warmth of the house enfolded her, and she inhaled

with relief, hardly noticing as he turned a wooden chair away from the table and placed her on it. Without speaking he turned on the hot water tap and let it run, then filled a dishpan, frequently checking the water and adjusting the temperature.

Well, she had reached her destination, and though she hadn't accomplished her arrival in quite the manner she had intended, she might as well get to the purpose of her visit. "I'm Mary Potter, the new schoolteacher."

"I know," he said briefly.

Her eyes widened as she stared at his broad back. "You know?"

"Not many strangers around."

She realized that he hadn't introduced himself and was suddenly unsure. Was she even at the right place? "Are... are you Mr. Mackenzie?"

He glanced over his shoulder at her, and she noticed that his eyes were as black as night. "I'm Wolf Mackenzie."

She was instantly diverted. "I suppose you know your name is uncommon. It's Old English—"

"No," he said, turning around with the dishpan in his hands. He placed it on the floor beside her feet. "It's Indian."

She blinked. "Indian?" She felt incredibly stupid. She should have guessed, given the blackness of his hair and eyes, and the bronze of his skin, but she hadn't. Most of the men in Ruth had weathered skin, and she had simply thought him darker than the others. Then she frowned at him and said in a positive tone, "Mackenzie isn't an Indian name."

He frowned back at her. "Scottish."

"Oh. Are you a half-breed?"

She asked the question with the same unconsciousness as if she had been asking directions, silky brows lifted in-

quiringly over her blue eyes. It set his teeth on edge.
"Yeah," he grunted. There was something so irritating
about the primness of her expression that he wanted to
shock her out of her prissiness. Then he noticed the shivers
shaking her body, and he pushed his irritation aside, at least
until he could get her warm. The clumsy way she had been
walking when he'd first seen her had told him that she was
in the first stages of hypothermia. He shrugged out of his
heavy coat and tossed it aside, then put on a pot of coffee.

Mary sat silently as he made coffee; he wasn't a very
talkative person, though that wasn't going to make her give
up. She was truly cold; she would wait until she had a cup
of that coffee, then begin again. She looked up at him as
he turned back to her, but his expression was unreadable.
Without a word he took the scarf from her head and began
unbuttoning her coat. Startled, she said, "I can do that,"
but her fingers were so cold that any movement was agony.
He stepped back and let her try for a moment, then brushed
her hands aside and finished the job himself.

"Why are you taking my coat off when I'm so cold?"
she asked in bewilderment as he peeled the coat down her
arms.

"So I can rub your arms and legs." Then he proceeded
to remove her shoes.

The idea was as alien to her as snow. She wasn't accustomed to anyone touching her, and didn't intend to become
accustomed. She started to tell him so, but the words vanished unsaid when he abruptly thrust his hands under her
skirt, all the way to her waist. Mary gave a startled shriek
and jerked back, almost oversetting the chair. He glared at
her, his eyes like black ice.

"You don't have to worry," he snapped. "This is Saturday. I only rape on Tuesdays and Thursdays." He
thought about throwing her back out into the snow, but he

couldn't let a woman freeze to death, not even a white woman who obviously thought his touch would contaminate her.

Mary's eyes grew so wide they eclipsed the rest of her face. "What's wrong with Saturdays?" she blurted, then realized that she had almost issued him an invitation, for pity's sake! She clapped her gloved hands to her face as a tide of red surged to her cheeks. Her brain must have frozen; it was the only possible explanation.

Wolf jerked his head up, not believing she had actually said that. Wide, horrified blue eyes stared at him from over black leather gloves, which covered the rest of her face but couldn't quite hide the hot color. It had been so long since he'd seen anyone blush that it took him a minute to realize she was acutely embarrassed. Why, she was a prude! It was the final cliché to add to the dowdy, old maid schoolteacher image she presented. Amusement softened his irritation. This was probably the highlight of her life. "I'm going to pull your panty hose off so you can put your feet in the water," he explained in a gruff voice.

"Oh." The word was muffled because her hands were still over her mouth.

His arms were still under her skirt, his hands clasped on her hips. Almost unconsciously he felt the narrowness of her, and the softness. Dowdy or not, she still had the softness of a woman, the sweet scent of a woman, and his heartbeat increased as his body began to respond to her nearness. Damn, he needed a woman worse than he'd thought if this frumpy little schoolteacher could turn him on.

Mary sat very still as one powerful arm closed around her and lifted her so he could strip the panty hose down her hips and legs; the position put his head close to her breasts and stomach, and she stared down at his thick, shiny

black hair. He had only to turn his head and his mouth
would brush against her breasts. She had read in books that
a man took a woman's nipples into his mouth and sucked
them as a nursing infant would, and she had always wondered why. Now the thought made her feel breathless, and
her nipples tingled. His roughly callused hands brushed
against her bare legs; how would *they* feel on her breasts?
She began to feel oddly warm, and a little dizzy.

Wolf didn't glance at her as he tossed the insubstantial
panty hose to the floor. He lifted her feet onto his thigh and
slid the dishpan into place, then slowly lowered her feet
into the water. He had made certain the water was only
warm, but he knew her feet were so cold even that would
be painful. She sucked in her breath but didn't protest,
though he saw the gleam of tears in her eyes when he
looked up at her.

"It won't hurt for long," he murmured reassuringly,
moving so that his legs were on each side of hers, clasping
them warmly. Then he carefully removed her gloves, struck
by the delicacy of her white, cold hands. He held them
between his warm palms for a moment, then made a decision and unbuttoned his shirt as he crowded closer to her.

"This will get them warm," he said, and tucked her
hands into the hollows of his armpits.

Mary was dumbstruck. She couldn't believe that her
hands were nestled in his armpits like birds. His warmth
seared her cold fingers. She wasn't actually touching skin;
he wore a T-shirt, but it was still the most intimate she had
ever been with another person. Armpits...well, everyone
had them, but she certainly wasn't accustomed to touching
them. She had never before been this *surrounded* by anyone, least of all a man. His hard legs were on each side of
hers, clasping them; she was bent forward a little, her hands
neatly tucked beneath his arms, while he briskly rubbed his

hands over her arms and shoulders, then down to her thighs. She made a little sound of surprise; she simply couldn't believe this was happening, not to Mary Elizabeth Potter, old maid schoolteacher *ordinaire*.

Wolf had been concentrating on his task but he looked up at the sound she made, into her wide blue eyes. They were an odd blue, he thought, not cornflower or that pure dark blue. There was just a hint of gray in the shade. Slate blue, that was it. Distantly he noticed that her hair was straggling down from the ungodly knot she'd twisted it into, framing her face in silky, pale brown wisps. She was very close, her face just inches from his. She had the most delicate skin he'd ever seen, as fine-grained as an infant's, so pale and translucent he could see the fragile tracery of blue veins at her temples. Only the very young should have skin like that. As he watched, another blush began to stain her cheeks, and unwillingly he felt himself become entranced by the sight. He wondered if her skin was that silky and delicate all over—her breasts, her stomach, her thighs, between her legs. The thought was like an electrical jolt to his system, overloading his nerves. Damn, she smelled sweet! And she would probably jump straight out of that chair if he lifted her skirt the way he wanted to and buried his face against her silky thighs.

Mary licked her lips, oblivious to the way his eyes followed the movement. She had to say something, but she didn't know what. His physical nearness seemed to have paralyzed her thought processes. My goodness, he was warm! And close. She should remember why she had come here in the first place, instead of acting like a ninny because a very good-looking, in a rough sort of way, very masculine person was too close to her. She licked her lips again, cleared her throat, and said, "Ah...I came to speak to Joe, if I may."

His expression changed very little, yet she had the impression that he was instantly aloof. "Joe isn't here. He's doing chores."

"I see. When will he be back?"

"In an hour, maybe two."

She looked at him a little disbelievingly. "Are you Joe's father?"

"Yes."

"His mother is...?"

"Dead."

The flat, solitary word jarred her, yet at the same time she was aware of a faint, shocking sense of relief. She looked away from him again. "How did you feel about Joe quitting school?"

"It was his decision."

"But he's only sixteen! He's just a boy—"

"He's Indian," Wolf interrupted. "He's a man."

Indignation mingled with exasperation to act as a spur. She jerked her hands from his armpits and planted them on her hips. "What does that have to do with anything? He's sixteen years old and he needs to get an education!"

"He can read, write and do math. He also knows everything there is to know about training horses and running a ranch. He chose to quit school and work here full-time. This is my ranch, and my mountain. One day it will be his. He decided what to do with his life, and it's train horses." He didn't like explaining his and Joe's personal business to anyone, but there was something about this huffy, dowdy little teacher that made him answer. She didn't seem to realize he was Indian; intellectually she knew it, but she obviously had no idea what it *meant* to be Indian, and to be Wolf Mackenzie in particular, to have people turn aside to avoid speaking to him.

"I'd like to talk to him anyway," Mary said stubbornly.

"That's up to him. He may not want to talk to you."

"You won't try to influence him at all?"

"No."

"Why not? You should at least have tried to keep him in school!"

Wolf leaned very close, so close that his nose was almost touching hers. She stared into his black eyes, her own eyes widening. "He's Indian, lady. Maybe you don't know what that means. Hell, how could you? You're an Anglo. Indians aren't welcome. What education he has, he got on his own, without any help from the Anglo teachers. When he wasn't being ignored, he was being insulted. Why would he want to go back?"

She swallowed, alarmed by his aggression. She wasn't accustomed to men getting right in her face and swearing at her. Truthfully, Mary admitted that she wasn't accustomed to men at all. When she had been young, the boys had ignored the mousy, bookish girl, and when she had gotten older the men had done the same. She paled a little, but she felt so strongly about the benefits of a good education that she refused to let him intimidate her. Big people often did that to smaller people, probably without even thinking about it, but she wasn't going to give in simply because he was bigger than she. "He was at the head of his class," she said briskly. "If he managed that on his own, think of what he could accomplish with help!"

He straightened to his full height, towering over her. "Like I said, it's up to him." The coffee had long since finished brewing, so he turned to pour a cup and hand it to her. Silence fell between them. He leaned against the cabinets and watched her sip daintily, like a cat. Dainty, yeah, that was a good word for her. She wasn't *tiny*, maybe five three, but she was slightly built. His eyes dropped to her breasts beneath that dowdy blue dress; they weren't big, but they looked nice and round. He wondered if her nipples would be a delicate shell pink, or rosy beige. He wondered if she would be able to take him comfortably, if she would be so tight he'd go wild—

Sharply he brought his erotic thoughts to a halt. Damn it, that particular lesson should have been etched into his soul! Anglo women might flirt with him and twitch themselves around him, but few of them really wanted to get down and dirty with an Indian. This prissy little frump wasn't even flirting, so why was he getting so turned on? Maybe it was because she *was* a frump. He kept imagining how the dainty body beneath that awful dress would look, stripped bare and stretched out on the sheets.

Mary set the cup aside. "I'm much warmer now. Thank you, the coffee did the trick." That, and the way he'd run his hands all over her, but she wasn't about to tell him that. She looked up at him and hesitated, suddenly uncertain when she saw the look in his black eyes. She didn't know what it was, but there was something about him that made her pulse rate increase, made her feel faintly uneasy. Was he actually looking at her *breasts*?

"I think some of Joe's old clothes will fit you," he said, face and voice expressionless.

"Oh, I don't need any clothes. I mean, what I have on is perfectly—"

"Idiotic," he interrupted. "This is Wyoming, lady, not New Orleans, or wherever you're from."

"Savannah," she supplied.

He grunted, which seemed to be one of his basic means of communication, and took a towel from a drawer. Going down on one knee, he lifted her feet from the water and wrapped them in a towel, rubbing them dry with a touch so gentle it was at odds with the thinly veiled hostility of his manner. Then, standing, he said, "Come with me."

"Where are we going?"

"To the bedroom."

Mary stopped, blinking at him, and a bitter smile twisted his mouth. "Don't worry," he said harshly. "I'll control my savage appetites, and after you get dressed, you can get the hell off my mountain."

Mary drew herself up to her full height and lifted her chin, her mouth setting itself in a prim line. "It isn't necessary to make fun of me, Mr. Mackenzie," she said calmly, but her even tone was hard won. She knew she fell short in the come-hither department; she didn't need sarcasm to remind her. Usually she wasn't disturbed by her mousiness, having accepted it as an unchangeable fact, much like having the sun rise in the east. But Mr. Mackenzie made her feel strangely vulnerable, and it was oddly painful that he should have pointed out how unappealing she was.

Wolf's straight black brows drew together over his high-bridged nose. "I wasn't making fun of you," he snapped. "I was dead serious, lady. I want you off of my mountain."

"Then I'll leave, of course," she replied steadily. "But it was still unnecessary to make fun of me."

He put his hands on his hips. "Make fun of you? How?"

A flush tinged her exquisite skin, but her gray-blue eyes never wavered. "I know I'm not an attractive woman, certainly not the type to stir a man's—er, savage appetites."

She was serious. Ten minutes ago he'd have agreed with her that she was plain, and God knew she was no fashion plate, but what astounded him was that she honestly didn't seem to realize what it meant that he was Indian, or what he'd meant by his sarcasm, or even that he had been strongly aroused by her closeness. A lingering throbbing in his loins reminded him that his reaction hadn't completely subsided. He gave a harsh laugh, the sound devoid of amusement. Why not put a little more excitement in her life? When she heard the flat truth, she wouldn't be able to get off his mountain fast enough.

"I wasn't joking or making fun," he said. His black eyes glittered at her. "Touching you like that, being so close to you that I could smell the sweetness, turned me on."

Astonished, she stared at him. "Turned you on?" she asked blankly.

"Yeah." She still stared at him as if he were speaking a different language, and impatiently he added, "Got me hot, however you want to describe it."

She pushed at a silky strand that had escaped from her hairpins. "You're making fun of me again," she accused. It was impossible. She had never made a man...aroused a man in her life.

He was already irritated, already aroused. He had learned to use iron control when dealing with Anglos, but something about this prim little woman got under his skin. Frustration filled him until he thought he might explode. He hadn't intended to touch her, but suddenly he had his hands on her waist, pulling her toward him. "Maybe you need a demonstration," he said in a rough undertone, and bent to cover her mouth with his.

Mary trembled in profound shock, her eyes enormous as he moved his lips over hers. His eyes were closed. She could see the individual lashes, and for a moment marveled at how thick they were. Then his hands, still clasped on her waist, drew her into firm contact with his muscled body, and she gasped. He took instant advantage of her opened mouth, probing inside with his tongue. She quivered again, and her eyes slowly closed as a strange heat began to warm her inside. The pleasure was unfamiliar, and so intense that it frightened her. A host of new sensations assailed her, making her dizzy. There was the firmness of his lips, his heady taste, the startling intimacy of his tongue stroking hers as if enticing it to play. She felt the heat of his body, smelled the warm muskiness of his skin. Her soft breasts were pressed against the muscular planes of his chest, and her nipples began to tingle in that strange, embarrassing way again.

Suddenly he lifted his mouth from hers, and sharp disappointment made her eyes fly open. His black gaze burned her. "Kiss me back," he muttered.

"I don't know how," Mary blurted, still unable to believe this was happening.

His voice was almost guttural. "Like this." He took her mouth again, and this time she parted her lips immediately, eager to accept his tongue and feel that odd, surging pleasure once more. He moved his mouth over hers, molding her lips with fierce pleasure, teaching her how to return the pressure. His tongue touched hers again, and this time she responded shyly in kind, welcoming his small invasion with gentle touches of her own. She was too inexperienced to realize the symbolism of her acceptance, but he began to breathe harder and faster, and his kiss deepened, demanding even more of her.

A frightening excitement exploded through her body, going beyond mere pleasure and becoming a hungry need. She was no longer cold at all, but burning inside as her heartbeat increased until her heart was banging against her ribs. So this was what he meant when he'd said she got him hot. He got her hot, too, and it stunned her to think he had felt this same restless yearning, this incredible wanting. She made a soft, unconscious sound and moved closer to him, not knowing how to control the sensations his experienced kisses had aroused.

His hands tightened painfully on her waist, and a low,

rough sound rumbled in his throat. Then he lifted her, pulled her closer, adjusted her hips against his and graphically demonstrated his response to her.

She hadn't known it could be like that. She hadn't known that desire could burn so hot, could make her forget Aunt Ardith's warnings about men and the nasty things they liked to do to women. Mary had quite sensibly decided that those things couldn't be too nasty, or women wouldn't put up with them, but at the same time she had never flirted or tried to attract a boyfriend. The men she had met at college and on the job had seemed normal, not slavering sex fiends; she was comfortable with men, and even considered some to be friends. It was just that she wasn't sexy herself; no man had ever beaten down doors to go out with her, or even managed to accomplish the dialing of her telephone number, so her exposure to men hadn't prepared her for the tightness of Wolf Mackenzie's arms, the hunger of his kisses, or the hardness of his manhood pushing against the juncture of her thighs. Nor had she known that she could want more.

Unconsciously she locked her arms around his neck and squirmed against him, tormented by increasing frustration. Her body was on fire, empty and aching and wanting all at once, and she didn't have the experience to control it. The new sensations were a tidal wave, swamping her mind beneath the overload from her nerve endings.

Wolf jerked his head back, his teeth locked as he relentlessly brought himself back under control. Black fire burned in his eyes as he looked down at her. His kisses had made her soft lips red and pouty, and delicate pink colored her translucent porcelain skin. Her eyes were heavy-lidded as she opened them and slowly met his gaze. Her pale brown hair had slipped completely out of its knot and tumbled silkily around her face and over her shoulders. Desire was on her face; she already looked tousled, as if he had done more than kiss her, and in his mind he had. She was light and delicate in his arms, but she had twisted against him with a hunger that matched his own.

He could take her to bed now; she was that far gone, and he knew it. But when he did, it would be because she had consciously made the decision, not because she was so hot she didn't know what she was doing. Her inexperience was obvious; he'd even had to teach her how to kiss—the thought stopped as abruptly as if he'd hit a mental wall, as he realized the full extent of her inexperience. Damn it, she was a *virgin*!

The thought staggered him. She was looking at him now with those grayish blue eyes both innocent and questioning, languid with desire, as she waited for him to make the next move. She didn't know what to do. Her arms were locked around his neck, her body pressed tightly to his, her legs opened slightly to allow him to nestle against her, and she was waiting for him because she didn't have a clue how to proceed. She hadn't even been kissed before. No man had touched those soft breasts, or taken her nipples in his mouth. No man had loved her at all before.

He swallowed the lump that threatened to choke him, his eyes still locked with hers. "God Almighty, lady, that nearly got out of hand."

She blinked. "Did it?" Her tone was prim, the words clear, but the dazed, sleepy look was still in her eyes.

Slowly, because he didn't want to let her go, and gently, because he knew he had to, he let her body slip down his until she was standing on her feet again. She was innocent of the ramifications, but he wasn't. He was Wolf Mackenzie, half-breed, and she was the schoolteacher. The good citizens of Ruth wouldn't want her associating with him; she was in charge of their young people, with untold influence on their forming morals. No parents would want their impressionable daughter being taught by a woman who was having a wild fling with an Indian ex-con. Why, she might even entice their sons! His prison record could be accepted, but his Indian blood would never go away.

So he had to let her go, no matter how much he wanted to take her to his bedroom and teach her all the things that went on between a man and a woman.

Her arms were still around his neck, her fingers buried in the hair at his nape. She seemed incapable of movement. He reached up to take her wrists and draw her hands away from him.

"I think I'll come back later."

A new voice intruded in Mary's dreamworld of newly discovered sensuality, and she jerked away, color burning her cheeks as she whirled to face the newcomer. A tall, dark-haired boy stood just inside the kitchen door, his hat in his hand. "Sorry, Dad. I didn't mean to barge in."

Wolf stepped away from her. "Stay. She came to see you, anyway."

The boy looked at her quizzically. "You could have fooled me."

Wolf merely shrugged. "This is Miss Mary Potter, the new schoolteacher. Miss Potter, my son, Joe."

Even through her embarrassment, Mary was jolted that he would call her "Miss Potter" after the intimacy they had just shared. But he seemed so calm and controlled, as if it hadn't affected him at all, while every nerve in her body was still jangling. She wanted to fling herself against him and give herself up to that encompassing fire.

Instead she stood there, her arms stiffly at her sides while her face burned, and forced herself to look at Joe Mackenzie. He was the reason she was here, and she wouldn't allow herself to forget it again. As her embarrassment faded, she saw that he was very like his father. Though he was only sixteen, he was already six feet tall and would likely match his father's height, just as his broad young shoulders showed the promise of being as powerful. His face was a younger version of Wolf's, as strong-boned and proud, the features precisely chiseled. He was calm and controlled, far too controlled for a sixteen-year-old, and his eyes, oddly, were pale, glittering blue. Those eyes held something in them, something untamed, as well as a sort of bitter acceptance and knowledge that made him old beyond his years. He was his father's son.

There was no way she could give up on him.

She held out her hand to him. "I'd really like to talk to you, Joe."

His expression remained aloof, but he crossed the kitchen to shake her hand. "I don't know why."

"You dropped out of school."

The statement hardly needed verification, but he nodded. Mary drew a deep breath. "May I ask why?"

"There was nothing for me there."

She felt frustrated by the calm, flat statement, because she couldn't sense any uncertainty in this unusual boy. As Wolf had said, Joe had made up his own mind and didn't intend to change it. She tried to think of another way to approach him, but Wolf's quiet, deep voice interrupted.

"Miss Potter, you can finish talking after you get into some sensible clothes. Joe, don't you have some old jeans that might be small enough to fit her?"

To her astonishment, the boy looked her over with an experienced eye. "I think so. Maybe the ones I wore when I was ten." For a moment amusement sparkled in his blue-diamond eyes, and Mary primmed her mouth. What did these Mackenzie men get out of needlessly pointing out her lack of attractiveness?

"Socks, shirt, boots and coat," Wolf added to the list. "The boots will be too big, but two pairs of socks will hold them on."

"Mr. Mackenzie, I really don't need extra clothes. What I have on will do until I get home."

"No, it won't. The high temperature today is about ten below zero. You aren't walking out of this house with bare legs and those stupid shoes."

Her sensible shoes were suddenly stupid? She felt like flying to their defense, but suddenly remembered the snow that had gotten inside them and frozen her toes. What was sensible in Savannah was woefully inadequate in a Wyoming winter.

"Very well," she assented, but only because it was, after all, the sensible thing to do. She still felt uncomfortable about taking Joe's clothes, even temporarily. She had never worn anyone else's clothes before, never swapped sweaters or blouses with chums as an adolescent. Aunt Ardith had thought such familiarity ill-bred.

"I'll see about your car while you change." Without even glancing at her again, he put on his coat and hat and walked out the door.

"This way," Joe said, indicating that she should follow him. She did so, and he looked over his shoulder. "What happened to your car?"

"A water hose blew."

"Where is it?"

She stopped. "It's on the road. Didn't you see it when you drove up?" An awful thought struck her. Had her car somehow slid off the mountain?

"I came up the front side of the mountain. It's not as steep." He looked amused again. "You actually tried driving up the back road in a car, when you're not used to driving in snow?"

"I didn't know that was the back road. I thought it was the only road. Couldn't I have made it? I have snow tires."

"Maybe."

She noticed that he didn't sound very confident in her ability, but she didn't protest, because she wasn't very confident herself. He led the way through a rustic but comfortable living room and down a short hallway to an open door. "My old clothes are boxed up in the storage room, but it won't take long for me to dig them out. You can change in here. It's my bedroom."

"Thank you," she murmured, stepping inside the room. Like the living room, it was rustic, with exposed beams and thick wooden walls. There was nothing in it to indicate it was inhabited by a teenage boy: no sports apparatus of any kind, no clothes on the floor. The full-size bed was neatly made, a homemade quilt smoothed on top. A straight chair stood in one corner. Next to his bed, bookshelves stretched from floor to ceiling; the shelves were obviously handmade, but weren't crude. They had been finished, sanded and varnished. They were crammed with books, and curiosity led her to examine the titles.

It took her a moment to realize that every book had to do with flight, from da Vinci's experiments through *Kitty Hawk* and space exploration. There were books on bombers, fighters, helicopters, radar planes, jets and prop planes, books on air battles fought in each war since pilots first shot at each other with pistols in World War I. There were books on experimental aircraft, on fighter tactics, on wing design and engine capability.

"Here are the clothes." Joe had entered silently and placed the clothes on the bed. Mary looked at him, but his face was impassive.

"You like planes," she said, then winced at her own banality.

"I like planes," he admitted without inflection.

"Have you thought about taking flying lessons?"

"Yes." He didn't add anything to that stark answer, however; he merely left the room and closed the door behind him.

She was thoughtful as she slowly removed her dress and pulled on the things Joe had brought. The collection of books indicated not merely an interest in flying, but an obsession. Obsessions were funny things; unhealthy ones could ruin lives, but some obsessions lifted people to higher planes of life, made them shine with a brighter light, burn with a hotter fire, and if those obsessions weren't fed, then the person withered, a life blighted by starvation of the soul. If she were right, she had a way to reach Joe and get him back in school.

The jeans fit. Disgusted at this further proof that she had the figure of a ten-year-old boy, she pulled on the too-big flannel shirt and buttoned it, then rolled the sleeves up over her hands. As Wolf had predicted, the worn boots were too big, but the two pairs of thick socks padded her feet enough that the boots didn't slip up and down on her heels too much. The warmth was heavenly, and she decided she would pinch pennies any way she could until she could afford a pair of boots.

Joe was adding wood to the fire in the enormous rock fireplace when she entered, and a little grin tugged at his mouth when he saw her. "You sure don't look like Mrs. Langdale, or any other teacher I've ever seen."

She folded her hands. "Looks have nothing to do with ability. I'm a very good teacher—even if I do look like a ten-year-old boy."

"Twelve. I wore those jeans when I was twelve."

"What a consolation."

He laughed aloud, and she felt pleased, because she had the feeling neither he nor his father laughed much.

"Why did you quit school?"

She had learned that if you kept asking the same question, you would often get different answers, and eventually the evasions would cease and the real answer would emerge. But Joe looked at her steadily and gave the same answer as before. "There was nothing for me there."

"Nothing more for you to learn?"

"I'm Indian, Miss Potter. A mixed-breed. What I learned, I learned on my own."

Mary paused. "Mrs. Langdale didn't—" She stopped, unsure of how to phrase her question.

"I was invisible." His young voice was harsh. "From the time I started school. No one took the time to explain anything to me, ask me questions, or include me in anything. I'm surprised my papers were even graded."

"But you were number one in your class."

He shrugged. "I like books."

"Don't you miss school, miss learning?"

"I can read without going to school, and I can help Dad a lot more if I'm here all day. I know horses, ma'am, maybe better than anyone else around here except for Dad, and I didn't learn about them in school. This ranch will be mine someday. This is my life. Why should I waste time in school?"

Mary took a deep breath and played her ace. "To learn how to fly."

He couldn't prevent the avid gleam that shone briefly in his eyes, but it was quickly extinguished. "I can't learn how to fly in Ruth High School. Maybe someday I'll take lessons."

"I wasn't talking about flying lessons. I was talking about the Air Force Academy."

His bronze skin whitened. This time she didn't see a gleam of eagerness, but a deep, anguished need so powerful it shook her, as if he'd been shown a glimpse of heaven. Then he turned his head, and abruptly he looked older. "Don't try to make a fool of me. There's no way."

"Why isn't there a way? From what I saw in your school records, your grade average will be high enough."

"I dropped out."

"You can go back."

"As far behind as I am? I'd have to repeat this grade, and I won't sit still while those jerks call me a stupid Indian."

"You aren't that far behind. I could tutor you, bring you up fast enough that you could start your senior year in the fall. I'm a licensed teacher, Joe, and for your information, my credentials are very good. I'm qualified to tutor you in the classes you need."

He took a poker and jabbed at a log, sending a shower of sparks flying. "What if I do it?" he muttered. "The Academy isn't a college where you take an entrance exam, pay your money and walk in."

"No. The usual way is to be recommended by your congressman."

"Yeah, well, I don't think my congressman is going to recommend an Indian. We're way down on the list of people it's fashionable to help. Dead last, as a matter of fact."

"I think you're making too much of your heritage," Mary said calmly. "You can keep blaming everything on being Indian, or you can get on with your life. You can't do anything about other people's reactions to you, but you *can* do something about your own. You don't know what your congressman will do, so why give up when you haven't even tried yet? Are you a quitter?"

He straightened, his pale eyes fierce. "I don't reckon."

"Then it's time to find out, isn't it? Do you want to fly bad enough that you'll fight for the privilege? Or do you want to die without ever knowing what it's like to sit in the cockpit of a jet doing Mach 1?"

"You hit hard, lady," he whispered.

"Sometimes it takes a knock on the head to get someone's attention. Do you have the guts to try?"

"What about you? The folks in Ruth won't like it if you spend so much time with me. It would be bad enough if I were alone, but with Dad, it's twice as bad."

"If anyone objects to my tutoring you, I'll certainly set him straight," she said firmly. "It's an honor to be accepted into the Academy, and that's our goal. If you'll agree to being tutored, I'll write to your congressman immediately. I think this time your heritage will work in your favor."

It was amazing how proud that strong young face could be. "I don't want it if they give it to me just because I'm Indian."

"Don't be ridiculous," she scoffed. "Of course you won't be accepted into the Academy just because you're half Indian. But if that fact catches the congressman's interest, I say, good. It would only make him remember your name. It'll be up to you to make the grade."

He raked his hand through his black hair, then restlessly walked to the window to look out at the white landscape. "Do you really think it's possible?"

"Of course it's possible. It isn't guaranteed, but it's possible. Can you live with yourself if you don't try? If *we* don't try?" She didn't know how to go about bringing someone to a congressman's attention for consideration for recommendation to the Academy, but she was certainly willing to write to every senator and representative Wyoming had seated in Congress, a letter a week, until she found out.

"If I agreed, it would have to be at night. I have chores around here that have to be done."

"Night is fine with me. Midnight would be fine with me, if it would get you back in school."

He gave her a quick look. "You really mean it, don't you? You actually care that I dropped out of school."

"Of course I care."

"There's no 'of course' about it. I told you, no other teacher cared if I showed up in class. They probably wished I hadn't."

"Well," she said in her briskest voice, "I care. Teaching is what I do, so if I can't teach and feel I'm doing some good, then I lose part of myself. Isn't that how you feel about flying? That you *have* to, or you'll die?"

"I want it so bad it hurts," he admitted, his voice raw.

"I read somewhere that flying is like throwing your soul into the heavens and racing to catch it as it falls."

"I don't think mine would ever fall," he murmured, looking at the clear cold sky. He stared, entranced, as if paradise beckoned, as if he could see forever. He was probably imagining himself up there, free and wild, with a powerful machine screaming beneath him and taking him higher. Then he shook himself, visibly fighting off the dream, and turned to her. "Okay, Miss Teacher, when do we start?"

"Tonight. You've already wasted enough time."

"How long will it take for me to catch up?"

She gave him a withering look. "Catch up? You're going to leave them in the dust. How long it takes depends on how much work you can do."

"Yes, ma'am," he said, grinning a little.

She thought that already he looked younger, more like a boy, than he had before. He was, in all ways, far more mature than the other boys his age in her classes, but he looked as if a burden had been lifted from him. If flying meant that much to him, how had it felt to set himself a course that would deny him what he wanted most?

"Can you be at my house at six? Or would you rather I come here?" She thought of that drive, in the dark and snow, and wondered if she'd make it if he wanted her to come here.

"I'll come to your house, since you aren't used to driving in snow. Where do you live?"

"Go down the back road and take a left. It's the first house on the left." She thought a minute. "I believe it's the first house, period."

"It is. There isn't another house for five miles. That's the old Witcher house."

"So I've been told. It was kind of the school board to arrange living quarters for me."

Joe looked dubious. "More like it was the only way they had of getting another teacher in the middle of the year."

"Well, I appreciated it anyway," she said firmly. She looked out the window. "Shouldn't your father be back by now?"

"Depends on what he found. If it was something he could fix right then, he'd do it. Look, here he comes now."

The black pickup roared to a stop in front of the house, and Wolf got out. Coming up on the porch, he stomped his feet to rid his boots of the snow caked on them and opened the door. His cool black gaze flickered over his son, then to Mary. His eyes widened fractionally as he examined every slim curve exhibited by Joe's old jeans, but he didn't comment.

"Get your things together," he instructed. "I have a spare hose that will fit your car. We'll put it on, then take you home."

"I can drive," she replied. "But thank you for your trouble. How much is the hose? I'll pay you for that."

"Consider it neighborly assistance to a greenhorn. And we'll still take you home. I'd rather you practiced driving in the snow somewhere other than on this mountain."

His dark face was expressionless, as usual, but she sensed that he'd made up his mind and wouldn't budge. She got her dress from Joe's room and the rest of her things from the kitchen. When she returned to the living room, Wolf held a thick coat for her to wear. She slipped into it; since it reached almost to her knees and the sleeves totally obscured her hands, she knew it had to be his.

Joe had on his coat and hat again. "Ready."

Wolf looked at his son. "Have you two had your talk?"

The boy nodded. "Yes." He met his father's eyes squarely. "She's going to tutor me. I'm going to try to get into the Air Force Academy."

"It's your decision. Just make sure you know what you're getting into."

"I have to try."

Wolf nodded once, and that was the end of the discussion. With her sandwiched between them, they left the warmth of the house, and once again Mary was struck by the bitter, merciless cold. She scrambled gratefully into the truck, which had been left running, and the blast of hot air from the heater vents felt like heaven.

Wolf got behind the wheel, and Joe got in beside her, trapping her between their two much bigger bodies. She sat with her hands primly folded and her booted feet placed neatly side-by-side as they drove down to an enormous barn with long stables extending off each side of it like arms. Wolf got out and entered the barn, then returned thirty seconds later with a length of thick black hose.

When they reached her car, both Mackenzies got out and

poked their heads under the raised hood, but Wolf told her, in that tone of voice she already recognized as meaning business, to stay in the truck. He was certainly autocratic, but she liked his relationship with Joe. There was a strong sense of respect between them.

She wondered if the townspeople were truly so hostile simply because the Mackenzies were half Indian. Something Joe had said tugged at her memory, something about it would be bad enough if it were just him involved, but it would be twice as bad because of Wolf. What about Wolf? He'd rescued her from an unpleasant, even dangerous, situation, he'd seen to her comfort, and now he was repairing her car.

He'd also kissed her silly.

She could feel her cheeks heat as she remembered those fierce kisses. No, the kisses, and remembering them, begot a different kind of heat. Her cheeks were hot because her own behavior was so appalling she could barely bring herself to think about it. She had never—never!—been so forward with a man. It was totally out of character for her.

Aunt Ardith would have had a conniption fit at the thought of her mousy, sedate niece letting a strange man put his tongue in her mouth. It had to be unsanitary, though it was also, to be honest, exciting in a primitive way.

Her face still felt hot when Wolf got back into the truck, but he didn't even look at her. "It's fixed. Joe will follow us."

"But doesn't it need more water and antifreeze?"

He cast her a disbelieving look. "I had a can of antifreeze in the back of the truck. Weren't you paying attention when I got it out?"

She blushed again. She hadn't been paying attention; she'd been lost in reliving those kisses he'd given her, her heart thundering and her blood racing. It was an extraordinary reaction, and she wasn't certain how to handle it. Ignoring it seemed the wisest course, but was it possible to ignore something like that?

His powerful leg moved against hers as he shifted gears, and abruptly she realized she was still sitting in the middle of the seat. "I'll get out of your way," she said hastily, and slid over by the window.

Wolf had liked the feel of her sitting next to him, so close that his arm and leg brushed her whenever he changed gears, but he didn't tell her that. Things had gotten way out of hand at the house, but he didn't have to let them go any further. This deal with Joe worried him, and Joe was more important to him than the way a soft woman felt in his arms.

"I don't want Joe hurt because your do-gooder instincts won't leave well enough alone." He spoke in a low, silky tone that made her jump, and he knew she sensed the menace in it. "The Air Force Academy! That's climbing high for an Indian kid, with a lot of people waiting to step on his fingers."

If he'd thought to intimidate her, he'd failed. She turned toward him with fire sparking in her eyes, her chin up. "Mr. Mackenzie, I didn't promise Joe he would be accepted into the Academy. He understands that. His grades were high enough to qualify him for recommendation, but he dropped out of school. He has no chance at all unless he gets back into school and gets the credits he needs. That's what I offered him: a chance."

"And if he doesn't make it?"

"He wants to try. Even if he isn't accepted, at least he'll know he tried, and at least he'll have a diploma."

"So he can do exactly what he would have done without the diploma."

"Perhaps. But I'm going to begin checking into the procedure and qualifications on Monday, and writing to people. The competition to get into the Academy is really fierce.''

''The people in town won't like you tutoring him.''

''That's what Joe said.'' Her face took on that prim, obstinate look. ''But I'll have something to say to anyone who kicks up about it. Just let me handle them, Mr. Mackenzie.''

They were already down the mountain that had taken her so long to drive up. Wolf was silent for the rest of the drive, so Mary was, too. But when he pulled up to the old house where she was living, he rested his gloved hands on the steering wheel and said, ''It isn't just Joe. For your sake, don't let on that you're doing it. It's better for you if no one knows you've ever even spoken to me.''

''Why ever not?''

His smile was wintry. ''I'm an ex-con. I did time for rape.''

Afterward, Mary kicked herself for simply getting out of the truck without saying a word in response to his bald statement, but at the time she had been shocked to the core and incapable of a response. Rape! The crime was repulsive. It was unbelievable. She had actually kissed him! She'd been so stunned that she'd merely nodded goodbye to him and told Joe that she'd see him that night, then gone in the house without thanking them for all their help and trouble.

Now reality set in. Standing alone in the old-fashioned kitchen, she watched Woodrow hungrily lapping milk from his saucer while she considered the man and his statement. She abruptly snorted. "Hogwash! If that man's a rapist, I'll boil you for supper, Woodrow."

Woodrow looked remarkably unconcerned, which to Mary indicated that the cat agreed with her judgment, and she had a high opinion of Woodrow's ability to know what was best for himself.

After all, Wolf hadn't said that he'd committed rape. He'd said that he had served time in prison for rape. When Mary thought of the way both Mackenzies automatically and bitterly accepted that they would be shunned because of their Indian blood, she wondered if perhaps the fact that Wolf was part Indian figured in his conviction. But he hadn't done it. She knew that as well as she knew her own face. The man who had helped her out of a bad situation, warmed her cold hands against his own body and kissed her with burning male hunger, simply wasn't the type of man who could hurt a woman like that. *He* was the one who had halted before those kisses had gone too far; she had already been putty in his hands.

It was ridiculous. There was no way he was a rapist.

Oh, perhaps it hadn't been any great hardship for him to stop kissing her; after all, she was mousy and inexperienced and would never be voluptuous, but... Her thoughts trailed off as remembered sensations intruded. She was inexperienced, but she wasn't stupid. He had been—well, hard. She had distinctly felt *it*. Perhaps he hadn't had an outlet for his physical appetites lately and she had been handy, but still he hadn't taken advantage of her. He hadn't treated her with a sailor's attitude that any port in a storm would suffice. What was that awful term she had heard one of her students use once? Oh, yes—horny. She could accept that Wolf Mackenzie had been in that condition and she had accidentally stirred his fire in some way that still remained a mystery to her, but the bottom line was that he hadn't pushed his advantage.

What if he had?

Her heart started a strong, heavy beat, and heat crept through her, while an achy, restless feeling settled low inside. Her breasts tightened and began throbbing, and automatically she pressed her palms over them before she realized what she was doing and jerked her hands down. But what if he had touched them? What if he had put his mouth on her? She felt as if she would melt now, just thinking about him. Fantasizing. She pressed her thighs together, trying to ease the hollow ache, and a whimper escaped her lips. The sound was low, but seemed inordinately loud in the silent house, and the cat looked up from his saucer, gave a questioning meow, then returned to the milk.

Would she have been able to stop him? Would she even have tried to stop him? Or would she now be standing here remembering making love instead of trying to imagine how it would be? Her body tingled, but from barely awakened instincts and needs rather than true knowledge.

She had never before known passion, other than the passion for knowledge and teaching. To find her body capable of such strong sensations was frightening, because she had thought she knew herself well. Suddenly her own flesh was alien to her, and her thoughts and emotions were abruptly unruly. It was almost like a betrayal.

Why, this was lust! She, Mary Elizabeth Potter, actually *lusted* after a man! Not just any man, either. Wolf Mackenzie.

It was both amazing and embarrassing.

Joe proved a quick, able student, as Mary had known he would be. He was prompt, arriving right on time, and thankfully alone. After stewing over the morning's events for the entire afternoon, she didn't think she could ever face Wolf Mackenzie again. What must he think of her? To her mind, she had practically attacked the man.

But Joe was alone, and in the three hours that followed, Mary found herself liking him more and more. He was hungry for knowledge and absorbed it like a dry sponge. While he worked on the assignments she had set out for him, she prepared a set of records in which to keep the time he spent on each subject, the matter covered and his test scores. The goal they had set for themselves was much higher than just a high school diploma. Though she hadn't promised it, she knew she wouldn't be satisfied unless Joe was accepted into the Air Force Academy. There had been something in his eyes that told her he would never be complete unless he could fly; he was like a grounded eagle, his soul yearning for the sky.

At nine o'clock she called a halt and noted the time in her records. Joe yawned as he rocked the chair onto its back legs. "How often do we do this?"

"Every night, if you can," she replied. "At least until you catch up with the rest of your class."

His pale, blue-diamond eyes glittered at her, and again she was struck by how old those eyes were. "Do I have to go back to regular classrooms next year?"

"It would help if you did. You'd be able to get much more work done, and we could do your advanced studies here."

"I'll think about it. I don't want to leave Dad in the lurch. We're expanding the ranch now, and it means a lot more work. We have more horses now than we've ever had before."

"Do you raise horses?"

"Quarter horses. Good ranch horses, trained to handle cattle. We not only breed them, but people bring their own horses to the ranch for Dad to train. He's not just good, he's the best. Folks don't mind that he's an Indian when it comes to training their horses."

Again the bitterness was apparent. Mary propped her elbows on the table and leaned her chin on her upraised, folded hands. "And you?"

"I'm Indian, too, Miss Potter. Half Indian, and that's more than enough for most people. It wasn't as bad when I was younger, but an Indian kid isn't much of a threat to anyone. It's when that kid grows up and starts looking at the white Anglo daughters that all hell breaks loose."

So a girl had been part of the reason Joe had quit school. Mary raised her eyebrows at him. "I imagine the white

Anglo daughters looked back, too,'' she said mildly. ''You're very good-looking.''

He almost grinned at her. ''Yeah. That and two bits will get me a cup of coffee.''

''So they looked back?''

''And flirted. One acted like she really cared something about me. But when I asked her to a dance, the door was slammed in my face right quick. I guess it's okay to flirt with me, sort of like waving a red flag at a bull from a safe distance, but there was no way she was actually going to go out with an Indian.''

''I'm sorry.'' Without thinking, Mary reached out and covered his strong young hand with her own. ''Is that when you quit school?''

''There didn't seem to be any point in going. Don't think I was serious about her, or anything like that, because it hadn't gotten that far. I was just interested in her. But the whole thing made it plain that I was never going to fit in, that none of those girls would ever go out with me.''

''So what did you plan on doing? Working on the ranch for the rest of your life and never dating, never getting married?''

''I'm sure not thinking of getting married!'' he said strongly. ''As for the rest of it, there are other towns, bigger towns. The ranch is doing pretty good now, and we have a little extra money.'' He didn't add that he'd lost his virginity two years before, on a trip to one of those bigger towns. He didn't want to shock her, and he was certain she would be shocked if she had any idea of his experience. The new teacher wasn't just prim, she was innocent. It made him feel oddly protective. That, and the fact that she was different from the other teachers he'd known. When she looked at him she saw *him*, Joe Mackenzie, not the bronzed skin and black hair of a half-breed. She had looked into his eyes and seen the dream, the obsession he'd always had with planes and flying.

After Joe had left, Mary locked the house and got ready for bed. It had been a tumultuous day for her, but it was a long time before she slept, and then she overslept the next morning. She deliberately kept herself busy that day, not giving herself time to moon over Wolf Mackenzie, or fantasize about things that hadn't happened. She mopped and waxed until the old house was shiny, then dragged out the boxes of books she had brought from Savannah. Books always gave a house a lived-in look. To her frustration, however, there was no place to put them. What she needed was some of that portable shelving; if all it required for assembly was a screwdriver, she should be able to put it up herself. With her customary decisiveness, she made plans to check at the general store the next afternoon. If they didn't have what she needed, she would buy some lumber and hire someone to build some shelves.

At lunch on Monday she made a call to the state board of education to find out what she had to do to make certain Joe's studies would be accepted toward his diploma. She knew she had the qualifications, but there was also a good deal of paperwork to be done before he could earn the necessary credits by private tutoring. She made the call on the pay phone in the tiny teacher's lounge, which was never used because there were only three teachers, each teaching four grades, and there was never any time for a break. Nevertheless it had three chairs and a table, a tiny, dented refrigerator, an automatic coffee maker and the pay phone. It was so unusual for any of the teachers to use the lounge that Mary was surprised when the door opened and Sharon Wycliffe, who taught grades one through four, poked her head in.

"Mary, are you feeling sick or anything?"

"No, I'm fine." Mary stood and dusted off her hands. The receiver had carried a gray coating, evidence of how often it was used. "I was making a call."

"Oh. I just wondered. You'd been in here a long time, and I thought you might not be feeling well. Who were you calling?"

The question was asked without any hesitancy. Sharon had been born in Ruth, had gone to school here, had married a local boy. Everyone in Ruth knew every one of the other one hundred and eighty inhabitants; they all knew each other's business and saw nothing unusual about it. Small towns were merely large extended families. Mary wasn't taken aback by Sharon's open curiosity, having already experienced it.

"The state board. I needed some information on teaching requirements."

Sharon looked alarmed. "Do you think you aren't properly certified? If there's any trouble, the school board will likely commit mass suicide. You don't know how hard it is to find a teacher with the proper qualifications willing to come to a town as small as Ruth. They were almost at the panic stage when you were located. The kids were going to have to start going to school over sixty miles away."

"No, it isn't that. I thought I might begin private tutoring, if any of the kids need it." She didn't mention Joe Mackenzie, because she couldn't forget the warnings both he and his father had given her.

"Thank goodness it isn't bad news," Sharon exclaimed. "I'd better get back to the kids before they get into trouble." With a wave and a smile she withdrew her head, her curiosity satisfied.

Mary hoped Sharon didn't mention it to Dottie Lancaster, the teacher who taught grades five through eight, but she knew it was a futile hope. Eventually, everything in Ruth became common knowledge. Sharon was warm and full of good humor with her young charges, and Mary's teaching style was rather relaxed, too, but Dottie was strict and abrupt with the students. It made Mary uncomfortable, because she sensed Dottie regarded her job as merely a job, something that was necessary but not enjoyed. She had even heard that Dottie, who was fifty-five, was thinking about an early retirement. For all Dottie's shortcomings, that would certainly upset the local school board, because as Sharon had pointed out, it was almost impossible to get a teacher to relocate to Ruth. The town was just too small and too far away from everything.

As she taught the last classes of the day, Mary found herself studying the young girls and wondering which one had daringly flirted with Joe Mackenzie, then retreated when he had actually asked her out. Several of the girls were very attractive and flirtatious, and though they had the shallowness typical of teenagers, they all seemed likable. But which one would have attracted Joe, who wasn't shallow, whose eyes were far too old for a sixteen-year-old boy? Natalie Ulrich, who was tall and graceful? Pamela Hearst, who had the sort of blond good looks that belonged on a California beach? Or maybe it was Jackie Baugh, with her dark, sultry eyes. It could be any of the eight girls in her classes, she realized. They were used to being pursued, having had the stupendous good luck to be outnumbered, nine to eight, by the boys. They were all flirts. So which one was it?

She wondered why it mattered, but it did. One of these girls, though she hadn't broken Joe's heart, had nevertheless dealt him what could have been a life-destroying blow. Joe had taken it as the final proof that he'd never have a place in the white man's world, and he'd withdrawn. He still might never re-enter this school, but at least he'd agreed to be tutored. If only he didn't lose hope.

When school was out, she swiftly gathered all the materials she would need that night, as well as the papers she had to grade, and hurried to her car. It was only a short drive to Hearst's General Store, and when she asked, Mr. Hearst kindly directed her to the stacks of shelving in a corner.

A few minutes later the door opened to admit another customer. Mary saw Wolf as soon as he entered the store; she had been examining the shelving, but it was as if her skin was an alarm system, signaling his nearness. Her nerves tingled, the hair at the nape of her neck bristled, she looked up, and there he was. Instantly she shivered, and her nipples tightened. Distress at that uncontrollable response sent blood rushing to her face.

With her peripheral vision she saw Mr. Hearst stiffen, and for the first time she truly believed the things Wolf had told her about the way he was regarded in town. He hadn't done anything, hadn't said anything, but it was obvious Mr. Hearst wasn't happy to have him in the store.

Quickly she turned back to the shelving. She couldn't look him in the eye. Her face heated even more when she thought of the way she'd acted, throwing herself at him like a sex-starved old maid. It didn't help her feelings that he probably thought she *was* a sex-starved old maid; she couldn't argue with the old maid part, but she had never paid much attention to the other until Wolf had taken her in his arms. When she thought of the things she had done...

Her face was on fire. Her body was on fire. There was no way she could talk to him. What must he think of her? With fierce concentration, she read the instructions on the box of shelving and pretended she hadn't seen him enter the store.

She had read the instructions three times before she realized she was acting just like the people he had described: too good to speak to him, disdaining to acknowledge knowing him. Mary was normally even-tempered, but suddenly rage filled her, and it was rage at herself. What sort of person was she?

She jerked the box of shelving toward her and nearly staggered under the unexpected weight. Just as she turned, Wolf laid a box of nails on the checkout counter and reached in his pocket for his wallet.

Mr. Hearst glanced briefly at Wolf; then his eyes cut to where Mary was struggling with the box. "Here, Miss Potter, let me get that," he said, rushing from behind the counter to grab the box. He grunted as he hefted it in his arms. "Can't have you wrestling with something this heavy. Why, you might hurt yourself."

Mary wondered how he thought she would get it from her car into her house if she didn't handle it herself, but refrained from pointing that out. She followed him back to the counter, squared her shoulders, took a deep breath, looked up at Wolf and said clearly, "Hello, Mr. Mackenzie. How are you?"

His night-dark eyes glittered, perhaps in warning. "Miss Potter," he said in brief acknowledgment, touching the brim of his hat with his fingers, but he refused to respond to her polite inquiry.

Mr. Hearst looked sharply at Mary. "You know him, Miss Potter?"

"Indeed I do. He rescued me Saturday when my car broke down and I was stranded in the snow." She kept her voice clear and strong.

Mr. Hearst darted a suspicious look at Wolf. "Hmmph," he said, then reached for the box of shelving to ring it up.

"Excuse me," Mary said. "Mr. Mackenzie was here first."

She heard Wolf mutter a curse under his breath, or at least she thought it was a curse. Mr. Hearst turned red.

"I don't mind waiting," Wolf said tightly.

"I wouldn't dream of cutting in front of you." She folded her hands at her waist and pursed her lips. "I couldn't be that rude."

"Ladies first," Mr. Hearst said, trying for a smile.

Mary gave him a stern look. "Ladies shouldn't take advantage of their gender, Mr. Hearst. This is an age of equal treatment and fairness. Mr. Mackenzie was here first, and he should be waited on first."

Wolf shook his head and gave her a disbelieving look. "Are you one of those women's libbers?"

Mr. Hearst glared at him. "Don't take that tone with her, Indian."

"Now, just a minute." Controlling her outrage, she shook her finger at him. "That was rude and entirely uncalled for. Why, your mother would be ashamed of you, Mr. Hearst. Didn't she teach you better than that?"

He turned even redder. "She taught me just fine," he mumbled, staring at her finger.

There was something about a schoolteacher's finger; it had an amazing, mystical power. It made grown men quail before it. She had noticed the effect before and decided that a schoolteacher's finger was an extension of Mother's finger, and as such it wielded unknown authority. Women grew out of the feeling of guilt and helplessness brought on by that accusing finger, perhaps because most of them became mothers and developed their own powerful finger, but men never did. Mr. Hearst was no exception. He looked as if he wanted to crawl under his own counter.

"Then I'm certain you'll want to make her proud of

you," she said in her most austere voice. "After you, Mr. Mackenzie."

Wolf made a sound that was almost a growl, but Mary stared at him until he jerked the money from his wallet and threw it on the counter. Without another word, Mr. Hearst rang up the nails and made change. Equally silent, Wolf grabbed the box of nails, spun on his heel and left the store.

"Thank you," Mary said, finally relenting and bestowing a forgiving smile on Mr. Hearst. "I knew you would understand how important it is to me that I be treated fairly. I don't wish to take advantage of my position as a teacher here." She made it sound as if being a teacher was at least as important as being queen, but Mr. Hearst only nodded, too relieved to pursue the matter. He took her money and dutifully carried the box of shelving out to her car, where he stored it in the trunk for her.

"Thank you," she said again. "By the way, Pamela—she *is* your daughter, isn't she?"

Mr. Hearst looked worried. "Yes, she is." Pam was his youngest, and the apple of his eye.

"She's a lovely girl and a good student. I just wanted you to know that she's doing well in school."

His face was wreathed in smiles as she drove away.

Wolf pulled over at the corner and watched his rearview mirror, waiting for Mary to exit the store. He was so angry he wanted to shake her until her teeth rattled, and that made him even angrier, because he knew he wouldn't do it.

Damn her! He'd warned her, but she hadn't listened. Not only had she made it plain they were acquainted, she had outlined the circumstances of their meeting and then championed him in a way that wouldn't go unnoticed.

Hadn't she understood when he'd told her he was an ex-con, and why? Did she think he'd been joking?

His hands clenched around the steering wheel. She'd had her hair twisted up in a knot again, and those big glasses perched on her nose, hiding the soft slate-blue of her eyes, but he remembered how she had looked with her hair down, wearing Joe's old jeans that had clung tightly to her slender legs and hips. He remembered the way passion had glazed her eyes when he'd kissed her. He remembered the softness of her lips, though she had had them pressed together in a ridiculously prim expression.

If he had any sense he'd just drive away. If he stayed completely away from her, there wouldn't be anything for people to talk about other than the fact that she was tutoring Joe, and that would be bad enough in their eyes.

But how would she get that box out of the car and into the house when she got home? It probably weighed as much as she did. He would just carry the box in for her, and at the same time peel a strip off her hide for not listening to him.

Oh, hell, who was he fooling? He'd had a taste of her, and he wanted more. She was a frumpy old maid, but her skin was as pale and translucent as a baby's, and her slender body would be soft, gently curving under his hands. He wanted to touch her. After kissing her, holding her, he hadn't gone to see Julie Oakes because he hadn't been able to get the feel of Miss Mary Potter out of his mind, off of his body. He still ached. His physical frustration was painful, and it was going to get worse, because if he'd ever known anything, it was that Miss Mary Potter wasn't for him.

Her car pulled out from in front of the store and passed him. Smothering another curse, he put the truck in gear and slowly followed her. She maintained a sedate pace, following the two-lane highway out of town, then turning off on the narrow secondary road that led to her house. She had to see his truck behind her, but she didn't give any indication that she knew she was being followed. Instead she drove straight to her house, carefully turned in at the snow-packed driveway and guided the car around to her customary parking spot behind the house.

Wolf shook his head as he pulled in behind her and got out of the truck. She was already out of her car, and she smiled at him as she fished the house key out of her purse. Didn't she remember what he'd told her? He couldn't believe that he'd told her he'd served time for rape and still she greeted him as calmly as if he were a priest, though they were the only two people for miles around.

"Damn it all, lady!" he barked at her, his long legs carrying him to her in a few strides. "Didn't you listen to anything I said Saturday?"

"Yes, of course I listened. That doesn't mean I agreed." She unlocked the trunk and smiled at him. "While you're here, would you please carry this box in for me? I'd really appreciate it."

"That's why I stopped," he snapped. "I knew you couldn't handle it."

His ill temper didn't seem to faze her. She merely smiled at him again as he lifted the box onto his shoulder, then led the way to the back door and opened it.

The first thing he noticed was that the house had a fresh, sweet smell to it, instead of the musty smell of an old house that had stood empty for a long time. His head lifted, and against his will he inhaled the faint scent. "What's that smell?"

She stopped and sniffed delicately. "What smell?"

"That sweet smell. Like flowers."

"Flowers? Oh, that must be the lilac sachet I put in all the drawers to freshen them. So many of the sachets are overpowering, but the lilacs are just right, don't you think?''

He didn't know anything about sachets, whatever they were, but if she put them in all the drawers, then her underwear must smell like lilacs, too. Her sheets would smell like lilacs and the warm scent of her body. His body responded strongly to the thought, and he cursed, then set the box down with a thud. Though the house was chilly, he felt sweat break out on his forehead.

''Let me turn up the heat,'' she said, ignoring his cursing. ''The furnace is old and noisy, but I don't have any wood for the fireplace, so it'll have to do.'' As she talked, she left the kitchen and turned down a hallway, her voice growing fainter. Then she was back, and she smiled at him again. ''It'll be warm in just a minute. Would you like a cup of tea?'' After giving him a measuring look she said, ''Make that coffee. You don't look like a tea-drinking man.''

He was already warm. He was burning up. He pulled off his gloves and tossed them on the kitchen table. ''Don't you know everybody in that town will be talking about you now? Lady, I'm Indian, and I'm an ex-con—''

''Mary,'' she interrupted briskly.

''What?''

''My name is Mary, not 'lady.' Mary Elizabeth.'' She added the second name out of habit because Aunt Ardith had always called her by both names. ''Are you certain you don't want coffee? I need something to warm up my insides.''

His hat joined the gloves, and he raked an impatient hand through his hair. ''All right. Coffee.''

Mary turned to run the water and measure the coffee, using the activity to hide the sudden color in her face. His hair. She felt stupid, but she'd hardly noticed his hair before. Maybe she'd been too upset, then too bemused, or maybe it was just that his midnight-black eyes had taken her attention, but she hadn't noticed before how long his hair was. It was thick and black and shiny, and touched his broad shoulders. He looked magnificently pagan; she had immediately pictured him with his powerful chest and legs bare, his body covered only by a breechclout or loincloth, and her pulse rate had gone wild.

He didn't sit down, but propped his long body against the cabinet beside her. Mary kept her head down, hoping her blush would subside. What was it about the man that the mere sight of him triggered erotic fantasies? She had certainly never had any fantasies before, erotic or otherwise. She had never before looked at a man and wondered what he looked like nude, but the thought of Wolf nude made her ache inside, made her hands itch to touch him.

"What the hell are you doing letting me even come in your house, let alone inviting me to have coffee?" he asked in a low, rough voice.

She blinked at him, her expression startled. "Why shouldn't I?"

He thought he might explode with frustration. "Lady—"

"Mary."

His big fists clenched. "*Mary.* Don't you have any better sense than to let an ex-con into your house?"

"Oh, that." She dismissed it with a wave of her hand. "It would be wise to follow your advice if you were truly a criminal, but since you didn't do it, I don't think that applies in this instance. Besides, if you *were* a criminal, you wouldn't give me that advice."

He couldn't believe the casual way she disregarded any possibility of his guilt. "How do you know I didn't do it?"

"You just didn't."

"Do you have any reason for your deduction, Sherlock, or are you going on good old feminine intuition?"

She jerked around and glared at him. "I don't believe a rapist would have handled a woman as tenderly as you—as you handled me," she said, her voice tapering off into a whisper, and the color surged back into her face. Mortified by the stupid way she continued to blush, she slapped her palms to her face in an effort to hide the betraying color.

Wolf clenched his teeth, partly because she was white and therefore not for him, partly because she was so damned innocent, and partly because he wanted so fiercely to touch her that his entire body ached. "Don't build any dreams because I kissed you Saturday," he said harshly. "I've been too long without a woman, and I'm—"

"Horny?" she supplied.

He was staggered by the incongruity of that word coming from her prim mouth. "What?"

"Horny," she said again. "I've heard some of my students say it. It means—"

"I know what it means!"

"Oh. Well, is that what you were? Still are, for all I know."

He wanted to laugh. The urge almost overpowered him, but he changed the sound into a cough. "Yeah, I still am."

She looked sympathetic. "I understand that can be quite a problem."

"It's hard on a guy."

It took a moment, but then her eyes widened, and before she could stop herself, her gaze had slid down his body. Instantly she jerked her head back up. "Oh. I see. I mean—I understand."

The need to touch her was suddenly so strong that he

had to give in to it, had to touch her in even the smallest way. He put his hands on her shoulders, savoring her softness, the delicacy of her joints under his palms. "I don't think you do understand. You can't associate with me and still work in this town. At best, you'd be treated like a leper, or a slut. You would probably lose your job."

At that, she pressed her lips together, and a militant light came into her eyes. "I'd like to see someone try to fire me for associating with a law-abiding, tax-paying citizen. I refuse to pretend I don't know you."

"There's knowing, and there's knowing. It would be bad enough for you to be friends with me. Sleeping with me would make your life here impossible."

He felt her stiffen under his hands. "I don't believe I've asked to sleep with you," she said, but the color rose in her face again. She hadn't actually said the words, but he knew she certainly had thought about what it would be like.

"You asked, all right, but you're so damned innocent you didn't realize what you were doing," he muttered. "I could crawl on top of you right now, sweetheart, and I'd do it if you had any real idea of what you're asking for. But the last thing I want is to have some prissy little Anglo screaming 'rape' at me. Believe me, an Indian doesn't get the benefit of the doubt."

"I wouldn't do anything like that!"

He smiled grimly. "Yeah, I've heard that before. I'm probably the only man who has ever kissed you, and you think you'd like more, don't you? But sex isn't pretty and romantic, it's hot and sweaty, and you probably wouldn't like the first time at all. So do me a favor and find some other guinea pig. I have enough troubles without adding you to the list."

Mary jerked away from him, pressing her lips firmly together and blinking her eyes as fast as she could to keep the tears from falling. Not for anything would she let him make her cry.

"I'm sorry I gave you that impression," she said, her voice stifled but even. "It's true I've never been kissed before, but I'm sure you aren't surprised by that. I'm obviously not Miss America material. If my—my response was out of line, I apologize. It won't happen again." She turned briskly to the cabinet. "The coffee is ready. How do you take yours?"

A muscle jerked in his jaw, and he grabbed his hat. "Forget the coffee," he muttered as he jammed the hat on his head and reached for his gloves.

She didn't look at him. "Very well. Goodbye, Mr. Mackenzie."

Wolf slammed out the door, and Mary stood there with an empty coffee cup in her hand. If it really was goodbye, she didn't know how she would be able to stand it.

Chapter Four

Mary wasn't weak-willed, and she refused to give in to the desolation that filled her every time she thought of that horrible day. During the days she prodded, cajoled and enticed her students toward knowledge; at night she watched Joe devour the facts she spread before him. His thirst for knowledge was insatiable, and he not only caught up with the students in her regular classes, he passed them.

She had written her letters to the Wyoming members of Congress, and had also written to a friend for all the information she could find on the Air Force Academy. When the package came, she gave it to Joe and watched his eyes take on that fiercely intent, enthralled look he got whenever he thought of flying. Working with Joe was a joy; her only problem was that he reminded her so strongly of his father.

It wasn't that she missed Wolf; how could she miss someone she had seen only twice? He hadn't imbedded himself in her daily routine so that her life seemed empty without him. But while she had been with him, she had felt more vividly alive than she ever had before. With Wolf, she hadn't been Mary Potter, old maid, she had been Mary Potter, woman. His intense masculinity had reached parts of her that she hadn't known existed, bringing to life dormant yearnings and emotions. She argued with herself that what she felt was plain old garden-variety lust, but that didn't stop the ache she felt whenever she thought of him. Even worse was her humiliation because her inexperience had been so obvious, and now she *knew* he thought of her as a sex-starved old maid.

It was April before the inevitable happened and word got out that Joe Mackenzie was spending a lot of time at the new teacher's house. At first Mary wasn't aware of the rumor flying through the town, though the kids in her classes had been watching her strangely, and there had been a lot of whispering. Sharon Wycliffe and Dottie Lancaster, the other two teachers, also took to giving her odd looks and whispering to each other. It didn't take Mary long to decide that the secret was no longer secret, but she went about her business with a serene smile. She had already received a favorable letter from a senator, signaling his interest in Joe, and despite her own arguments for caution, her spirits were high.

The school board's regular meeting was scheduled for the third week in April. The afternoon of the meeting, Sharon, with elaborate casualness, asked Mary if she planned to attend. Mary looked at her in surprise. "Of course. I thought all of us were expected to attend on a regular basis."

"Well, yes. It's just that—I thought—"

"You thought I would avoid the meeting now that everyone knows I've been teaching Joe Mackenzie?" Mary asked directly.

Sharon's mouth fell open. "What?" Her voice was weak.

"You didn't know? Well, it isn't an earth-shattering secret." She shrugged. "Joe thought people would be upset if I tutored him, so I haven't said anything. From the way everyone has been acting, I thought the cat was out of the bag."

"I think it was the wrong cat," Sharon admitted sheepishly. "His truck was seen at your house at night and people—um—got the wrong idea."

Mary felt blank. "What wrong idea?"

"Well, he's big for his age and all."

Still Mary didn't understand, until Sharon blushed hotly. Then comprehension burst on her brain like a flash, and horror filled her, followed swiftly by anger. "They think I'm having an affair with a *sixteen-year-old boy*?" Her voice rose with each word.

"It was late at night when his truck was seen," Sharon added, looking miserable.

"Joe leaves promptly at nine o'clock. Someone's idea of 'late' differs from mine." Mary stood and began shoving papers into her tote, her nostrils flaring, her cheeks white. The awful thing was that she had to simmer until seven o'clock that night, but she didn't think waiting would cool her temper. If anything, pressure would build. She felt savage, not only because her reputation had been impugned, but because Joe had also been attacked. He was trying desperately to make his dreams come true, and people were trying to tear him down. She wasn't a hen fussing with one chick; she was a tigress with one cub, and that cub had been threatened. It didn't matter that the cub was seven inches taller than she and outweighed her by almost eighty pounds; Joe, for all his unusual maturity, was still young and vulnerable. The father had disdained her protection, but there was no power on earth that could stop her from defending the son.

Evidently word had spread, because the school board meeting was unusually crowded that night. There were six members of the board: Mr. Hearst, who owned the general store; Francie Beecham, an eighty-one-year-old former teacher; Walton Isby, the bank president; Harlon Keschel, who owned the combination drugstore/hamburger joint; Eli

Baugh, a local rancher whose daughter, Jackie, was in Mary's class; and Cicely Karr, who owned the service station. All of the board members were solid members of the small community, all of them property owners, and all of them except Francie Beecham had stony faces.

The board meeting was held in Dottie's classroom, and extra desks were brought from Mary's classroom so there would be enough seats for everyone, an indication of how many people felt it necessary to attend. Mary was certain that at least one parent of each of her students was present. As she entered the room, every eye turned toward her. The women looked indignant; the men looked both hostile and speculative, and that made Mary even angrier. What right did they have to look down on her for her supposed sins, while at the same time they were wondering about the details?

Leaning against the wall was a tall man in a khaki deputy sheriff's uniform, watching her with narrowed eyes, and she wondered if they meant to have her arrested for sexual misconduct. It was ridiculous! If she had looked anything other than exactly what she was, a slight, mousy old maid, their suspicions would at least have made more sense. She poked an errant strand of hair back into the knot at the back of her head, sat down and folded her arms, intending to let them make the first move.

Walton Isby cleared his throat and called the meeting to order, no doubt feeling the importance of his position with so many people present to watch the proceedings. Mary drummed her fingers on her arm. The board went through the routine of its normal business, and suddenly she decided she wasn't going to wait. The best defense, she'd read, was an attack.

When the normal business was finished, Mr. Isby cleared his throat again, and Mary took it as a signal that they were about to get down to the real purpose of the meeting. She rose to her feet and said clearly, "Mr. Isby, before you continue, I have an announcement to make."

He looked startled, and his florid face turned even redder. "This is—uh, well, irregular, Miss Potter."

"It's also important." She kept her voice at the level she used when lecturing and turned so she could see the entire room. The deputy straightened from his position against the wall as everyone's attention locked on her like a magnet to a steel bar. "I'm certified to tutor pupils privately, and the credits they earn in private lessons are as legitimate as those earned in a public classroom. For the past month, I've been tutoring Joe Mackenzie in my home—"

"I'll just bet you have," someone muttered, and Mary's eyes flashed.

"Who said that?" she demanded crisply. "It was incredibly vulgar."

The room fell silent.

"When I saw Joe Mackenzie's school records, I was outraged that a student of his intelligence had quit school. Perhaps none of you know it, but he was at the top of his class. I contacted him and persuaded him to take lessons to catch up to his classmates, and in one month he has not only caught them, he has surpassed them. I have also been in contact with Senator Allard, who has expressed an interest in Joe. Joe's strong academic standing has made him a candidate for recommendation to the Air Force Academy. He's an honor to the community, and I know all of you will give him your support."

She was gratified to see the stunned looks in the room and sat down with the cool poise Aunt Ardith had tirelessly drummed into her. Only rabble got into brawls, Aunt Ardith had said; a lady could make her point in other ways.

Whispers rustled through the room as people put their

heads together, and Mr. Isby shuffled the three sheets of paper in front of him as he searched for something to say. The other members of the board put their heads together, too.

She looked around the room, and a shadow in the hall beyond the open door caught her attention. It was only a slight movement; if she hadn't looked at precisely that second, she would have missed it. As it was, it took her a moment to make out the outline of a tall man, and her skin tingled. Wolf. He was out in the hall, listening. It was the first time she had seen him since the day he'd come to her house, and even though all she could see was a darker outline against the shadows, her heart began to pound.

Mr. Isby cleared his throat, and the murmuring in the room settled down. "That is good news, Miss Potter," he began. "However, we don't think you've given the best appearance as an example to our young people—"

"Speak for yourself, Walton," Francie Beecham said testily, her voice cracking with old age.

Mary stood again. "In precisely what way have I given the wrong appearance?"

"It doesn't look right to have that boy in your house all hours of the night!" Mr. Hearst snapped.

"Joe leaves my home at exactly nine o'clock, after three hours of lessons. What is your definition of 'all hours of the night'? However, if the board doesn't approve of the location, I take it all are agreed that the schoolhouse will be used for night classes? I have no objection to moving the lessons here."

Mr. Isby, who was at heart a good-natured soul, looked harassed. The board members put their heads together again.

After a minute of heated consultation, they looked up again. Harlon Keschel wiped his perspiring face with a handkerchief. Francie Beecham looked outraged. This time it was Cicely Karr who spoke. "Miss Potter, this is a difficult situation. The odds against Joe Mackenzie being accepted into the Air Force Academy are high, I'm sure you'll admit, and the truth is that we don't approve of your spending so much time alone with him."

Mary's chin lifted. "Why is that?"

"Because you're a newcomer to this area, I'm sure you don't understand the way things are around here. The Mackenzies have a bad reputation, and we fear for your safety if you continue to associate with the boy."

"Mrs. Karr, that's hogwash," Mary replied with inelegant candor. Aunt Ardith wouldn't have approved. She thought of Wolf standing out in the hallway listening to these people slandering both him and his son, and she could almost feel the heat of his temper. He wouldn't let it hurt him, but it hurt her to know he was hearing it.

"Wolf Mackenzie helped me out of a dangerous situation when my car broke down and I was stranded in the snow. He was kind and considerate, and refused payment for repairing my car. Joe Mackenzie is an outstanding student who works hard on their ranch, doesn't drink or carouse—" she hoped that was true "—and has never been anything but respectful. I consider both of them my friends."

In the hallway, the man standing in the shadows knotted his fists. Damn the little fool, didn't she know this would probably cost her her job? He knew that if he stepped into that room all the hostility would instantly be focused on him, and he started to move, to draw their attention away from her, when he heard her speaking again. Didn't she know when to shut up?

"I would be as concerned if any of your children dropped out of school. I can't bear to see a young person give up on the future. Ladies and gentlemen, I was hired to teach. I intend to do that to the best of my ability. All of you are good people. Would any of you want me to give up if it were *your* child?"

Several people looked away and cleared their throats. Cicely Karr merely raised her chin. "You're sidestepping the point, Miss Potter. This isn't one of our children. This is Joe Mackenzie. He's…he's—"

"Half Indian?" Mary supplied, lifting her brow in question.

"Well, yes. That's part of it. The other part is his father—"

"What about his father?"

Wolf had to stifle a curse, and he started to step forward again when Mary asked scornfully, "Are you concerned because of his prison sentence?"

"That's cause enough, I should think!"

"Should you? Why?"

"Cicely, sit down and hush," Francie Beecham snapped. "The girl has a point, and I agree. If you start trying to think at this stage of your life, it could bring on hot flashes."

Just for a moment there was stunned silence in the room; then it exploded in thunderous laughter. Rough ranchers and their hard-working wives held their stomachs as they bent double, tears running down their faces. Mr. Isby turned so red his face was almost purple; then he burst into a great whooping laugh that sounded like a hysterical crane laying eggs, or so Cicely Karr told him. Her face was red, too, from anger. Big Eli Baugh actually rolled out of his chair, he was laughing so hard. Cicely grabbed his hat from the back of his chair and hit him over the head with it. He continued to howl with laughter as he protected his head with his arms.

"You can buy your motor oil from some other place from now on!" Cicely roared at Mr. Baugh, continuing to bash him with his hat. "And your gas! Don't you or any of your hands set foot on my property again!"

"Now, Cicely," Eli choked as he tried to dodge his hat.

"Folks, let's have some order in here," Harlon Keschel pleaded, though he looked as if he were enjoying the spectacle of Cicely bashing Eli with his own hat. Certainly everyone else in the room was. Almost everyone, Mary thought, as she spotted Dottie Lancaster's cold face. Suddenly she realized that the other teacher would have been glad to see her fired, and she wondered why. She'd always tried to be friendly with Dottie, but the older woman had rebuffed all overtures. Had *Dottie* seen Joe's truck at Mary's house and started the gossip? Would Dottie have been out driving around at night? There were no other houses on Mary's road, so no one would have been driving past to visit a neighbor.

The uproar had died down, though there was still an occasional chuckle heard around the room. Mrs. Karr continued to glare at Eli Baugh, having for some reason made him the focal point of her embarrassed anger rather than turning it on Francie Beecham, who had started it all.

Even Mr. Isby was still grinning as he raised his voice. "Let's see if we can get back to business here, folks."

Francie Beecham piped up again. "I think we've handled enough business for the night. Miss Potter is giving the Mackenzie boy private school lessons so he can go to the Air Force Academy, and that's that. I'd do the same thing if I were still teaching."

Mr. Hearst said, "It still don't look right—"

"Then she can use the classroom. Everyone agreed?" Francie looked at the other board members, her wrinkled face triumphant. She winked at Mary.

"It's okay by me," Eli Baugh said as he tried to reshape his hat. "The Air Force Academy—well, that's something. I don't reckon anyone from this county has ever been to any of the academies."

Mr. Hearst and Mrs. Karr disagreed, but Mr. Isby and Harlon Keschel sided with Francie and Eli. Mary stared hard at the shadowed hallway, but couldn't see anything now. Had he left? The deputy turned his head to see what she was looking at, but he didn't see anything, either, because he gave a slight shrug and looked back at her, then winked. Mary was startled. More people had winked at her that night than in the rest of her life total. What was the proper way to handle a wink? Were they ignored? Should she wink back? Aunt Ardith's lectures on proper behavior hadn't covered winking.

The meeting broke up with a good deal of teasing and laughter, and more than a few of the parents took a moment to shake Mary's hand and tell her she was doing a good job. It was half an hour before she was able to get her coat and make it to the door, and when she did, she found the deputy waiting for her.

"I'll walk you to your car," he said in an easy tone. "I'm Clay Armstrong, the local deputy."

"How do you do? Mary Potter," she replied, holding out her hand.

He took it, and her small hand disappeared in his big one. He set his hat on top of dark brown curly hair, but his blue eyes still twinkled, even in the shadow of the brim. She liked him on sight. He was one of those strong, quiet men who were rock steady, but who had a good sense of humor. He'd been delighted by the uproar.

"Everyone in town knows who you are. We don't often have a stranger move in, especially a young single woman from the South. The first day you were here, the whole county heard about your accent. Haven't you noticed that all the girls in school are trying to drawl?''

"Are they?" she asked in surprise.

"They sure are." He slowed his walk to keep pace with her as they walked to her car. The cold air rushed at her, chilling her legs, but the night sky was crystal clear, and a thousand stars winked overhead in compensation.

They reached her car. "Would you tell me something, Mr. Armstrong?"

"Anything. And call me Clay."

"Why did Mrs. Karr get so angry at Mr. Baugh, instead of at Miss Beecham? It was Miss Beecham who started the whole thing."

"Cicely and Eli are first cousins. Cicely's folks died when she was young, and Eli's parents took her to raise. Well, Cicely and Eli are the same age, so they grew up together and fought like wildcats the whole time. Still do, I guess, but some families are like that. They're still pretty close."

That kind of family was strange to Mary, but it sounded warm and secure, too, to be able to fight with someone and know he still loved you.

"So she hit him for laughing at her?"

"And because he was convenient. No one is going to get too angry with Miss Beecham. She taught all the adults in this county, and we all still think a lot of that old lady."

"That sounds so nice," Mary said, smiling. "I hope I'm still here when I'm that old."

"Are you planning to raise cain at school board meetings, too?"

"I hope so," she repeated.

He leaned down to open the car door for her. "I hope so, too. Be careful driving home." After she got in, he closed the door and touched his fingers to his hat brim, then strode away.

He was a nice man. Most of the people in Ruth were nice. They were blind where Wolf Mackenzie was concerned, but basically they weren't vicious people.

Wolf. Where had he gone?

She hoped Joe wouldn't decide to stop his lessons because of this. Though she knew it was foolish to count her chickens prematurely, she felt a growing certainty that he would be accepted into the Academy and was inordinately proud that she could be part of getting him there. Aunt Ardith would have said that pride goeth before a fall, but Mary had often thought that a person would never fall if he didn't first try to stand. On more than one occasion she had countered Aunt Ardith's cliché of choice with her own "nothing ventured, nothing gained." It had always made Aunt Ardith huffy when her favorite weapon was turned against her. Mary sighed. She missed her acerbic aunt so much. Her supply of clichés might wither from lack of use without Aunt Ardith to sharpen her wits against.

When she turned into her driveway, she was tired, hungry and anxious, afraid that Joe would try to be noble and stop his lessons so she wouldn't have any more trouble because of him. "I'll teach him," she muttered aloud as she stepped out of the car, "if I have to follow him around on horseback."

"Who are you following around?" Wolf demanded irritably, and she jumped so violently that she banged her knee against the car door.

"Where did you come from?" she demanded just as irritably. "Darn it, you scared me!"

"Probably not enough. I parked in the barn, out of sight."

She stared up at him, drinking in the sight of his proud,

chiseled face and closed expression. The starlight was colorless, revealing his features in stark angles and shadows, but it was enough for her. She hadn't realized how starved she had been for the sight of him, the heart-pounding nearness of him. She couldn't even feel the cold now, the way blood was racing through her veins. This was probably what "being in heat" meant. It was breathtaking and a little scary, but she decided she liked it.

"Let's go in," he said when she made no effort to move, and Mary silently led the way to the back door. She'd left it unlocked so she wouldn't have to fumble with a key in the dark, and Wolf's black brows drew together when she turned the knob and pushed the door open.

They entered, and Mary closed the door behind them, then turned on the light. Wolf stared down at her, at the silky brown hair escaping from its knot, and he had to clench his fists to keep from grabbing her. "Don't leave your door unlocked again," he ordered.

"I don't think I'll be burgled," she countered, then admitted honestly, "I don't have anything a self-respecting burglar would want."

He'd sworn he wouldn't touch her, but even though he'd known it would be difficult to keep his hands to himself, he hadn't realized quite *how* difficult. He wanted to grab her and shake some sense into her, but he knew if he touched her in any way at all, he wouldn't want to stop. Her female scent teased his nostrils, beckoning him closer; she smelled warm and delicately fragrant, so feminine it made his entire body ache with longing. He moved away from her, knowing it was safer for them both if he put some distance between them.

"I wasn't thinking about a burglar."

"No?" She considered that, then realized what he'd meant and what she'd said in response. She cleared her throat and marched to the stove, hoping he wouldn't see her red face. "If I make a pot of coffee, will you drink a cup this time or storm out like you did before as soon as it's made?"

The tart reproach in her voice amused him, and he wondered how he had ever thought her mousy. Her clothes were dowdy, but her personality was anything but timid. She said exactly what she thought and didn't hesitate to take someone to task. Less than an hour before she had taken on the entire county on his behalf. The memory of it sobered him.

"I'll drink the coffee if you insist on making it, but I'd rather you just sat down and listened to me."

Turning, Mary slid into a chair and primly folded her hands on the table. "I'm listening."

He pulled the chair next to her away from the table and turned it to the side, facing her, before he sat down. She turned an unsmiling gaze on him. "I saw you in the hall tonight."

He looked grim. "Damn. Did anyone else notice me?" He wondered how she had seen him, because he'd been very careful, and he was good at not being seen when he didn't want to be.

"I don't think so." She paused. "I'm sorry they said those things."

"I'm not worried about what the good people of Ruth think about me," he said in a hard tone. "I can handle them, and so can Joe. We don't depend on them for our living, but you do. Don't go to bat for us again, unless you don't like your job very much and you're trying to lose it, because that's damn sure what will happen if you keep on."

"I won't lose my job for teaching Joe."

"Maybe not. Maybe they'll have some tolerance for Joe, especially since you threw the Academy at them, but I'm another story."

"Nor will I lose my job for being friendly with you. I have a contract," she explained serenely. "An ironclad contract. It isn't easy to get a teacher in a place as small and isolated as Ruth, especially in the middle of winter. I can lose my job only if I'm judged incompetent, or break the law, and I defy anyone to prove me incompetent."

He wondered if that meant she didn't rule out breaking the law, but didn't ask her. The kitchen light was shining directly down on her head, turning her hair to a silvery halo and distracting him with its glitter. He knew her hair was brown, but it was such a pale, ash brown that it had no red tones, and when light struck it the strands actually looked silver. She looked like an angel, with her soft blue eyes and translucent skin, and her silky hair slipping from its confining knot to curl around her face. His insides knotted painfully. He wanted to touch her. He wanted her naked beneath him. He wanted to be inside her, to gently ride her until she was all soft and wet, and her nails were clawing at his back—

Mary reached out and put her slim hand on his much larger one, and just that small touch burned him. "Tell me what happened," she invited softly. "Why were you sent to prison? I know you didn't do it."

Wolf was a hard man, by nature as well as necessity, but her simple, unquestioning faith in him shook him to the bone. He had always stood alone, isolated by his Indian blood from Anglos and by his Anglo blood from Indians. Not even his parents had been close to him, though they had loved him and he had loved them in return. They had simply never truly known him, never been admitted into his private thoughts. Nor had he been close to his wife, Joe's mother. They had slept together, he'd been fond of her, but she, too, had been kept at a distance. Only with Joe had his reserve been breached, and Joe knew him as no other person on earth did. They were part of each other, and he fiercely loved the boy. Only the thought of Joe had gotten him through the years in prison alive.

It was more than alarming that this slight Anglo woman had a knack for touching nerves he'd thought completely insulated; he didn't want her close to him, not in any emotional way. He wanted to have sex with her, but he didn't want her to matter to him. Angrily he realized that she already mattered to him, and he didn't like it at all.

He stared at her fragile hand on his, her touch light and soft. She didn't shrink from touching him, as if he were dirty; nor was she grasping at him as some women did, rapaciously, wanting to use him, to see if the savage could satisfy their shallow, greedy appetites. She had simply reached out to touch him because she cared.

Ever so slowly he watched his hand turn and engulf hers, enfolding the pale, slim fingers within his callused palm as if to protect them.

"It was nine years ago." His voice was low, harsh; she had to lean forward to hear him. "No—almost ten years. Ten years this June. Joe and I had just moved here. I was working for the Half Moon Ranch. A girl from the next county was raped and killed, and her body dumped just within the far boundary of Half Moon. I was picked up and questioned, but hell, I'd been expecting it from the minute I heard about the girl. I was new to the area, and Indian. But there was no evidence against me, so they had to let me go.

"Three weeks later, another girl was raped. This one was from the Rocking L Ranch, just to the west of town. She was stabbed, like the other girl, but she lived. She'd seen the rapist." He paused for a minute, the expression in his black eyes shuttered as he looked back at those long-ago years. "She said he looked like an Indian. He was dark, with black hair, and he was tall. Not many tall Indians around. I was picked up again before I even knew another girl had been raped. They put me in a lineup with six dark-haired Anglos. The girl identified me, and I was charged. Joe and I lived on Half Moon, but somehow no one remembered seeing me at home the night that girl was raped, except Joe, and a six-year-old Indian kid's word didn't carry much weight."

Her chest hurt when she thought of how it had been for him, and for Joe, who had been only a small child. How much worse had it been for Wolf because of Joe, worrying what would happen to his son? She didn't know of anything she could say now to lessen that ten-year-old outrage, so she didn't try; she just tightened her fingers around his, letting him know he wasn't alone.

"I was put on trial and found guilty. I'm lucky they weren't able to tie me to the first rape, the girl who'd been murdered, or I'd have been lynched. As it was, everyone thought I'd done it."

"You went to prison." It was so hard to believe, even though she knew it was true. "What happened to Joe?"

"He was made a ward of the state. I survived prison. It wasn't easy. A rapist is considered fair game. I had to be the roughest son of a bitch in there just to live from one night to the next."

She had heard tales about what happened to men in prison, and her pain increased. He had been locked up, away from the sun and the mountains, the clear fresh air, and she knew it had been like caging a wild animal. He was innocent, but his freedom and his son had been taken from him, and he'd been thrown in with the dregs of humanity. Had he slept soundly even once the entire time he'd been in prison, or had he merely dozed, his senses attuned to attack?

Her throat was tight and dry. All she could manage was a whisper. "How long were you in?"

"Two years." His face was hard, his eyes full of menace as he stared at her, but she knew the menace was directed inward, at his bitter memories. "Then a series of rapes and murders from Casper to Cheyenne were tied together and the guy was caught. He confessed, seemed proud of his accomplishments, but a little put out that they hadn't given him complete credit. He admitted to the two rapes in this area, and gave them details no one but the rapist could have known."

"Was he Indian?"

His smile was flinty. "Italian. Olive-skinned, curly haired."

"So you were released?"

"Yeah. My name was cleared, and they said 'Sorry about that,' and turned me loose. I'd lost my son, my job, everything I'd owned. I found out where they'd put Joe and hitched there to get him. Then I rodeoed for a while to get some money and lucked out. I did pretty well. I won enough to come back here with something in my pocket. The old guy who had owned Half Moon had died with no heirs, and the land was about to be sold for taxes. It wiped me out, but I bought the land. Joe and I settled here, and I began training horses and building up the ranch."

"Why did you come back?" She couldn't understand it. Why return to the place where he'd been so mistreated?

"Because I was tired of always moving on, never having a place of my own. Damn tired of being looked down on as a trashy, shiftless Indian. Tired of my son not having a home. And because there was no way in hell I was going to let the bastards get the best of me."

The aching in her intensified. She wished she could ease the anger and bitterness in him, wished she dared take him in her arms and soothe him, wished he could become a part of the community instead of a thorn in its side.

"They're not all illegitimate," she said, and wondered why his mouth suddenly twitched as if he might smile. "Any more than all Indians are trashy or shiftless. People are just people, good and bad."

"You need a keeper," he replied. "That Pollyanna attitude is going to get you in trouble. Teach Joe, do what you can for him, but stay the hell away from me, for your own sake. These people didn't change their minds about me just because I was released."

"You haven't tried to change their minds. You've just kept rubbing their noses in their guilt," she pointed out, her tone acerbic.

"Am I supposed to forget what they did?" he asked just as sharply. "Forget that their 'justice' consisted of putting me in a lineup with six Anglos and telling that girl to 'pick out the Indian'? I spent two years in hell. I still don't know what happened to Joe, but it was almost three months after I got him back before he spoke a word. Forget that? Like hell."

"So, they won't change their minds, you won't change your mind, and I won't change mine. I believe we have a stalemate."

His dark eyes burned with frustration as he glared at her, and suddenly he seemed to realize he was still holding her hand. He released her abruptly and stood. "Look, you can't be my friend. *We* can't be friends."

Now that her hand was free, Mary felt abandoned and cold. She clasped her hands in her lap and looked up at him. "Why? Of course, if you simply don't like me…" Her voice trailed off, and she bent her head to examine her hands as if she'd never seen them before.

Not like her? He couldn't sleep, his temper was frayed,

he got hard whenever he thought about her, and he thought about her too damn much. He was so physically frustrated that he thought he might go mad, but he couldn't even ease himself with Julie Oakes or any other woman now, because all he could think about was baby-fine brown hair, slate-blue eyes and skin like translucent rose petals. It was all he could do to keep from taking her, and only the knowledge of how the good townspeople of Ruth would turn on her if he made her his woman kept him from grabbing her. Her stubborn principles hadn't prepared her for the pain and trouble she would face.

Suddenly his frustration boiled over, and he was filled with rage at having to walk away from the one woman he wanted to the point of madness. Before he could stop himself, he reached down and grasped her wrists, hauling her to her feet. "No, damn it, we can't be friends! Do you want to know why? Because I can't be around you without thinking of stripping you naked and taking you, wherever we happen to be. Hell, I don't know if I'd take the time to strip you! I want your breasts in my hands, your nipples in my mouth. I want your legs around my waist, or your ankles on my shoulders, or any position at all if I can just get inside you." He'd pulled her so close that his warm breath brushed her cheeks as he rasped the low, harsh words at her. "So, sweetheart, there's no way we can be *friends*."

Mary shivered as her body responded to his words. Though they'd been spoken in anger, they told her that he felt the same way she did, and described actions she could only half imagine. She was too inexperienced and honest to hide her feelings from him, so she didn't even try. Her eyes were filled with painful longing. "Wolf?"

Just that, but the way she said his name, with an aching little inflection at the end, made his grip on her wrists tighten. "No."

"I—I want you."

Her whispered, trembly confession left her completely vulnerable to him, and he knew it. He groaned inwardly. Damn it, didn't she have any sense of self-protection at all? Didn't she know what it did to a man to have the woman he wanted offer herself like that, with no qualifications or holding back? His control was stretched hair-thin, but he grimly held on to it because the hard truth was that she truly didn't know. She was a virgin. She was old-fashioned, strictly raised, and had only the vaguest idea of what she was inviting.

"Don't say that," he finally muttered. "I've told you before—"

"I know," she interrupted. "I'm too inexperienced to be interesting, and you…you don't want to be used as a guinea pig. I remember." She seldom cried, but she felt the salty wetness burning her eyes, and he winced at the hurt he saw there.

"I lied. God, how I lied."

Then his control broke. He had to hold her, feel her in his arms just for a little while, have her taste on his mouth again. He drew her wrists up and placed her hands around his neck, then bent his head even as he locked his arms around her and drew her up tight against him. His mouth covered hers, and her eager response seared him. She knew what to do now; her lips parted, allowing his tongue entrance, where she met him with soft, welcoming touches from her own tongue. He had taught her that, just as he'd taught her to melt against him, and the knowledge drove him almost as crazy as the feel of her soft breasts flattening against his chest.

Mary drowned in the sheer ecstasy of being in his arms again, and the tears that she'd held back spilled past her lashes. This was too painful, and too wonderful, to be mere lust. If this was love, she didn't know if she could bear it.

His mouth was hungry and hard, taking long, deep kisses that left her clinging to him mindlessly. His hand moved surely up her stomach and closed over her breast, and all she could do was make a soft sound of pleasure low in her throat. Her nipples burned and throbbed; his touch both assuaged the pain and intensified it, making her want more. She wanted it the way he had described it, with his mouth on her breasts, and she twisted feverishly against him. She was empty and needed to be filled. She needed to be his woman.

He jerked his head up and pressed her face against his shoulder. "I have to stop. Now." He groaned the words. He was shaking, as hot as any teenage stud in the back seat of his daddy's car.

Mary briefly weighed all of Aunt Ardith's strictures against the way she felt and accepted that she was in love, because this mingled glory and torment could be nothing else. "I don't want to stop," she said raggedly. "I want you to love me."

"No. I'm Indian. You're white. The people in this town would destroy you. Tonight was just a taste of what you'd have to go through."

"I'm willing to risk it!" she cried desperately.

"I'm not. I can take it, but you—you hang on to your Pollyanna principles, sweetheart. I can't offer you anything in return." If he'd thought there was even a fifty-fifty chance of living here in peace, Wolf would have taken the risk, but he knew there wasn't, not the way things were. Other than Joe, she was the only human being in the world he'd ever wanted to protect, and it was the hardest thing he'd ever done.

Mary lifted her head from his shoulder, revealing her wet cheeks. "All I want is you."

"I'm the one thing you can't have. They'd tear you apart." Very gently he pulled her arms down and turned to leave.

Her voice came behind him, low and strained as she fought against tears. "I'll risk it."

He stopped, his hand on the doorknob. "I won't."

For the second time she watched him walk away, and this time was far worse than the first.

Joe was unusually distracted; he was normally the most attentive of students, applying himself to the subject at hand with almost phenomenal concentration, but tonight he had something else on his mind. He'd accepted without comment their move to the school for lessons and never even hinted that he'd learned the subject of the school board meeting that had resulted in the change of locations. As it was the beginning of May, and the day had been unseasonably warm, Mary was half inclined to put his restlessness down to spring fever. It had been a long winter, and she was restless herself.

Finally she closed the book before her. "Why don't we go home early tonight?" she suggested. "We're not getting much done."

Joe closed his own book and pushed his fingers through his thick black hair, identical to his father's. Mary had to look away. "Sorry," he said on a long exhalation. It was typical that he didn't offer an explanation. Joe didn't often feel the need to justify himself.

But in the weeks she'd been tutoring him, they had had a lot of personal conversations between the prepared lessons, and Mary never hesitated when she thought one of her students might be troubled. If it were only spring fever gnawing at him, then she wanted him to say so. "Is something bothering you?"

He gave her a wry smile, one that was too adult to belong to a sixteen-year-old boy. "You could say that."

"Ah." That smile relieved her, because now she thought she knew the cause of his restlessness. It was indeed spring fever, after a fashion. As Aunt Ardith had often lectured her niece, "When a young man's sap rises, a girl should look out. I declare, they seem to run mad." Evidently Joe's sap was rising. Mary wondered if women had sap, too.

He picked up his pen and fiddled with it for a moment before tossing it aside as he made up his mind to say more. "Pam Hearst asked me to take her to a movie."

"*Pam?*" This was a surprise, and possible trouble. Ralph Hearst was one of the townspeople most adamantly opposed to the Mackenzies.

Joe's ice-blue eyes were hooded as he glanced at her. "Pam is the girl I told you about before."

So, it *was* Pam Hearst. She was pretty and bright, and her slim young body had a form guaranteed to affect a young man's sap. Mary wondered if Pam's father knew she had been flirting with Joe and that was one reason for his hostility.

"Are you going to go?"

"No," he said flatly, surprising her.

"Why?"

"There aren't any movie houses in Ruth."

"So?"

"That's the whole point. We'd have to go to another town. No one we know would be likely to see us. She wanted me to pick her up behind the school, after it got dark." He leaned back in his chair and looped his hands behind his head. "She was too ashamed to go to the dance with me, but I'm good enough for her to sneak around and see. Maybe she thought that even if we were seen, the idea that I might go to the Academy would keep her from getting in too much trouble. Folks seem taken with the idea.'' His tone was ironic. "I guess it makes a difference when the Indian wears a uniform.''

Suddenly her impulsive announcement at the school board meeting didn't seem like such a good idea. "Do you wish I hadn't told them?''

"You had to, considering," he replied, and by that she knew he was aware of the subject of that meeting. "It puts extra pressure on me to get into the Academy, because if I don't they'll all say that the Indian just couldn't cut it, but that's not a bad thing. If it will push me to do more, then I'm that much closer to getting in.''

Privately, Mary didn't think Joe needed any added incentive; he wanted it so badly now that the need burned in him. She returned the conversation to Pam. "Does it bother you, that she asked now?''

"It made me mad. And it *really* made me mad having to turn her down, because I sure would like to get my hands on her." He stopped abruptly and gave Mary another of those too-adult looks before a little grin tugged at his lips. "Sorry. I didn't mean to get too personal. Let's just say that I'm attracted to her physically, but that's all it is, and I can't afford to fool with that kind of situation. Pam's a nice girl, but she doesn't figure in my plans.''

Mary understood what he meant. No woman figured in his plans, other than to provide physical release, for a long time, if ever. There was something solitary about him, as there was about Wolf, and in addition, Joe was so possessed by the specter of flight that part of him was already gone. Pam Hearst would marry some local boy, settle down in Ruth or nearby, and raise her own family in the same calm setting where she'd grown up; she wasn't meant for the brief attention Joe Mackenzie could give her before he moved on.

"Do you have any idea who started the gossip?" Joe asked, his pale eyes hard. He didn't like the idea of anyone hurting this woman.

"No. I haven't tried to find out. It could have been anyone who drove by and saw your truck at my house. But most people seemed to have forgotten about it now, except for—" She stopped, her eyes troubled.

"Who?" Joe demanded flatly.

"I don't mean that I think she started the gossip," Mary said hastily. "I just feel uneasy around her. She dislikes me, and I don't know why. Maybe she's this way with everyone. Has Dottie Lancaster—"

"Dottie Lancaster!" He gave a harsh laugh. "Now there's a thought. Yeah, she could have started the gossip. She's had a rough life, and I kind of feel sorry for her, but she did her best to make my life hell when I was in her classes."

"Rough? How?"

"Her husband was a truck driver, and he was killed years ago when her son was just a baby. He was on a run in Colorado, and a drunk driver ran him off the side of a cliff. The drunk was an Indian. She never got over it and blames all Indians, I guess."

"That's irrational."

He shrugged, as if to say a lot of things were irrational. "Anyway, she was left alone with her kid, and she had a hard time. Not much money. She started teaching, but she had to pay someone to take care of the kid, and he needed special training when he was old enough to start school, which took even more money."

"I didn't know Dottie had any children," Mary said, surprised.

"Just Robert—Bobby. He's about twenty-three or four,

I guess. He still lives with Mrs. Lancaster, but he doesn't go around other people much.''

"What's wrong with him? Does he have Down's syndrome, or a learning disability?''

"He's not retarded. Bobby's just different. He likes people, but not in groups. A lot of people together make him nervous, so he pretty much stays to himself. He reads a lot, and listens to music. But once he had a summer job at the building supply store, and Mr. Watkins told Bobby to fill a wheelbarrow full of sand. Instead of pushing the wheelbarrow to the sandpile and shoveling the sand in, Bobby would get a shovelful of sand and carry it back to the wheelbarrow. It's things like that. He'd have trouble getting dressed, because he'd put his shoes on first, and then he couldn't get his jeans on.''

Mary had seen people like Bobby, who had trouble with practical problem-solving. It was a learning disability, and took a lot of patient, specialized training to handle. She felt sorry for him, and for Dottie, who couldn't have had a happy life.

Joe pushed his chair back and stood up, stretching his cramped muscles. "Do you ride?" he asked suddenly.

"No. I've never even been on a horse." Mary chuckled. "Will that get me thrown out of Wyoming?"

His tone was grave. "It could. Why don't you come up on the mountain some Saturday and I'll give you riding lessons? School will be out for the summer soon, and you'll have a lot of time to practice.''

He couldn't know how appealing the idea was, not only to ride but to see Wolf again. The only thing was, it would hurt just as much to see him as it did not to see him, because he was still out of her reach. "I'll think about it," she promised, but she doubted she would ever take him up on the offer.

Joe didn't push it, but he didn't intend to let it drop, either. He'd get Mary up on the mountain one way or another. He figured Wolf had about reached the limits of his restraint. Parading her right under his nose would be like leading a mare in heat in front of a stallion. His pretty, tart-tongued little teacher would be lucky if his dad didn't have her flat on her back before she had the hello out of her mouth. Joe had to hide his smile. He'd never seen anyone get to Wolf the way Miss Mary Elizabeth Potter had. She had Wolf so tied in knots he was as dangerous as a wounded cougar.

He mentally hummed a few bars of "Matchmaker."

When Mary got home the next Friday afternoon, there was a letter in the mailbox from Senator Allard, and her fingers trembled as she tore it open. If it was bad news for Joe, if Senator Allard had declined to recommend him to the Academy, she didn't know what she would do. Senator Allard wasn't their only possibility, but he had seemed the most receptive, and a turndown from him would really be discouraging.

The senator's letter to her was brief, thanking her for her efforts in bringing Joe to his attention. He had decided to recommend Joe for admittance to the Academy, for the freshman class beginning after Joe's graduation from high school. From there on, it would be up to Joe to pass the rigorous academic and physical examinations.

Enclosed was a private letter of congratulations to Joe.

Mary hugged the letters to her breast, and tears welled in her eyes. They had done it, and it hadn't even been that difficult! She had been prepared to petition every congressman every week until Joe was given his chance, but it hadn't been necessary. Joe's grades and credits had done it for him.

It was news too good to wait, so she got back into her car and drove up Mackenzie's Mountain. The drive was much different now; the snow had melted, and wildflowers bloomed beside the road. After the harsh winter cold, the spring warmth felt like a blessing on her skin, though it still wasn't nearly as warm as the springs she had known in Savannah. She was so excited and happy that she didn't even notice the steep drop on the side of the road as it wound higher, but she did notice the wild grandeur of the mountains, stretching magnificently toward the dark blue heavens. She drew a deep breath and realized that the spring did make up for the winter. It felt like home, a new home, a place dear and familiar.

The tires threw out a spray of gravel as she slid to a stop at the kitchen door of Wolf's one-story frame house, and before the vehicle had rocked back on its springs she was bounding up the steps to pound on the door. "Wolf! Joe!" She knew she was yelling in a very unladylike manner, but she was too happy to care. Some situations just called for yelling.

"Mary!"

The call came from behind her, and she whirled. Wolf was coming from the barn at a dead run, his powerful body surging fluidly. Mary yelped in excitement and launched herself from the steps, her skirt flying up as she bolted down the graveled drive toward the barn. "He got it!" she screamed, waving the letters. "He got it!"

Wolf skidded to a halt and watched the sedate teacher literally skipping and leaping toward him, her skirt kicking up around her thighs with each step. He just had time to realize there was nothing wrong, that she was laughing, when, three steps away, she went airborne. He braced himself and caught her weight against his chest, his brawny arms wrapping around her.

"He got it!" she shrieked again, and threw her arms around his neck.

Wolf could think of only one thing, and it made his mouth go dry. "He got it?"

She waved the letters under his nose. "He got it! Senator Allard—the letter was in my mailbox—I couldn't wait—where's Joe?" She knew she was almost incoherent and made an effort to compose herself, but she just couldn't stop grinning.

"He's in town picking up a load of fencing. Damn it, are you sure that's what it says? He still has a year of school—"

"Not a year, not at the rate he's going. But he'll have to be seventeen, anyway. The senator has recommended him for the freshman class starting after he graduates. Less than a year and a half!"

Fierce pride filled Wolf's face, the warrior's pride he'd inherited from both Comanche and Celt. His eyes glittered with black fire, and exultantly he lifted her high, his hands under her armpits, and twirled around with her. She threw back her head, shrieking with laughter, and suddenly Wolf felt his entire body clench with desire. It was as powerful as a blow to the gut, knocking the wind out of him. She was soft and warm in his arms, her laughter was as fresh as the spring, and he wanted her out of the prim little shirtwaist she wore.

Slowly his face changed to a harder, more primitive cast. She was still laughing as he lowered her, her hands braced on his shoulders, but he stopped when her breasts were level with his face. The laughter died in Mary's throat as he deliberately brought her closer to him and buried his face between her breasts. His grip shifted, one arm locking around her buttocks and the other around her back, and his hot mouth searched for her nipple. He found it, his mouth clamping down on it through the barriers of her dress and bra, but the sensation was still so exquisite that her breath caught on a moan and her back arched, pushing her breast against him.

It wasn't enough. She burrowed her fingers through his hair, digging into his skull to push him harder against her, but it wasn't enough. She wanted him with sudden, fierce desperation. The layers of cloth that kept him from her drove her mad, and she squirmed against him, low whimpers coming from her throat. "Please," she begged. "Wolf—"

He lifted his head, his eyes savage with need. His blood was thundering through his veins, and he was breathing hard. "Do you want more?" The words were guttural, a normal tone beyond him.

She squirmed against him again, her hands clutching desperately. "Yes."

Very gently he let her slide down his body, deliberately rubbing her over the hardened bulge in his jeans, and both of them shuddered. Wolf was beyond thinking of all his reasons for not becoming involved with her, beyond anything but the urge to mate. To hell with what anyone thought.

He looked around, gauging the distance to both house and barn. The barn was closer. Clamping his hand around her wrist, he strode toward the big open double doors that revealed the dim interior.

Mary could barely get her breath as she was all but dragged in his wake. Her senses bewildered by the sudden cessation of pleasure, she was confused by his actions and wanted to ask what he was doing, but she didn't have enough oxygen in her lungs to form the question. Then they were inside the barn, and she was swamped by the perceptions of dim light, animal warmth and the earthy smells of dust, hay, leather and horses. She heard soft nickers and the muffled stamping of hooves on straw. Wolf led her into an empty stall and dragged her down onto the fresh hay. She sprawled on her back, and he came down on top of her, his muscled weight pressing her even deeper into the hay.

"Kiss me," she whispered, reaching up to thrust her fingers into his long hair and pull him down to her.

"I'll kiss you all over before I'm through with you," he muttered, and bent his head. Her mouth opened under the force of his, and his tongue moved into her in a deep rhythm that she instinctively recognized and accepted, responded to eagerly. He was heavy, but it was so natural that she bear his weight that she rejoiced in the pressure of his body. She wrapped her arms around his thickly muscled shoulders and hugged him even tighter to her; she wanted to be as close as she could to him, and to that end her hips undulated slightly, adjusting to the carnal pressure of his loins.

The slow movements of her hips beneath him made him feel as if his head would explode from the rush of blood through his body. He made a low, rough sound in his throat and reached for the zipper at the back of her dress. He thought he would die if he didn't feel her silky skin under his hands, if he didn't sheathe his throbbing flesh inside her.

It was startlingly new to her, bringing a delicate flush to her cheeks, but it was still so *right* that she didn't even think of protesting. She didn't want to protest. She wanted Wolf. She was female to his male, warm and sexual, intensely aware of being a woman and offering herself to the man she loved. She wanted to be naked for him, so she helped him by pulling her arms free of the sleeves as he tugged the dress from her shoulders and let it fall to her waist. She had felt racy, daring to buy a bra with a single front clasp, but as he looked down at her breasts, barely covered by the thin, flesh-colored material, she was so glad she had done it. He deftly opened the clasp with one hand, a trick she hadn't learned yet, and watched the edges pull back to bare her soft curves, stopping before her nipples were revealed.

He made that rough sound again, almost like a growl, and bent to nuzzle the bra aside. His mouth, warm and wet, slid across her breast and clamped on the tightly beaded nipple. She jumped, her entire body reacting to a pleasure so intense it bordered on pain, as he sucked strongly at her. Mary's eyes closed, and she moaned. She couldn't bear it; it felt *too* good, a hot river of pleasure-pain impulses running from breast to loin, where an empty ache made her press her legs together and arch beneath him, silently begging for the release her body had never known, but sensed with ancient wisdom.

Wolf felt her move beneath him again, and the last shred of control he'd retained, vanished. Roughly he jerked her skirt to her waist and kneed her thighs apart, settling himself between the vulnerable V of her legs. She opened her eyes, a little shocked by what she could feel down there, but eager to know more. "Take off your clothes," she whispered frantically, and tore at the buttons on his shirt.

He reared back on his knees and tore his shirt open, then off. His naked skin glistened with a fine patina of sweat; in the dim light, filled with floating dust motes, the overlay of sleek bronze skin on powerful muscles gave him the look of live art sculpted by a master's hand. Mary's gaze moved hungrily, feverishly, over him. He was perfect, strong and male, the scent of his body hot and faintly musky. She reached out for him, her hands sliding over his broad chest, lightly haired in a diamond pattern stretching from nipple to nipple. She touched those tight little buds, and he froze, a massive shiver of pleasure rippling through his muscles.

He groaned aloud and dropped his hands to his belt. He unbuckled the wide band of leather, then unsnapped his jeans and jerked the zipper down, the hissing of the metal teeth blending with their harsh breathing. With some last desperate fragment of willpower, he kept himself from lowering his pants. She was a virgin; he couldn't allow himself to forget that, even in his urgency. Damn it, he had to regain some control, or he'd both scare and hurt her, and he would die before he turned her first time into a nightmare.

Mary's slim fingers curled in the hair on his chest and tugged lightly. "Wolf," she said. Just his name, just that one word, but her voice was warm and low and drugged sounding, and it beckoned him more powerfully than anything he'd known before.

"Yes," he said in response. "Now." He leaned forward to cover her again, then froze as a distant sound came to his ears.

He swore quietly and sank back on his heels, battling desperately to control his body and his frustration.

"Wolf?" Now her tone was hesitant, consternation and self-consciousness creeping into it. That inflection made him feel murderous, because she hadn't been self-conscious before. She had been warm and loving, willing to give herself without reserve.

"Joe will be here in a few minutes," he said flatly. "I can hear his truck coming up the mountain."

She was still so far out of it that she merely looked confused. "Joe?"

"Yes, Joe. Remember him? My son, the reason you're up here in the first place."

Her cheeks flooded with color, and she jerked into an

upright position, as far as she could, because her thighs were still draped over his. "Oh my God," she said. "Oh my God. I'm naked. You're naked. Oh my God."

"We're not naked," Wolf muttered, wiping his sweaty face. "Damn it."

"Almost!"

"Not enough." Even her breasts were rosy with embarrassment now. He looked at them with regret, remembering her sweet taste and the way her velvety little nipple had bloomed in his mouth. But the sound of the truck was much closer now, and with a low, obscene comment on his son's rotten timing, he got to his feet and effortlessly lifted Mary to hers.

Tears blurred her vision as she turned her back to fumble with that blasted space-age clasp on her bra. What ever had possessed her to buy such a contraption? Aunt Ardith would have been outraged. Aunt Ardith would have fallen on the ground in a hissy fit if she'd even thought of her niece *rolling naked in the hay* with a man. And, darn it, she hadn't even been able to finish her rolling!

"Here, I'll do it," Wolf said in a far gentler tone than she'd ever before heard from him. He turned her around and deftly handled the diabolical clasp. Mary kept her head down, unable to look him in the eye, but the contrast of his sun-bronzed hands against her pale breasts made her feel hot again. She swallowed and looked at his belt buckle. He'd zipped his jeans back up and buckled his belt, but the visible swell of his loins told her he wasn't completely unaffected by this interruption. That made her feel better, and she blinked the tears from her eyes as he helped her back into her dress and turned her around to zip it.

"You have hay in your hair," he teased, and picked the straw from the tangled tresses, then brushed it from her dress.

Mary put up both hands to discern the state of her hair and found it had come completely down. "Leave it," Wolf said. "I like it down. It looks like silk."

Nervously she combed her fingers through the strands and watched as he leaned down to pick up his shirt from the hay. "What will Joe think?" she blurted as the truck pulled to a stop outside the barn.

"That he's lucky he's my son, or I'd have killed him," Wolf muttered grimly, and Mary wasn't certain he was teasing. He put his shirt on but didn't bother buttoning it before stepping into the open door. Taking a deep breath, Mary braced herself to get through the embarrassment and followed him.

Joe had just gotten out of the truck, and now he stood beside the door, his ice-blue eyes moving from his father to Mary and back, taking in Wolf's stone face and open shirt, and Mary's tousled hair. "Damn it!" he swore and slammed the door shut. "If it had just taken me fifteen minutes longer—"

"My feelings exactly," Wolf concurred.

"Hey, I'll leave—"

Wolf sighed. "No. She came to see you anyway."

"That's what you said the first time." Joe grinned hugely.

"And I just said it again." He turned to Mary, and some of the enjoyment of her stunning news returned to his eyes. "Tell him."

She couldn't think. "Tell him?"

"Yeah. Tell him."

Slowly her dazed mind registered what he was saying. She looked in bewilderment at her empty hands. What had happened to the letters? Had they lost them in the hay? How mortifying it would be to have to search through the hay for them! Not knowing what else to do, she spread her hands and said simply, "You're in. I got the letter today."

Blood drained from Joe's face as he stared at her, and he reached out blindly to rest his hand on the truck as if to steady himself. "I got in? The Academy? I got into the Academy?" he asked hoarsely.

"You got the recommendation. It's up to you to pass the exams."

He threw back his head and screamed, an exultant, spine-chilling sound like that of a hunting panther, then leaped at Wolf. The two of them pounded each other's backs, laughing and yelling, then finally just hugging each other in a way two weaker men couldn't have done. Mary folded her hands and watched them, smiling, so happy her heart swelled to the point of pain. Then suddenly an arm reached out and snagged her, and she found herself sandwiched between the two Mackenzies, almost smashed flat by their celebration.

"You're smothering me!" she protested in a gasping voice, wedging her hands against two broad chests and pushing. One of those chests was bare, exposed by an unbuttoned shirt, and the touch of his warm skin made her go weak in the knees. Both of them laughed at her protest, but both of them immediately gentled their embrace.

Mary patted her hair down and smoothed her dress. "The letters are here somewhere. I must have dropped them."

Wolf gave her a wicked look. "You must have."

His teasing made her happy deep inside, and she smiled at him. It was a quietly intimate smile, the sort that a woman gives the man she loves after she has been in his arms, and it warmed him. To cover his reaction, he turned to look for the dropped letters and spotted one on the drive, while the other had fallen close to the barn door. He retrieved both of them, and gave Joe the one addressed to him.

The boy's hands shook as he read the letter, even though he already knew the contents. He couldn't believe it. It had happened so fast. A dream come true should have been harder to attain; he should have had to sweat blood to get it. Oh, he wasn't driving one of those twenty-million dollar babies yet, but he would. He had to, because he would be only half alive without wings.

Mary was watching him with proud indulgence when she felt Wolf stiffen beside her. She looked at him inquiringly. His head was lifted as if he scented danger, and his face was suddenly as impassive as stone. Then she heard the sound of an engine and turned as a deputy sheriff's car rolled to a stop behind Joe's truck.

Joe turned, and his face took on the same stony look as Wolf's as Clay Armstrong got out of the county car.

"Ma'am." Clay spoke to her first, tipping his hat.

"Deputy Armstrong." Two hundred years of strict training on social behavior were in her voice. Aunt Ardith would have been proud. But she sensed some threat to Wolf, and it was all she could do not to put herself between him and the deputy. Only the knowledge that he wouldn't appreciate the action kept her standing at his side.

Clay's friendly blue eyes weren't friendly at all now. "Why are you up here, Miss Potter?"

"Why are you asking?" she shot back, putting her hands on her hips.

"Just skip to the good part, Armstrong," Wolf snapped.

"Fine," Clay snapped back. "You're wanted for questioning. You can come with me now, the easy way, or I can get a warrant for your arrest."

Joe stood frozen, fury and hell in his eyes. This had happened before, and he'd lost his father for two nightmarish years. It seemed even more terrible this time, because just moments before they had been celebrating, and he'd been on top of the world.

Wolf began buttoning his shirt. In a voice like gravel he asked, "What happened this time?"

"We'll talk about that at the sheriff's office."

"We'll talk about it now."

Black eyes met blue, and abruptly Clay realized this man wouldn't move a foot unless he had some answers. "A girl was raped this morning."

Sulfuric rage burned in those night-dark eyes. "So naturally you thought of the Indian." He spat the words like bullets from between clenched teeth. God, this couldn't be happening again. Not twice in one lifetime. The first time had almost killed him, and he knew he'd never go back to that hellhole, no matter what he had to do.

"We're just questioning some people. If you have an alibi, there's no problem. You'll be free to go."

"I suppose you picked up every rancher in this area? Do you have Eli Baugh at the sheriff's office answering questions?"

Clay's face darkened with anger. "No."

"Just the Indian, huh?"

"You have priors." But Clay looked uncomfortable.

"I don't have...one...single...prior conviction," Wolf snarled. "I was *cleared*."

"Damn it, man, I know that!" Clay suddenly yelled. "I was told to pick you up, and I'm going to do my job."

"Well, why didn't you just say so? I wouldn't want to stop a man from doing his job." After that sarcastic jab, Wolf strode to his truck. "I'll follow you."

"You can ride in the car. I'll bring you back."

"No, thanks. I'd rather have my own wheels, just in case the sheriff decides a walk would do me good."

Swearing under his breath, Clay went to the car and got in. Dust and gravel flew from his tires as he headed back down the mountain, with Wolf behind him slinging even more dust and gravel.

Mary began shaking. At first it was just a tremor, but it swiftly escalated into shudders that rattled her entire body. Joe was standing as if turned to stone, his fists clenched. Suddenly he whirled and slammed his fist into the hood of his truck. "By God, they won't do it to him again," he whispered. *"Not again."*

"No, they certainly won't." She was still shaking, but she squared her shoulders. "If I have to get every judge and court in this country involved, I will. I'll call newspapers, I'll call television networks, I'll call—oh, they don't have any idea of who all I can call." The network of Old Family contacts she had left behind in Savannah was still there, and more favors would be called in than the sheriff of this county could count. She'd hang him out to dry!

"Why don't you go home?" Joe suggested in a flat tone.

"I want to stay."

He'd expected her to quietly walk to her car, but at her words he looked at her for the first time. Deep inside, part of him had thought she wouldn't be able to leave fast enough, that he and Wolf would be alone again, as they had always been. They were used to being alone. But Mary stood her ground as if she had no intention of budging off this mountain, her slate-blue eyes full of fire and her fragile chin lifted in the way that he'd learned meant others could just get out of her path.

The boy, forced by circumstance to grow up hard and fast, put his strong arms around the woman and held her, desperately absorbing some of her strength, because he was deathly afraid he'd need it. And Mary held him. He was Wolf's son, and she'd protect him with every ounce of fight she had.

It was after nine when they heard Wolf's truck, and both of them froze with mingled tension and relief: tension because they dreaded to hear what had happened, and relief because he was home instead of locked in jail. Mary couldn't imagine Wolf in jail, even though he'd spent two years in prison. He was too wild, like a lobo that could never be tamed. Imprisoning him had been an act so cruel as to be obscene.

He came in the back door and stood there staring at her, his dark face expressionless. She and Joe sat at the kitchen table, nursing cups of coffee. "Why are you still here? Go home."

She ignored the flatness of his tone. He was so angry she could almost feel the heat from across the room, but she knew it wasn't directed against her. Getting up, she dumped her lukewarm coffee into the sink and got another cup from the cabinet, then poured fresh coffee into both cups. "Sit down, drink your coffee and tell us what happened," she said in her best schoolteacher voice.

He did reach for the coffee, but he didn't sit down. He was too angry to sit. The rage boiled in him, robbing his movements of their usual fluidity. It was starting all over again, and he'd be damned if he'd go to prison again for something he hadn't done. He'd fight any way he could and with any weapon he could, but he'd die before he'd go back to prison.

"They let you go," Joe said.

"They had to. The girl was raped around noon. At noon I was delivering two horses to the Bar W R. Wally Rasco verified it, and the sheriff couldn't figure out a way I could have been in two different places, sixty miles apart, at the same time, so he had to let me go."

"Where did it happen?"

Wolf rubbed his forehead, then pinched his nose between his eyes as if he had a headache, or maybe he was just tired. "She was grabbed from behind when she got in her car, parked in her own driveway. He made her drive almost an hour before telling her to pull off on the side of the road. She never saw his face. He wore a ski mask. But she could tell he was tall, and that was enough of a description for the sheriff."

"The side of the road?" Mary blurted. "That's...weird. It doesn't make sense. I know there's not much traffic, but still, someone could have come by at any time."

"Yeah. Not to mention that he was waiting for her in her driveway. The whole thing is strange."

Joe drummed his fingers on the table. "It could have been someone passing through."

"How many people 'pass through' Ruth?" Wolf asked dryly. "Would a drifter have known whose car it was, or when she was likely to come out of the house? What if the car belonged to a man? That's a big chance to take, especially when rape seems to have been the only thing on his mind, because he didn't rob her, even though she had money."

"Are they keeping her identity secret?" Mary asked.

He looked at her. "It won't stay a secret, because her father was in the sheriff's office waving a rifle and threatening to blow my guts out. He attracted a lot of attention, and people talk."

His face was still expressionless, but Mary sensed the bitter rage that filled him. His fierce pride had been dragged in the dust—again. How had he endured being forced to sit there and listen to insults and threats? Because she knew he'd been insulted, by vile words describing his mixed heritage as well as by the very fact he'd been picked up for questioning. He was holding it all in, controlling it, but the rage was there.

"What happened?"

"Armstrong stopped it. Then Wally Rasco got there and cleared me, and the sheriff let me go with a friendly warning."

"A *warning*?" Mary jumped to her feet, her eyes flashing. "For what?"

He pinched her chin and gave her a coldly ferocious smile. "He warned me to stay away from white women, sweetcake. And that's just what I'm going to do. So you go on home now, and stay there. I don't want you on my mountain again."

"You didn't feel that way in the barn," she shot back, then darted a look at Joe and blushed. Joe just quirked an eyebrow and looked strangely self-satisfied. She decided to ignore him and turned back to Wolf. "I can't believe you're letting that mush-brain sheriff tell you who you can see."

He narrowed his eyes at her. "Maybe it hasn't dawned on you yet, but it's all starting again. It doesn't matter that Wally Rasco cleared me. Everyone is going to remember what happened ten years ago, and the way they felt."

"You were cleared of that, too, or doesn't that count?"

"With some people," he finally admitted. "Not with most. They're already afraid of me, already distrust and dislike me. Until this bastard is caught, I probably won't be able to buy anything in that town, not groceries, gas or feed. And any white woman who has anything to do with me could be in real danger of being tarred and feathered.''

So that was it. He was still trying to protect her. She stared at him in exasperation. ''Wolf, I refuse to live my life according to someone else's prejudices. I appreciate that you're trying to protect me—''

She could hear an audible click as his teeth snapped together. ''Do you?'' he asked with heavy sarcasm. ''Then go home. Stay home, and I'll stay here.''

''For how long?''

Instead of answering her question, he made an oblique statement. ''I'll always be a half-breed.''

''And I'll always be what *I* am, too. I haven't asked you to change,'' she pointed out, pain creeping into her voice. She looked at him with longing plain in her eyes, as no woman had ever looked at him before, and the rage in him intensified because he couldn't simply reach out and take her in his arms, proclaim to the world that she was his woman. The sheriff's warning had been clear enough, and Wolf knew well that the hostility toward him would rapidly swell to explosive proportions. It could easily spill over onto Mary, and now he wasn't just worried that she would lose her job. A job was nothing compared to the physical danger she could suffer. She could be terrorized in her own home, her property vandalized; she could be cursed and spat upon; she could be physically attacked. For all her sheer determination, she was still just a rather slight woman, and she would be helpless against anyone who wanted to hurt her.

''I know,'' he finally said, and despite himself, he reached out to touch her hair. ''Go home, Mary. When this is over—'' He stopped, because he didn't want to make promises he might not be able to keep, but what he'd said was enough to put a glowing light in her eyes.

"All right," she murmured, putting her hand on his. "By the way, I want you to get a haircut."

He looked startled. "A haircut?"

"Yes. You want me to wear my hair down, and I want you to get a haircut."

"Why?"

She gave him a shrewd look. "You don't wear it long because you're Indian. You wear it long just to upset people, so they'll never forget your Indian blood. So get it cut."

"Short hair won't make me less Indian."

"Long hair won't make you more Indian."

She looked as if she would stand there until doomsday unless he agreed to get a haircut. He gave in abruptly, muttering, "All right, I'll get a haircut."

"Good." She smiled at him and went on tiptoe to kiss the corner of his mouth. "Good night. Good night, Joe."

"Goodnight, Mary."

When she was gone, Wolf wearily ran his hand through his hair, then frowned as he realized he'd just agreed to cut it off. He looked up to find Joe watching him steadily.

"What are we going to do?" the boy asked.

"Whatever we have to," Wolf replied, his expression flinty.

When Mary bought groceries the next morning, she found everyone in the store huddling together in small groups of two or three and whispering about the rape. The girl's identity was quickly revealed; it was Cathy Teele, whose younger sister, Christa, was in Mary's class. The entire Teele family was devastated, according to the whispers Mary heard as she gathered her groceries.

Next to the flour and cornmeal, she encountered Dottie Lancaster, who was flanked by a young man Mary assumed was Dottie's son. "Hello, Dottie." Mary greeted the woman pleasantly, even though it was possible Dottie had started the rumor about her and Joe.

"Hello." Dottie wore a distressed expression, rather than her habitual sour one. "Have you heard about that poor Teele girl?"

"I haven't heard anything else since I entered the store."

"They arrested that Indian, but the sheriff had to let him go. I hope now you'll be more careful about the company you keep."

"Wolf wasn't arrested." Mary managed to keep her voice calm. "He was questioned, but he was at Wally Rasco's ranch when the attack occurred, and Mr. Rasco backed him up. Wolf Mackenzie isn't a rapist."

"A court of law said he was and sentenced him to prison."

"He was also cleared when the true rapist was caught and confessed to the crime for which Wolf had been convicted."

Dottie drew back, her face livid. "That's what that Indian said, but as far as we know, he just got out on parole. It's easy to see whose side you're on, but then, you've been running with those Indians since the day you came to Ruth. Well, miss, there's an old saying that if you sleep with dogs, you're bound to get fleas. The Mackenzies are dirty Indian trash—"

"Don't you say another word," Mary interrupted, color high in her cheeks as she took a step toward Dottie. She was furious; her hand itched to slap the woman's self-righteous face. Aunt Ardith had said that a lady never brawled, but Mary was ready to forever relinquish any claim she had to the title. "Wolf is a decent, hard-working man, and I won't let you or anyone else say he isn't."

Dottie's color was mottled, but something in Mary's eyes

made her refrain from saying anything else about Wolf. Instead she leaned closer and hissed, "You'd better watch yourself, Miss Goody-Goody, or you'll find yourself in a lot of trouble."

Mary leaned closer, too, her jaw set. "Are you threatening me?" she demanded fiercely.

"Mama, please," the young man behind her whispered in a frantic tone, and tugged at Dottie's arm.

Dottie looked around at him, and her face changed. She drew back, but told Mary contemptuously, "You just mark my words," and stalked away.

Her son, Bobby, was so distressed he was wringing his hands as he hurried after Dottie. Immediately, Mary was sorry she had let the horrid little scene develop; from what Joe had told her, Bobby had a hard enough time handling everyday problems without adding more.

She took a few deep breaths to regain her composure, but almost lost it again when she turned and found several people standing in the aisle, staring at her. They had all obviously heard every word, and looked both shocked and avid. She had no doubt the tale would be all over town within the hour: two of the schoolteachers brawling over Wolf Mackenzie. She groaned inwardly as she picked up a bag of flour. Another scandal was just what Wolf needed.

In the next aisle, she met Cicely Karr. Remembering the woman's comments during the school board meeting, Mary couldn't stop herself from saying, "I've received a letter from Senator Allard, Mrs. Karr. He's recommending Joe Mackenzie for admission to the Academy." She sounded challenging even to her own ears.

To her surprise, Mrs. Karr looked excited. "He is? Why, I never would've believed it. Until Eli explained it to me, I didn't quite realize what an honor it is." Then she sobered. "But now this terrible thing has happened. It's awful. I—I couldn't help overhearing you and Dottie Lancaster. Miss Potter, you can't imagine what it was like ten years ago. People were frightened and angry, and now the same nightmare has started again.''

"It's a nightmare for Wolf Mackenzie, too," Mary said hotly. "He was sent to prison for a rape he didn't commit. His record was cleared, but still he was the first person the sheriff picked up for questioning. How do you think he feels? He'll never get back the two years he spent in prison, and now it looks as if everyone is trying to send him there again."

Mrs. Karr looked troubled. "We were all wrong before. The justice system was wrong, too. But even though Mackenzie proved he didn't rape Cathy Teele, don't you see why the sheriff wanted to question him?"

"No, I don't."

"Because Mackenzie had reason to want revenge."

Mary was aghast. "So you thought he'd take revenge by attacking a young woman who was just a child when he was sent to prison? What sort of man do you think he is?" She was horrified by both the idea and the feeling that everyone in Ruth would agree with Mrs. Karr.

"I think he's a man who hates," Mrs. Karr said firmly. Yes, she believed Wolf capable of such horrible, obscene revenge; it was in her eyes.

Mary felt sick; she began shaking her head. "No," she said. "No. Wolf is bitter about the way he was treated, but he doesn't hate. And he would never hurt a woman like that." If she knew anything in this world, she knew that. She had felt urgency in his touch, but never brutality.

But Mrs. Karr was shaking her head, too. "Don't tell me he doesn't hate! It's in those black-as-hell eyes every time he looks at us, any of us. The sheriff found out he'd been in Vietnam, in some special assassination group, or something. God only knows how it warped him! Maybe he didn't rape Cathy Teele, but this would be a perfect opportunity for him to get revenge and have it blamed on whoever *did* rape her!''

"If Wolf wanted revenge, he wouldn't sneak around to get it," Mary said scornfully. "You don't know anything about the kind of man he is, do you? He's lived here for years, and none of you *know* him.''

"And I suppose you do?" Mrs. Karr was getting red in the face. "Maybe we're talking about a different kind of 'knowing.' Maybe that rumor about you carrying on with Joe Mackenzie was half right, after all. You've been carrying on with *Wolf* Mackenzie, haven't you?''

The scorn in the woman's voice enraged Mary. "Yes!" she half shouted, and honesty impelled her to add, "But not as much as I'd like.''

A chorus of gasps made her look around, and she stared into the faces of the townspeople who had stopped in the aisle to listen. Well, she'd really done it now; Wolf had wanted her to distance herself from him, and instead she'd all but shouted from the rooftops that she'd been "carrying on" with him. But she couldn't feel even the tiniest bit of shame. She felt proud. With Wolf Mackenzie she was a woman, not a dowdy, old maid schoolteacher who even owned a cat, for heaven's sake. She didn't feel dowdy when she was with Wolf; she felt warm, wanted. If she had any regrets, it was that Joe hadn't been fifteen minutes later returning the day before, or even five minutes, because more than anything she wanted to be Wolf's woman in every way, to lie beneath his thrusting body, eagerly accepting the force of his passion and giving him her own. If for that, for loving him, she was ostracized, then she counted society well lost.

Mrs. Karr said icily, "I believe we'll have to have another school board meeting."

"When you do, consider that I have an ironclad contract," Mary shot back, and turned on her heel. She hadn't gathered all of the groceries she needed, but she was too angry to continue. When she plunked the items down on the counter, the clerk looked as if she wanted to refuse to ring them up, but she changed her mind under Mary's glare.

She stormed home and was gratified when the weather seemed to agree with her, if the gray clouds forming overhead were any indication. After storing her groceries, she checked on the cat, who had been acting strange lately. A horrid thought intruded: surely no one would have poisoned the cat? But Woodrow was sunning himself peacefully on the rug, so she dismissed the idea with relief.

When this is over...

The phrase echoed in her memory, tantalizing her and stirring an ache deep inside. She longed for him so intensely that she felt as if she were somehow incomplete. She loved him, and though she understood why he thought it better for her to stay away from him right now, she didn't agree. After what had happened that morning with Dottie Lancaster and Cicely Karr, there was no point in allowing this exile. She might as well have stood in the middle of the street and shouted it: she was Wolf Mackenzie's woman.

Whatever he wanted from her, she was willing to give. Aunt Ardith had raised her to believe that intimacy belonged only in marriage, if a woman for some reason felt she simply *couldn't* live without a man, though Aunt Ardith had made it plain she couldn't imagine what such a reason would be. While Mary had accepted that people obviously were intimate outside of marriage, she had never been tempted to it herself—until she'd met Wolf. If he wanted her for only a short time, she counted that as better than nothing. Even one day with him would be a bright and shining memory to treasure during the long, dreary years without him, a small bit of warmth to comfort her. Her dream was to spend a lifetime with him, but she didn't allow herself to expect it. He was too bitter, too wary; it was unlikely he would permit an Anglo to get that close to him. He would give her his body, perhaps even his affection, but not his heart or his commitment.

Because she loved him, she knew she wouldn't demand more. She didn't want anger or guilt between them. For as long as she could, in whatever way, she wanted to make Wolf happy.

He had asked her to wear her hair down, and the silky weight of it lay around her shoulders. She had been surprised, looking in the mirror that morning, how the relaxed hairstyle softened her face. Her eyes had glowed, because leaving her hair down was something she could do for him. She looked feminine, the way he made her feel.

There was no point in trying to make people think her neutral now, not after those arguments she'd gotten into. When she told him what had happened, he'd see the uselessness of trying to maintain the sham. She even felt relieved, because her heart hadn't been in it.

She had started to change into one of her shapeless housedresses when she caught sight of herself in the mirror and paused. In her mind she relived that moment the day she'd first met Wolf, when he'd seen her in Joe's old jeans and his eyes had momentarily widened with a look so hot and male it had the power, even now, to make her shake. She wanted him to look at her like that again, but he wasn't likely to as long as she kept wearing these—these *feed sacks*!

Suddenly she was dissatisfied with all her clothing. Her

dresses were, without exception, sturdy and modest, but they were also too drab and loose-fitting. Her slight build would be better displayed in delicate cottons and light, cheerful colors, or even hip-hugging jeans. She turned and looked at her bottom in the mirror; it was slim and curvy. She could see no reason why she should be ashamed of it. It was a very nice bottom, as bottoms went.

Muttering to herself, she zipped herself back into her serviceable ''good'' dress and grabbed her purse. Ruth wouldn't offer much in the way of new clothes, but she could certainly buy some jeans and sassy little tops, as well as some neat skirts and blouses that, above all, actually fit her.

And she never wanted to see another ''sensible'' shoe in her life.

The gray clouds lived up to their promise, and it began to rain as she made the drive into town. It was a steady rain, just the sort ranchers and farmers everywhere loved, rather than a downpour that simply ran off instead of soaking into the ground. Aunt Ardith wouldn't have set foot out of the house during a rain, but Mary ignored it. She stopped first at the one store in Ruth that dealt exclusively in women's clothing, though by necessity the clothes weren't hot from a fashion show in Paris. She bought three pairs of jeans, size six, two lightweight cotton sweaters, and a blue chambray shirt that made her feel like a pioneer. A snazzy denim skirt, paired with a ruby-red sweater, flattered her so much she spun on her heel in delight, just like a child. She also chose a brown skirt, which fit so well she couldn't turn it down despite the color, and teamed a crisp pink blouse with it. Her final choice was a pale lavender cotton skirt and matching top, which sported a delicate lace collar. Still in a fit of defiance and delight, she picked out a pair of dressy white sandals as well as a pair of track shoes. When the saleswoman rang them up and called out the total, Mary didn't even blink an eye. This had been too long in coming.

Nor was she finished. She locked her packages in the car and dashed through the rain to Hearst's general store, where everyone bought boots. Since Mary planned to be spending most of her time on Wolf's mountain, she figured she'd need a pair.

Mr. Hearst was almost rude to her, but she stared him down and briefly thought of shaking her schoolteacher's finger at him. She discarded the idea because the finger lost its power if used too often, and she might really need it sometime in the future. So she ignored him and tried on boots until she finally found a pair that felt comfortable on her feet.

She couldn't wait to get home and put on her jeans and chambray shirt; she might even wear her boots around the house to get them broken in, she thought. Woodrow wouldn't know her. She thought of that look in Wolf's eyes and began to shiver.

Her car was parked up the street, a block away, and it was raining hard enough now that she made a disgusted noise at herself for not driving from the clothing store to Hearst's. Ruth didn't have sidewalks, and already huge puddles were standing on the pavement. Well, she had on her sensible shoes; let them earn their keep!

Putting her head down and holding the box containing her boots up in an effort to ward off part of the rain, she darted from the sheltering overhang of the roof and immediately got wet to the ankles when she stepped into a puddle. She was still grumbling to herself about that when she passed the small alley that ran between the general store and the next building, which had formerly been a barbershop but now stood empty.

She didn't hear anything or see a flurry of movement; she had no warning at all. A big hand, wet with rain, clamped over her mouth, and an arm wrapped around the front of her body, effectively holding her arms down as her attacker began hauling her down the alley, away from the street. Mary fought instinctively, wriggling and kicking while she made muffled sounds behind the man's palm. His hand was so tight on her face that his fingers dug painfully into her cheek.

The tall, wet weeds in the alley stung her legs, and the pounding rain stung her eyes. Terrified, she kicked harder. This couldn't be happening! He couldn't just carry her off in broad daylight! But he could; he had done it to Cathy Teele.

She got one arm free and reached back, clawing for his face. Her desperate fingers found only wet, woolly cloth. He cursed, his voice low and raspy, and hit her on the side of the head with his fist.

Her senses blurred as her head was rocked with pain, and her struggles grew aimless. Vaguely she was aware when they reached the end of the alley and he dragged her behind the abandoned building.

His breathing was fast and harsh in her ear as he forced her down on her stomach in the gravel and mud. She managed to get her arm free again and put her hand out to break her fall; the gravel scraped her palm, but she barely felt it. His hand was still over her mouth, suffocating her; he ground her face into the wet dirt and held her down with his heavy weight on her back.

He scrabbled with his other hand for her skirt, pulling it up. Wildly she clawed at his hand, trying to pull it free so she could scream, and he hit her again. She was terrified and kept clawing. Cursing, he forced her legs apart and thrust himself against her. She could feel him through his pants and her undergarments, pushing at her, and began gagging. *God, no!*

She heard her clothing tear, and overpowering revulsion gave her strength. She bit savagely at his hand and reached back for his eyes, her nails digging for flesh.

There was a roaring in her ears, but she heard a shout. The man on top of her stiffened, then braced his hand beside her head and used it to balance himself as he leaped to his feet. Her vision blurred by rain and mud, she saw only a blue sleeve and a pale, freckled hand before he was gone. From above and behind her came a loud boom, and vaguely she wondered if now she would be struck by lightning. No, lightning came before the thunder.

Running footsteps pounded the ground, going past her. Mary lay still, her body limp and her eyes closed.

She heard low cursing, and the footsteps returned. "Mary," a commanding voice said. "Are you all right?"

She managed to open her eyes and looked up at Clay Armstrong. He was soaked to the skin, his blue eyes furious, but his hands were gentle as he turned her onto her back and lifted her in his arms.

"Are you all right?" The words were sharper now.

The rain stung her face. "Yes," she managed, and turned her head into his shoulder.

"I'll get him," Clay promised. "I swear to you, I'll get the bastard."

There was no doctor in town, but Bessie Pylant was a registered nurse, and Clay carried Mary to Bessie's house. Bessie called the private practitioner for whom she worked and got him to drive over from the next town. In the meantime she carefully cleaned Mary's scrapes and put ice on the bruises, and began pouring hot, too-sweet tea down her.

Clay had disappeared. Bessie's house was suddenly full

of women; Sharon Wycliffe came and assured Mary that she and Dottie could handle things on Monday if Mary didn't feel like working; Francie Beecham told tales of her own teaching days, her purpose obvious, and the other women took their cues from her. Mary sat quietly, clutching so tightly at the blanket Bessie had wrapped around her that her knuckles were white. She knew the women were trying to divert her, and was grateful to them; with rigid control she concentrated on their commonplace chatter. Even Cicely Karr came and patted Mary's hand, despite the argument they'd had only a few hours before.

Then the doctor arrived, and Bessie led Mary into a bedroom for privacy while the doctor examined her. She answered his questions in a subdued voice, though she winced when he probed the sore place on the side of her head where the man had struck her with his fist. He checked her pupil response and her blood pressure, and gave her a mild sedative.

"You'll be all right," he finally said, patting her knee. "There's no concussion, so your headache should go away soon. A good night's sleep will do more for you than anything I can prescribe."

"Thank you for driving out here," Mary said politely.

Desperation was growing in her. Everyone had been wonderful, but she could feel a fine wire inside her being coiled tighter and tighter. She felt dirty and exposed. She needed privacy and a shower, and more than anything she needed Wolf.

She left the bedroom and found that Clay had returned. He came to her immediately and took her hand. "How are you feeling?"

"I'm all right." If she had to say that one more time, she thought she would scream.

"I need a statement from you, if you think you can do it now."

"Yes, all right." The sedative was taking effect; she could feel the spreading sensation of remoteness as the drug numbed her emotions. She let Clay lead her to a chair and pulled the blanket tight around her once more. She felt chilled.

"You don't have to be afraid," Clay soothed. "He's been picked up. He's in custody now."

That aroused her interest, and she stared at him. "Picked up? You know who it is?"

"I saw him." The iron was back in Clay's voice.

"But he was wearing a ski mask." She remembered that, remembered feeling the woolly fabric under her fingers.

"Yeah, but his hair was hanging out from under the mask in back."

Mary stared up at him, the numbness in her changing into a kind of horror. His hair was long enough to hang out from under the mask? Surely Clay didn't think—surely not! She felt sick. "Wolf?" she whispered.

"Don't worry. I told you he's in custody."

She clenched her fists so tightly that her nails dug crescents in her palms. "Then let him go."

Clay looked stunned, then angry. "Let him go! Damn, Mary, can't you get it through your head that he attacked you?"

Slowly she shook her head, her face white. "No, he didn't."

"I saw him," Clay said, spacing out each word. "He was tall and had long black hair. Damn it, who else could it have been?"

"I don't know, but it wasn't Wolf."

The women were silent, sitting frozen as they listened to

the argument. Cicely Karr spoke up. "We did try to warn you, Mary."

"Then you warned me about the wrong man!" Her eyes burning, Mary stared around the room, then turned her gaze back to Clay. "I saw his hands! He was a white man, an *Anglo*. He had freckled hands. *It wasn't Wolf Mackenzie!*"

Clay's brow creased in a frown. "Are you certain about that?"

"Positive. He put his hand on the ground right in front of my eyes." She reached out and grabbed his sleeve. "Get Wolf out of jail, right now. Right now, do you hear me! And he'd better not have a bruise on him!"

Clay got up and went to the telephone, and once again Mary looked at the women in the room. They were all pale and worried. Mary could guess why. As long as they had suspected Wolf, they had had a safe target for their fear and anger. Now they had to look at themselves, at someone who was one of them. A lot of men in the area had freckled hands, but Wolf didn't. His hands were lean and dark, bronzed by the sun, callused from years of hard manual work and riding. She had felt them on her bare skin. She wanted to shout that Wolf had no reason to attack her, because he could have her any time he wanted, but she didn't. The numbness was returning. She just wanted to wait for Wolf, if he came at all.

An hour later he walked into Bessie's house as if he owned it, without knocking. An audible gasp rose when he appeared in the doorway, his broad shoulders reaching almost from beam to beam. He didn't even glance at the other people in the room. His eyes were on Mary, huddled in her blanket, her face colorless.

His boots rang on the floor as he crossed to her and hunkered down. His black eyes raked her from head to toe; then he touched her chin, turning her head toward the light so he could see the scrape on her cheek and the bruises where hard fingers had bitten into her soft flesh. He lifted her hands and examined her raw palms. His jaw was like granite.

Mary wanted to cry, but instead she managed a wobbly smile. "You got a haircut," she said softly, and linked her fingers together to keep from running them through the thick, silky strands that lay perfectly against his well-shaped head.

"First thing this morning," he murmured. "Are you all right?"

"Yes. He—he didn't manage to...you know."

"I know." He stood. "I'll be back later. I'm going to get him. I promise you, I'll get him."

Clay said sharply, "That's a matter for the law."

Wolf's eyes were cold black fire. "The law isn't doing a very good job." He walked out without another word, and Mary felt chilled again. While he had been there, life had begun tingling in her numb body, but now it was gone. He had said he would be back, but she thought she should go home. Everyone was very kind, too kind; she felt as if she would scream. She couldn't handle any more.

Though he was stunned by Wolf's changed appearance, it took Clay only a moment to follow him. As he had suspected, Wolf stopped his truck at the alley where Mary had been attacked. By the time Clay parked the county car and entered the alley, Wolf was down on one knee, examining the muddy ground. He didn't even glance up when Clay approached. Instead he continued his concentrated examination of every weed and bit of gravel, every scuff mark, every indentation.

Clay said, "When did you get a haircut?"

"This morning. At the barbershop in Harpston."

"Why?"

"Because Mary asked me to," Wolf said flatly, and returned his attention to the ground.

Slowly he moved down the alley and to the back of the buildings, pausing at the spot where Mary's attacker had thrust her to the ground. Then he moved on, following exactly the path the attacker had taken, and it was in the next alley that he gave a grunt of satisfaction and knelt beside a blurred footprint.

Clay had been over the ground himself, and so had many other people. He said as much to Wolf. "That print could belong to anyone."

"No. It's made by a soft-soled shoe, not a boot." After examining the print awhile longer, he said, "He toes in slightly when he walks. I'd guess he weighs about one seventy-five, maybe one eighty. He isn't in very good shape. He was already tired when he got this far.''

Clay felt uneasy. Some people would have simply passed off that kind of tracking ability as part of Wolf's Indian heritage, but they would have been wrong. There were excellent trackers of wildlife who could follow a man's footsteps in the wilderness as easily as if he had wet paint on the bottoms of his boots, but the details Wolf had discerned would have been noted only by someone who had been trained to hunt other men. Nor did he doubt what Wolf had told him, because he had seen other men, though not many, who could track like that.

"You were in Nam." He already knew that, but suddenly it seemed far more significant.

Wolf was still examining the footprint. "Yes. You?"

"Twenty-first Infantry. What outfit were you with?"

Wolf looked up, and a very slight, unholy smile touched his lips. "I was a LRRP."

Clay's uneasy feeling became a chill. The LRRPs, pronounced "lurp," were men on long-range reconnaissance patrol. Unlike the regular grunts, the LRRPs spent weeks in the jungles and hill country, living off the land, hunting and being hunted. They survived only by their wits and ability to fight, or to fade away into the shadows, whichever the situation demanded. Clay had seen them come in from the bush, lean and filthy, smelling like the wild animals they essentially were, with death in their eyes and their nerves so raw, so wary, that it was dangerous to touch them unexpectedly, or walk up to their backs. Sometimes they hadn't been able to bear the touch of another human being until their nerves settled down. A smart man walked lightly around a LRRP fresh in from the field.

What was in Wolf's eyes now was cold and deadly, an anger so great Clay could only guess at its force, though he understood it. Wolf smiled again, and in the calmest tone imaginable, one almost gentle, he said, "He made a mistake."

"What was that?"

"He hurt *my* woman."

"It's not your place to hunt him. It's a matter for the law."

"Then the law had better stay close to my heels," Wolf said, and walked away.

Clay stared after him, not even surprised by the blunt words claiming Mary as his woman. The chill ran down his back again and he shivered. The town of Ruth had made a mistake in judging this man, but the rapist had made an even bigger one, one that might prove fatal.

Mary stoically ignored all the protests and pleas when she announced her intention of driving home. They meant well, and she appreciated their concern, but she couldn't stay another moment. She was physically unharmed, and the doctor had said her headache would fade in the next few hours. She simply had to go home.

So she drove alone in the misting rain, her movements automatic. Afterward, she could never recall a moment of the drive. All she was aware of when she let herself into the creaky old house was a feeling of intense relief, and it so frightened her that she pushed it away. She couldn't afford to let herself relax, not now. Maybe later. Right now she had to hold herself together very tightly.

Woodrow looped around her ankles several times, meowing plaintively. Mary stirred herself to feed him, though he was as fat as a butterball already, then found herself exhausted by that brief effort. She sat down at the table and folded her hands in her lap, holding herself motionless.

That was how Wolf found her half an hour later, just as

the gray daylight began to fade. "Why didn't you wait for me?" he asked from the doorway, his tone a low, gentle growl.

"I had to come home," Mary explained.

"I would have brought you."

"I know."

He sat down at the table beside her and took her cold, tightly clasped hands in his. She looked at him steadily, and his heart clenched like a fist in his chest.

He would have given anything never to have seen that look in her eyes.

She had always been so indomitable, with her "damn the torpedoes" spirit. She was slight and delicately made, but in her own eyes she had been invincible. Because the very idea of defeat was foreign to her, she had blithely moved through life arranging it to suit herself and accepted it as only natural that shopkeepers quaked before her wagging finger. That attitude had sometimes irritated, but more often entranced, him. The kitten thought herself a tiger, and because she acted like a tiger, other people had given way.

She was no longer indomitable. A horrible vulnerability was in her eyes, and he knew she would never forget the moments when she had been helpless. That scum had hurt her, humiliated her, literally ground her into the dirt.

"Do you know what really horrified me?" she asked after a long silence.

"What?"

"That I wanted the first time to be with you, and he was going to—" She stopped abruptly, unable to finish.

"But he didn't."

"No. He pulled up my skirt and pushed against me, and he was tearing my clothes when Clay—I think Clay shouted. He might have fired a shot. I remember hearing a roaring sound, but I thought it was thunder."

Her flat little monotone bothered him, and he realized she was still in shock. "I won't let him get near you again. I give you my word."

She nodded, then closed her eyes.

"You're going to take a shower," Wolf said, urging her to her feet. "A long, warm shower, and while you're taking it, I'll fix something for you to eat. What would you like?"

She tried to think of something, but even the thought of food was repugnant. "Just tea."

He walked upstairs with her; she was steady, but the steadiness seemed fragile, as if she were barely holding herself under control. He wished that she would cry, or yell, anything that would break the tension encasing her.

"I'll just get my nightgown. You don't mind if I get my nightgown, do you?" She looked anxious, as if afraid she was being too troublesome.

"No." He started to reach out and touch her, to slide his arm around her waist, but dropped his hand before contact was made. She might not want anyone to touch her. A sick feeling grew in him as he realized she might find his, and any other man's, touch disgusting now.

Mary got her nightgown and stood docilely in the old-fashioned bathroom while Wolf adjusted the water. "I'll be downstairs," he said as he straightened and stepped back. "Leave the door unlocked."

"Why?" Her eyes were big and solemn.

"In case you faint, or need me."

"I won't faint."

He smiled a little. No, Miss Mary Elizabeth Potter wouldn't faint; she wouldn't allow herself to be so weak. Maybe it wasn't tension holding her so straight; it might be the iron in her backbone.

He knew he wouldn't be able to coax her to eat much, if anything, but he heated a can of soup anyway. His timing was perfect; the soup had just boiled and the tea finished steeping when Mary entered the kitchen.

She hadn't thought to put on a robe; she wore only the nightgown, a plain white cotton eyelet garment. Wolf felt himself begin to sweat, because as demure as the nightgown was, he could still see the darkness of her nipples through the fabric. He swore silently as she sat down at the table like an obedient child; now wasn't the time for lust. But telling himself that didn't stop it; he wanted her, under any circumstances.

She ate the soup mechanically, without protest, and drank the tea, then thanked him for making it. Wolf cleared the table and washed up the few dishes; when he turned, Mary was still sitting at the table, her hands folded and her eyes staring at nothing. He froze briefly and muttered a curse. He couldn't bear it another minute. Swiftly he lifted her out of the chair and sat down in it, then settled her on his lap.

She was stiff in his arms for a moment; then a sigh filtered between her lips as she relaxed against his chest. "I was so frightened," she whispered.

"I know, honey."

"How can you know? You're a man." She sounded faintly truculent.

"Yeah, but I was in prison, remember?" He wondered if she would know what he was talking about, and he saw her brow furrow as she thought.

Then she said, "Oh." She began scowling fiercely. "If anyone hurt you—" she began.

"Hold it! No, I wasn't attacked. I'm good at fighting, and everyone knew it." He didn't tell her how he'd established a reputation for himself. "But it happened to other prisoners, and I knew it could happen to me, so I was always on guard." He'd slept only in light naps, with a knife made from a sharpened spoon always in his hand; his cell had hidden a variety of weapons, a lot of which the guards had seen and not recognized for what they were. It would have taken another LRRP to have seen some of the things he'd done and the weapons he'd carried. Yeah, he'd been on guard.

"I'm glad," she said, then suddenly bent her head against his throat and began to cry. Wolf held her tightly, his fingers laced through her hair to press against her skull and hold her to him. Her soft, slender body shook with sobs as she wound her arms around his neck. She didn't say anything else, and neither did he, but they didn't need words.

He cradled her until finally she sniffed and observed dazedly, "I need to blow my nose."

He stretched to reach the napkin holder and plucked a napkin from it to place in her hands. Mary blew her nose in a very ladylike manner, then sat still, searching in her depths for the best way to handle what had happened. She knew it could have been much worse, but it had been bad enough. Only one thought surfaced: she didn't want to be alone tonight. She hadn't been able to tolerate the women fussing around her, but if Wolf would just stay with her, she'd be all right.

She looked up at him. "Will you stay with me tonight?"

Every muscle in his big body tensed, but there was no way he could deny her. "You know I will. I'll sleep on the—"

"No. I mean—if you could sleep with me tonight, and hold me so I won't be alone, just for tonight, I think I'll be all right tomorrow."

He hoped it would be that easy for her, but he doubted it. The memories would linger on, springing out from dark corners to catch her when she least expected it. Until the day she died, she would never entirely forget, and for that he wanted to catch her assailant and break the guy's neck. Literally.

"I'll call Joe and let him know where I am," he said, and lifted her from his lap.

It was still early, but her eyelids were drooping, and after he called Joe he decided there was no point in putting it off. She needed to be in bed.

He turned out the lights and put his arm around her as they climbed the narrow stairs together. Her flesh was warm and resilient beneath the thin cotton, and the feel of her made his heart begin a slow, heavy beat. His jaw clenched as blood throbbed through his body, pooling in his groin. He was in for a miserable night, and he knew it.

Her bedroom was so old-fashioned it looked turn-of-the-century, but he hadn't expected anything else. The delicate lilac smell he associated with Mary was stronger up here. The ache in his loins intensified.

"I hope the bed is big enough for you," she said, worrying as she eyed the double bed.

"It'll do." It wasn't big enough, but it would do. He'd have to spend the night curled around her. Her bottom would be nestled against him, and he would quietly go insane. Suddenly he didn't know if he could do it, if he could lie with her all night and not take her. No matter what his mind said, his body knew exactly what it wanted; he was already so hard it was all he could do to keep from groaning.

"Which side do you want?"

What did it matter? Torment was torment, no matter what side he was on. "The left."

Mary nodded and turned back the covers. Wolf wanted to look away as she climbed into bed, but his eyes wouldn't obey. He saw the curve of her buttocks as the nightgown was momentarily pulled tight. He saw her pale, slim legs and immediately pictured them clasped around his waist. He saw the outline of her pretty breasts with their rosy nipples, and he remembered the feel of her breasts in his hands, her nipples in his mouth, her smell and taste.

Abruptly he bent down and pulled the sheet up over her. "I have to take a shower."

He saw the brief dart of fear at being alone in her eyes, but then she conquered it and said, "The towels are in the closet next to the bathroom door."

He was swearing savagely to himself as he stood in the bathroom, jerking his clothes off. A cold shower wouldn't help; he'd had a lot of them lately, and the effect was remarkably short-lived. He needed Mary—naked, beneath him, sheathing his swollen and throbbing flesh. She would be so tight that he wouldn't last a minute—

Damn. He couldn't leave her, not tonight. No matter what it cost him.

His entire body was aching as he stood under the warm, beating water. He couldn't crawl into bed with her like this. The last thing she needed right now was to have him poking at her all night. She needed comfort, not lust. Not only that, he wasn't entirely certain of his control. He'd been too long without a woman, had wanted *her* for too long.

He couldn't leave her, but he couldn't go to her like this. He knew what he had to do, and his soapy hand slid down his body. At least this would give him some modicum of control, because he would rather slit his own throat than see that fear and vulnerability in Mary's eyes again.

She was lying very still when he rejoined her, and she didn't move as he turned out the light. It wasn't until his weight depressed the mattress that she shifted to lie on her side. He positioned himself on his side, too, and hooked an arm around her waist to pull her firmly back into the cradle of his body. She sighed, and he felt the tension slowly ebb from her body as she relaxed against him.

"This is nice," she whispered.

"You aren't afraid?"

"Of you? No. Never of you." Her tone was liquid with tenderness. She lifted her hand to reach back and cup his jaw in her palm. "I'll be all right in the morning, wait and see. I'm just too tired right now to deal with it. Will you hold me all night?"

"If you want me to."

"Please."

He brushed her hair to one side and pressed a kiss into the nape of her neck, delighting in the delicate little shiver that rippled through her body when he did so. "My pleasure," he said gently. "Good night, sweetheart."

It was the storm that woke her. It was barely dawn, the light still dim, though the black clouds contributed to the grayness. The storm was fierce, reminding her of the ferocious thunderstorms in the South. Lightning ripped the dark sky apart, and the booming thunder made the very air vibrate. She lazily counted the seconds between the lightning flashes and the thunder to see how far away the storm was: seven miles. But it was pouring rain, the sound loud on the old tin roof. It was wonderful.

She felt both acutely alive and deeply calm, as if she were waiting for something. Yesterday was, by its very definition, in the past. It could no longer hurt her. Today was the present, and the present was Wolf.

He wasn't in the bed, but she knew he had been there during the night. Even in sleep she had sensed him, felt his strong arms holding her. Sleeping together was a joy so deep she couldn't express it, as if it had been meant to be. Perhaps it had been. She couldn't stop herself from hoping.

Where was he? She thought she smelled coffee and got out of bed. She visited the bathroom, brushed her hair and teeth, and returned to the bedroom to dress. Oddly she felt suddenly constrained by the bra she put on and discarded it. A subtle pulsating sensation had enveloped her entire body, and the sense of waiting increased. Even underpants were too much. She simply pulled on a loose cotton house-dress over her nude body and went downstairs in her bare feet.

He wasn't in the parlor, or the kitchen, though the empty coffeepot and the cup in the sink explained the lingering scent. The kitchen door was open, the screen door no barrier to the cool damp air, and the fresh smell of rain mingled with that of the coffee. His truck was still parked at the back porch steps.

It took only a few minutes to boil water and steep a tea bag, and she drank the tea while sitting at the kitchen table, watching the rain sheet down the window. It was cool enough that she should have been chilled, wearing only the thin dress, but she wasn't, even though she could feel how her nipples had tightened. Once that would have embarrassed her. Now she thought only of Wolf.

She was halfway between the table and the sink, empty cup in hand, when suddenly he was there, standing on the other side of the screen door, watching her through the wire mesh. His clothing was plastered to his skin, rainwater dripping off of his face. Mary froze, her head turned to stare at him.

He looked wild, primitive, his eyes narrow and glittering, his feet braced apart. She could see every breath that swelled his chest, see the pulse that throbbed at the base of his throat. Though he was very still, she could feel his entire body pulsating with tension. In that moment she knew he was going to take her, and she knew that was why she had waited.

"I'll always be a half-breed," he said in a low, harsh voice, barely audible over the drumming rain. "There will always be people who look down on me because of it. Think long and hard before you agree to be my woman, because there's no going back."

Softly, clearly, she said, "I don't want to go back."

He opened the screen door and entered the kitchen, his movements slow and deliberate. Mary's hand shook as she reached out to place her cup on the cabinet; then she turned to face him.

He put his hands on her waist and gently drew her up against him; his clothes were wet, and immediately the front of her dress absorbed the moisture until the damp fabric was molded to her body. Mary slid her hands up his shoulders to join at the back of his neck and lifted her mouth to his. His kiss was slow and deep, making her toes curl as hot excitement began to dart through her. She knew how to kiss now and welcomed his tongue while she teased him with her own. His chest lifted with a deep, sharp intake of breath, and his grip on her tightened. Suddenly the kiss was no longer slow, but hungry and urgent, and the pressure of his mouth was almost painful.

She felt him gathering her skirt in his hand to lift it; then his callused palm was sliding up her thigh. He reached her hip and paused, shuddering with violent arousal as he realized she was naked under the dress; then his hand moved to her bare buttocks and caressed them. It was surprisingly pleasurable, and she moved her bottom against his hand. He had opened up an entire new world for her, the world of sensual pleasure, and he was constantly expanding the limits.

He couldn't wait much longer, and he lifted her in his arms. His face was hard and intent as he looked down at her. "Unless the house catches on fire, I won't stop this time," he said quietly. "I don't care if the phone rings, or if anyone drives up, or even knocks on the bedroom door. This time, we finish it."

She didn't reply, but gave him a slow, sweet smile that made him burn to take her right there. His arms tightened as he carried her up the narrow, creaky stairs and into her bedroom, where he carefully placed her on the bed.

He stood looking down at her for a moment, then walked to the window and raised it. "Let's let the storm in," he said, and then it was with them, filling the half-dark room with sound and vibration. The rain-chilled air washed over her, cool and fresh on her heated skin. She sighed, the small sound drowned out by the din of thunder and rain.

There by the window, with the dim gray light outlining the bulge and plane of powerful muscle, Wolf removed his wet clothing. Mary lay quietly on the bed, her head turned to watch him. The shirt went first, revealing his sleek, heavy shoulders and washboard stomach. She knew from touching him that he was unbelievably hard, with no give beneath his smooth skin. He bent down to tug off his boots and socks, then straightened and unbuckled his belt. The noise of the storm made his movements a pantomime, but she imagined the small pop as he unsnapped his jeans, then the hissing of the zipper as metal teeth pulled apart. Without hesitation he pushed down his jeans and underwear and stepped free of them.

He was naked. Her heart jerked painfully in her chest as she stared at him, for the first time feeling remarkably small and helpless beside him. He was big, he was strong, and he was undeniably male. She couldn't look away from his hard manhood. She was going to take him inside her, accept his heavy weight as they joined in the act of mating, and she was a little frightened.

He saw it in her eyes as he eased down beside her. "Don't be afraid," he whispered, brushing her hair away from her face. His hands were gentle as he reached under her and unzipped her dress.

"I know what's going to happen," she murmured, turning her face against his shoulder. "The mechanics of it, anyway. But I just don't see how it's possible."

"It is. I'll take it slow and easy."

"All right." She whispered her acquiescence and let him lift her so he could pull the dress off of her shoulders. Her breasts were bare, and she could feel them tightening, swelling, her nipples puckering. He bent to kiss both nipples, wetting them with his tongue, and her back arched as heat spread through her. He quickly stripped the dress down her hips and legs, the need to have her bare under his hands too urgent for him to ignore it any longer.

Mary quivered, then lay still. It was the first time since babyhood that anyone but herself had seen her completely nude; her cheeks heated, and she closed her eyes as she struggled with the sensations of embarrassment and painful exposure. He touched her breasts, gently squeezing them; then his rough palm slowly moved down her stomach until his fingers touched her silky triangle of curls. She made a small sound, and her eyes flew open to find him watching her with such a fierce, heated expression that she forgot her embarrassment. She was suddenly proud that he wanted her so intensely, that her body aroused him. Her legs relaxed, and one finger delved between her soft folds, lightly stroking the ultra-sensitive flesh he found. Mary's entire body tensed again, and she moaned. She hadn't known anything could feel like that, but she sensed there was more, and she didn't know if she could survive it. This was pleasure too intense to be borne.

"Do you like that?" Wolf murmured.

She gasped, her slender body beginning to writhe slowly on the sheets in a rhythm as old as the ages. He opened her legs farther with his hand, then returned to his sensual exploration, and at the same time bent to hungrily cover her mouth with his own. Mary's head spun, and her nails dug into his shoulders as she clung to him. She couldn't believe how he was touching her, how it made her feel, but she never wanted it to stop. He was causing a fever inside her, one that spread and intensified until she was aware of nothing but her own body and his. His stroking fingers raised her to delirium while his mouth muffled the small moans she made.

She tore her mouth away from his. "Wolf, please," she begged, frantic with need.

"Just a minute longer, sweetheart. Look at me. Let me see your face when I—ahh."

She whimpered. He was touching her even more intimately, finding her damp and swollen. His black gaze was locked with hers as he slowly slid his finger inside her, and they both shuddered convulsively.

Wolf knew he couldn't wait any longer. His entire body was throbbing. She was soft and wet and incredibly tight, and she was writhing on the verge of ecstasy. Her pale, translucent skin intoxicated him, enthralled him; just touching her made him wild. The textures of her body excited him more than anything he'd ever known before. Everything about her was soft and silky. Her hair was baby-fine, her skin delicate and satiny; even the curls between her legs were soft, rather than springy. He wanted her more than he wanted his next breath.

He moved between her legs, spreading them to make

room for his hips to nestle against her. She inhaled sharply as she felt him, hard and burning. Their eyes met again as he reached down between their bodies and guided himself into position, then began entering her.

The storm was right over them now. The lightning cracked, and the almost simultaneous thunder boomed, rattling the old house. The sharply gusting wind blew the curtains straight out into the room, spattering rain on the floor in front of the open window and carrying a fine mist over their bodies. Mary cried, her tears mingling with the mist on her face, as she accepted his slow penetration.

He was braced over her on his forearms, his face just an inch from hers. He licked the tears away, then kissed her mouth, and she tasted salt. She could feel burning pain as her body stretched to admit him, and enormous pressure. More tears seeped from the corners of her eyes. He deepened the kiss as his buttocks flexed, exerting more pressure, and suddenly her body's barrier gave way. He pushed deep into her, burying himself to the hilt with a deep, almost tortured groan of pleasure.

There was pain, but there was also a lot more. He'd told her that making love was hot and sweaty, and that she probably wouldn't like it, and he was both right and wrong. It *was* hot and sweaty, and raw, and primitive. It was so powerful that it swept her along with its rhythms. Despite the pain, she felt exalted by his possession. She could feel the tension and savage excitement in his powerful body as she cradled him with her legs and arms, her soft depths filled with him. She loved him, and he needed her. She had never really lived before, until this moment when she gave herself to the man she loved.

She couldn't keep it back, not that it mattered. He had to know already. Mary had never worn an emotional mask. Her hands moved over his sleek, wet shoulders and into his thick hair. "I love you," she said, her soft voice barely audible over another booming roll of thunder.

If he replied, she didn't hear him. He reached down between their bodies again, but this time his hand was on her, and he began moving. Heat shimmered through her again, making the discomfort fade; her body arched, hips lifting in an effort to take him even deeper, and she told him again that she loved him. Sweat beaded his taut face as he tried to control his thrusts, but the storm was in the room, in their bodies. Her hips undulated, rolling, driving him mad. They strained together, their movements punctuated by the thunder, by the thudding of the headboard against the wall, and by the creaking of the bedsprings beneath them. Low groans and soft cries; wet flesh and trembling muscles; hands clutching frantically; harsh, rapid breathing and urgent thrusts—she knew all of that, felt it, heard it, and felt herself being consumed by the fever.

"Wolf?" Her questioning cry was thin, frantic. Her nails dug into the flexing muscles of his back.

"Don't fight it, baby. Let it go." He was groaning, feeling his own completion approaching, and he had no more control left. He removed his hand from between them and gripped her hips, lifting them, fitting himself more solidly to her and rocking against her loins.

Mary felt the tension and fever increase to unbearable levels, and then her senses exploded. She cried out, her entire body shuddering and clenching. It was the sweetest madness imaginable, a pleasure beyond description, and it continued until she thought she might die of it. He held her until she quietened, then began thrusting hard and fast. His guttural cries blended with the thunder as he crushed her against the mattress, his body convulsing as the powerful jetting of completion emptied him.

They were silent afterward, as if words would be an intrusion between them. Their mating had been so compelling and urgent that nothing else had existed. Even the storm, as violent as it was, had been only an accompaniment. Slowly, reluctantly, Mary felt reality return, but she was content to lie beneath him and do nothing more than stroke his hair.

Their breathing had long since steadied and the storm moved away when he disengaged their bodies and shifted onto his side. He cradled her for a time, but now that their skin had cooled, the mist-dampened bed was distinctly uncomfortable. When she began to shiver, he got out of bed and crossed to the window to close it. She watched as his muscles alternately bunched and relaxed with each movement of his nude body. Then he turned, and she was instantly, helplessly, fascinated. She wished for the nerve to run her hands all over him, especially his loins. She wanted to inspect him, like an exploration, going over uncharted territory.

"Like what you see?" His voice was low and filled with amusement.

Things had gone too far between them for her to be embarrassed now. She looked up at him and smiled. "Very much. I imagined you once in a loincloth, but this is much better."

He reached down and plucked her from the bed as easily as if she were a feather. "We'd better get dressed before you get cold, and before I forget my good intentions."

"What good intentions?"

"Not to keep at you until you're so sore you can't walk."

She looked gravely at him. "You made it wonderful for me. Thank you."

"It was pretty damn wonderful for me, too." One side

of his mouth quirked upward, and he slid his hands into her silvery brown hair. "No bad moments?"

She understood what he meant and leaned her head against his chest. "No. That was an entirely different thing."

But she hadn't forgotten, either, and he knew it. She was still shaky and vulnerable inside, though she kept her chin proudly lifted. He intended for someone to pay for the damage done to her indomitable spirit.

He'd spent years living quietly on the fringes, maintaining the sort of armed truce that had existed between him and the citizens of Ruth, but no more. For Mary, he would find the creep who had attacked her, and if the townspeople didn't like it, that was just too bad.

She threw Wolf's wet clothes into the dryer, then prepared a late breakfast. Neither of them talked much. Despite her determination to overcome her shock, she couldn't quite forget those horrifying moments when she had been helpless at the hands of a madman, for he certainly was mad. No matter what she was doing or thinking, a lightning flash of memory would catapult her back to the attack, just for a minute, until she could regain control and put it from her again.

Wolf watched her, knowing what she was experiencing by the way her slight body would tense, then slowly relax. He'd lived through flashbacks, of Vietnam, of prison, and he knew how they worked, as well as the toll they took. He wanted to take her to bed again, to keep the shadows at bay for her, but knew from the occasional gingerness of her movements that she was too new to lovemaking for another bout right now to be anything other than abusive. When she was used to him... A very slight smile curved his lips as he thought of the hours of pleasure and all the different ways he would take her.

But first he had to find the man who had attacked her.

When his clothes were dry, he dressed and pulled Mary out to the back porch with him. The rain had diminished to a drizzle, so he figured they wouldn't get too wet. "Come out to the barn with me," he said, taking her hand.

"Why?"

"I want to show you something."

"I've been in the barn. There's nothing interesting in there."

"There is today. You'll like it."

"All right." They hurried through the drizzle to the old barn, which was dark and musty, without the warmth and rich, animal smells of his barn. Dust tickled her nose. "It's too dark to see anything."

"There's enough light. Come on." Still holding her hand, he led her into a stall where a couple of boards were missing from the wall, letting in the dreary light. After the darkness of the inner barn, she could see fairly well.

"What is it?"

"Look under the feed trough."

She bent down and looked. Curled up, in a nest of dusty straw and an old towel she recognized, was Woodrow. Curled against Woodrow's belly were four little rat-looking things.

She straightened abruptly. "Woodrow's a father!"

"Nope. Woodrow's a mother."

"A mother!" She stared at the cat, who stared back at her enigmatically before beginning to lick the kittens. "I was specifically told that Woodrow is male."

"Well, Woodrow is female. Didn't you look?"

Mary gave him a severe look. "I don't make a habit of looking at an animal's private parts."

"Just mine, right?"

She blushed, but couldn't deny the charge. "Right."

He slipped his arms around her waist and pulled her close for a slow, warm kiss. She sighed and softened against him, reaching up to clasp the back of his neck as his mouth moved over hers. The strength of his big body reassured her, made her feel safe. When his hard arms were around her, nothing could harm her.

"I have to go home," he murmured when he lifted his mouth from hers. "Joe will do as much as he can, but it takes both of us to get everything done."

She had thought she could handle it, but panic seized her at the thought of being alone. Quickly she controlled herself and let her arms drop from around his neck. "Okay." She started to ask if she'd see him later, but kept the words unsaid. Oddly, now that their relationship was so intimate, she felt far less sure of herself than she had before. Letting him get that close, letting him enter her body, had exposed a vulnerability she hadn't known was there. That kind of intimacy was a little scary.

"Get a jacket," he said as they left the barn.

"I already have a jacket."

"I meant, get one now. You're going with me."

She gave him a quick look, then dropped her gaze away from the awareness in his. "I have to be alone sometime," she said quietly.

"But not today. Go on, get that jacket."

She got the jacket and climbed up into his truck, feeling as if she had been reprieved from execution. Maybe by the time night came she would have her fears under control.

Joe came out of the barn as they drove up and walked to the passenger side of the truck. When Mary opened the door, he reached in and lifted her from the truck, then hugged her tightly. "Are you all right?" His young voice was gruff.

She hugged him in return. "He didn't hurt me. I was just scared."

Over her head Joe looked at his father and saw the cold, controlled rage in those black eyes as they lingered on the slight woman in his son's arms. Someone had dared to hurt her, and whoever it was would pay. Joe felt a deep primitive anger, and knew it was only a fraction of what Wolf felt. Their eyes met, and Wolf gave a slight shake of his head, indicating that he didn't want Joe to pursue the subject. Mary was here to relax, not relive the attack.

Wolf approached and looped his arm over her shoulder, using the pressure to turn her toward the stable. "Feel up to helping with the chores?"

Her eyes lit. "Of course. I've always wanted to see how a ranch works."

He automatically shortened his long stride to match hers as the three of them walked toward the stable. "This isn't a ranch, exactly. I run a small herd, but more for training and our personal beef than any other reason."

"What sort of training?"

"Training the horses to work a herd. That's what I do. I break and train horses. Quarter horses mostly, for ranchers, but sometimes I handle the odd show horse or Thoroughbred, or a fractious pleasure mount."

"Don't Thoroughbred owners have their own trainers?"

He shrugged. "Some horses are harder to train than others. An expensive horse isn't worth a damn if no one can get near him." He didn't elaborate, but Mary knew that he got the horses no one else was able to handle.

The long stable jutted out to the right of the barn. When they entered, Mary inhaled the rich earth scents of horses, leather, manure, grain and hay. Long satiny necks poked over the stall doors, and inquisitive whickers filled the air. She had never been around horses much, but she wasn't afraid of them. She moved down the line, patting and stroking, murmuring to the animals. "Are these all quarter horses?"

"No. That one in the next stall is a Canadian cutting horse—that's a type, not a breed. He belongs to a rancher in the next county north. Down in the last stall is a saddle-bred, for some big rancher's wife in Montana. He's going to give her the horse for her birthday in July. The rest of them are quarter horses.''

They were all young horses, and as playful as children. Wolf treated them as such, talking to them in a low, crooning tone, gentling them like overgrown babies. Mary spent the entire afternoon in the stables with Wolf and Joe, watching them attend to the endless chores of cleaning and feeding, checking shoes, grooming. The drizzle finally stopped in the late afternoon, and Wolf worked with a couple of the young quarter horses in the pen behind the stable, slowly and gently getting them accustomed to bits and saddles. He didn't rush them, or lose his patience when a fractious young horse shied away from him whenever Wolf tried to lift a saddle onto his back. He just soothed the colt and reassured him before trying again. Before the afternoon was over, the colt was ambling around the pen as if he'd been wearing a saddle for years.

Mary was enthralled, partly by his low, velvety voice, and partly by the way his strong hands moved over the young animals, teaching and soothing all at once. He had done that with her, but his hands had also excited her. She shivered as memories washed over her, and her breasts tightened.

''I've never seen anyone like him,'' Joe said beside her, keeping his tone low. ''I'm good, but not near as good as he is. I've never seen a horse he couldn't settle down. We had a stallion brought to us a couple of years ago. He'd been put out to stud, but he was so damn vicious the handlers couldn't control him. Dad just put him in a stall and left him alone, but every so often he'd leave sugar cubes, apples or carrots on the top of the stall door and stand there until the stallion got a good look at him. Then he'd walk off, and the stallion would get whatever he'd left on the door.

"The stallion started watching for him and snorting at him if Dad was taking his time about getting the food over there. Then Dad stopped moving away, and the stallion, Ringer, had to come up to the door while Dad was there if he wanted the food. The first few times, he tried to tear the stall apart, but finally he gave in and got the food. Next he had to eat out of Dad's hand if he wanted his treat. Dad switched completely to carrots then, to make sure he didn't lose any fingers. Finally Ringer was hanging his head over the stall, and he'd nuzzle Dad's shirt like a kid hunting candy. Dad petted him and groomed him—Ringer loved being brushed—and gradually broke him to the saddle and started riding him. I worked with him, too, after Dad had him settled down, and I guess he finally decided he didn't have to fight all the time.

"We had a mare come in heat, and Dad called Ringer's owner to ask if he wanted us to try Ringer on our mare. The guy gave his okay, Ringer performed like a real gentleman, and everybody was happy. The owner got his expensive stud civilized, and we got a hefty fee, as well as a hell of a colt out of the mare Ringer covered."

Mary blinked at all this talk of being "in heat" and "covered," and cleared her throat. "He's wonderful," she agreed, and cleared her throat again. Her skin felt hot and sensitive. She couldn't take her eyes off Wolf, tall and lean and broad-shouldered, the weak sunlight glinting off his black hair.

"When we get through here, maybe we could do a few lessons tonight, since I missed Friday night," Joe said, interrupting her thoughts.

She didn't like thinking about why he had missed Friday night, about the long hours spent waiting to hear if Wolf had been jailed. This afternoon had been a small oasis of calm, with the semblance of normality, but it would be a long time before things were back to normal in the county. A young girl had been raped, and Mary had been attacked the very next day. People would be enraged and wary, looking at their neighbors and wondering. God help any stranger who happened to wander through, at least until the man was caught.

Tires crunched on the gravel, and Joe left his post to see who had ventured up on Mackenzie's Mountain. He was back in a moment, with Clay Armstrong behind him. It was a replay of Friday afternoon, and Mary felt her heart lurch; surely Clay wasn't going to arrest Wolf now?

"Mary." Clay nodded at her and touched the brim of his hat. "You doing okay?"

"Yes." She said it firmly.

"I thought I'd find you up here. Do you feel like going over it again with me?"

Wolf pulled off his gloves as he approached. His eyes were flinty. "She went over it with you yesterday."

"Sometimes people remember little things after the shock has passed."

Because she sensed Wolf was about to throw Clay off his property, she turned and put her hand on his arm. "It's okay. *I'm* okay."

She was lying, and he knew it, but her mouth had taken on that stubborn set that meant she wouldn't back down. He felt a tinge of amusement; his kitten was getting back some of her confidence, after all. But no way was he going to let Clay question her alone. He looked at Joe. "Put the horse up. I'm going with Mary."

"That isn't necessary," Clay said.

"It is to me."

Mary felt dwarfed between the two big men as they walked up to the house; she thought she might soon find such protectiveness smothering. A smile touched her lips.

Clay probably felt he had to protect her from Wolf as well as from another attack, while Wolf was determined to protect her, period. She wondered what Clay would think if he knew that she didn't want to be protected from Wolf. Aunt Ardith would say Wolf had taken advantage of her, and Mary earnestly hoped he would do so again. Soon.

Wolf caught her sidelong glance and stiffened as he felt her interest and warmth. Damn it, didn't she know how he'd react, and that it could get embarrassing? Already he could feel the tension in his loins. But, no, she didn't know. Despite their early morning lovemaking, she was still too innocent about sex in general, and the effect she had on him in particular, to know what that look did to him. He hurried his step. He needed to sit down.

When they entered the kitchen, Mary moved around making coffee as naturally as she would have in her own house, emphasizing to Clay that she and Wolf were a couple. Folks in the county were just going to have to get used to it.

"Let's go through it from the beginning," Clay said.

Mary paused fractionally, then resumed her steady movements as she measured coffee into the percolator. "I'd just bought new boots at Hearst's store and was walking back to my car—my boots! I dropped them! Did you see them? Did anyone pick them up?"

"I saw them, but I don't know what happened to them. I'll ask around."

"He must have been standing against the side of Hearst's store, because I'd have seen him if he had been on the other side of the alley. He just grabbed me and put his hand over my mouth. He held my head arched back, so I couldn't move it at all, and started dragging me down the alley. I got one hand free and reached back, trying to scratch his face, but he had on a ski mask. He hit me in the head with his fist and I—I really don't remember much after that until he pushed me down. I kept scratching him, and I think I clawed his hand, because he hit me again. Then I bit him on the hand, but I don't know if I drew blood.

"Someone yelled, and he got up and ran. He put his hand on the ground right in front of my face when he got up. His sleeve was blue, and he had freckles on his hand. A lot of freckles. Then...you were there."

She fell silent and moved to look out the kitchen window, her back to the men sitting at the table, so she didn't see the murderous look in Wolf's eyes, or the way his big fists clenched, but Clay did, and it worried him.

"I was the one who yelled. I saw the package lying on the ground and went over to see what it was, and then I heard scuffling from the back of the building. When I saw him, I yelled and pulled my revolver, and fired over his head to try to stop him."

Wolf looked savage. "You should have shot the son of a bitch. That would have stopped him."

In retrospect Clay wished he'd shot the guy, too. At least then they wouldn't be racking their brains trying to put an ID to him, and the townspeople wouldn't be so jittery. Women were carrying an assortment of weapons with them wherever they went, even outside to hang the wash to dry. The mood people were in, it would be dangerous for a stranger to stop in the county.

That was what bothered him, and he said as much. "It looks like someone would have noticed a stranger. Ruth is a small town, and people pretty well know everyone in the county. A stranger would have been noticed right off, especially one with long black hair."

Wolf gave a wintry smile. "Everyone would have thought it was me."

At the window, Mary stiffened. She had been trying not

to listen, trying to push away the memories that had been called up by her recounting of what had happened. She didn't turn around, but suddenly all her attention was focused on the conversation behind her. What Wolf had said was true. On seeing her attacker's long black hair, Clay had immediately had Wolf arrested.

But that long black hair, so distinctive, didn't fit with the wealth of rust-colored freckles she'd seen on the man's hand. And his skin had been pale. Fair people freckled. The black hair didn't fit.

Unless it was a disguise. Unless the object had been to frame Wolf.

Her spine prickled, and she felt both hot and cold. Whoever had done it hadn't known that Wolf had had his hair cut. But the choice of victim was puzzling; it didn't make sense. Why attack her? Surely no one would think Wolf would attack the one person in town who'd championed him, and she'd made it plain how she felt. Unless she had been a random choice, *it just didn't make sense*. After all, there was no link between herself and Cathy Teele, no common ground. It could all be chance.

Still without turning around, she asked, "Wolf, do you know Cathy Teele? Have you ever spoken to her?"

"I know her by sight. I don't speak to little Anglo girls." His tone was ironic. "Their parents wouldn't like it."

"You're right about that," Clay said wearily. "A few months back Cathy told her mother you were the best-looking man around, and that she wouldn't mind dating Joe if he weren't younger than she was. The whole town heard about it. Mrs. Teele pitched a fit."

That chill ran down Mary's spine again. There was a link, after all: Wolf. Nor could she dismiss it as coincidence, though something about the whole thing was skewed.

She twisted her hands together, and turned to face them. "What if someone is deliberately trying to frame Wolf?"

Wolf's face went hard and blank, but Clay looked startled. "Damn," he muttered. "Why did you think of that?"

"The long black hair. It could have been a wig. The man had freckles on his hand, a lot of freckles, and his skin was pale."

Wolf got to his feet, and though Mary knew she never had anything to fear from him, she fell back a step at the expression in his eyes. He didn't say anything; he didn't have to. She had seen him angry before, but this was different. He was enraged, but it was an icy rage, and he was in perfect control of himself. Perhaps that was what alarmed her.

Then Clay said, "Sorry, but I don't think it'll wash. Once we had all thought about it, it didn't make sense that Wolf would have attacked you, of all people. You've stood up for him right from the beginning, when the rest of the people in town—"

"Wouldn't spit on me if I were on fire," Wolf finished.

Clay couldn't deny it. "Exactly."

The coffee had finished brewing, and Mary poured three cups. They were silent and thoughtful as they sipped, all of them turning things around in their minds, trying to make the pieces fit. The truth was that no matter how things were arranged, something was always off, unless they went with the idea that a criminal had chosen Mary and Cathy at random, and had perhaps used a long black wig for disguise by pure coincidence.

Everything in Mary rejected the idea of coincidence. So that meant someone was deliberately trying to implicate Wolf. But why choose *her* as a victim?

To punish Wolf by hurting the people who had championed him?

It was all supposition, without a shred of evidence. Wolf had lived here for years without anything like this happening, even though his presence was like salt on the wound of the town's conscience. They didn't like him, and he didn't let them forget. Still, they had all existed under a silent truce.

So what had triggered the violence?

She rubbed her temples as a sudden twinge of pain threatened to become a full-scale headache. Since she seldom had headaches, she supposed the tension was getting to her, and determined not to let it. She'd never been a Nervous Nellie and didn't intend to start now.

Clay sighed and pushed his empty cup back. "Thanks for the coffee. I'll get the report finished tomorrow. I'll bring the papers by the school for you to sign—uh, are you planning to go to work, or stay home?"

"Why, work, of course."

"Of course," Wolf muttered, and scowled at her. Mary lifted her chin at him. She saw no reason why she should suddenly become an invalid.

Clay left soon afterward, and Joe came up from the stables to join in the dinner preparations. It felt right, the three of them together, working together as comfortably as if they had done so for years. Joe winked at her once, and she blushed, because it was fairly easy to read the expression in his young-old eyes. Awareness, amusement and approval were all there. Was he simply assuming she and Wolf had become intimate because Wolf had spent the night at her house, which she supposed was the commonsense thing to assume, or was there something different about her? What if everyone in town could just look at her and know?

Wolf curved his hand around her waist. She had been standing motionless for several minutes, the pan in her hand forgotten, as she both frowned and blushed. The blush told him what she was thinking, and the familiar tension in his body made his fingers tighten until they dug into her ribs. She looked up at him, her gray-blue eyes wide and startled; then awareness shot into them, and her eyelids dropped to half veil the desire she couldn't disguise.

Joe reached to take the pan from her nerveless fingers. "I think I'll go see a movie somewhere," he announced.

Mary jerked her head around, tearing herself from the sensual spell Wolf spun about her so easily. "No! Your lessons, remember?"

"Another night won't hurt."

"Another night will hurt," she insisted. "The Academy isn't something you can take for granted just because Senator Allard is going to recommend you. You can't afford to let up for a minute."

Wolf released her. "She's right, son. You can't let your grades slip." He could wait. Barely.

It was after nine when Mary closed the books she and Joe had been using and stretched her arms over her head. "Could you take me home now?" she asked Wolf, barely suppressing a yawn. It had been an eventful day.

His face was impassive. "Why don't you stay here." It was more of a command than a suggestion.

"I can't do that!"

"Why not?"

"It isn't proper."

"I stayed with you last night."

"That's different."

"How?"

"I was upset."

"Your bed's too small. Mine's bigger."

"I'm getting out of here," Joe said, and suited the action to the words.

Mary got huffy. "Did you have to say that in front of him?"

"He knew anyway. Remember what I said about no going back?"

She stilled and said, "Yes." That warm look entered her eyes again. "I don't want to go back. But I can't stay here tonight. I have to go to work in the morning."

"No one would think any less of you if you didn't."

"*I* would." She had that look again, the stubborn, determined expression of a fierce will.

Wolf got to his feet. "All right. I'll take you home." He went into his bedroom and several minutes later reappeared with a small shaving kit in his hand and a change of clothes slung over his shoulder. He knocked briefly on Joe's door as he passed it. "I'll be home in the morning."

The door opened. Joe was barefoot and shirtless, having been preparing to take a shower. "Okay. Are you going to take her to school, or do you want me to?"

"I don't need anyone to take me to work," Mary interrupted.

"That's tough." Wolf turned back to his son. "Baugh is bringing a couple of horses up in the morning, so I'll have to be here. You take her to school, and I'll get her in the afternoon."

"I'm driving my own car, and you can't stop me!"

"That's okay. You'll just have an escort." Wolf crossed the floor to her and took her arm. "Ready?"

Realizing that he'd made up his mind and there wasn't anything she could do about it, Mary walked with him out to the truck. The night air was growing cold, but his big body radiated heat, and she moved closer to him. As soon as they were in the truck, he roughly took her in his arms and bent his head to hers. She opened her mouth beneath his onslaught and thrust her fingers into his thick hair. The warm taste of his mouth filled her; the pressure of his arms around her rib cage, of his hard-muscled chest on her breasts, drugged her more surely than any sedative. If he had pulled her down onto the seat and taken her right then, she wouldn't have objected.

As it was, when he put her from him, her entire body was throbbing. She sat silently on the drive down the mountain, thinking of their lovemaking that morning, aching for it to be repeated. A thought echoed in her mind: so this was what it meant to be a woman.

Woodrow was waiting patiently on the back doorstep. Mary fed him—her!—while Wolf showered and shaved. He didn't have a heavy beard, but two days' growth had darkened his jaw, and her face burned a little from contact with his when they had kissed. She felt that deep, almost painful sense of waiting again as she climbed the stairs to her bedroom.

He silently entered and stood for a moment watching her before she sensed his presence and turned. "The shower's yours."

He was naked, and slightly damp from the humidity in the bathroom. His black hair glistened under the light, and glittering droplets of water were caught in the dark curls of hair on his chest. He was already aroused. The throbbing in her body became acute.

She showered, and afterward, for the first time, sprayed perfume on her pulse points. She had never bought perfume in her life, but luckily one of her students in Savannah had given her the bottle for Christmas. The scent was sweetly exotic.

She opened the bathroom door, then gasped and fell back. Wolf was waiting for her in the doorway, his eyes narrow and fierce as they raked her. She had boldly left off her nightgown, and under his perusal the deep throbbing intensified. He put his big hands on her breasts and lifted them slightly so that they were plumped in his palms. Her nipples tightened even before he began rubbing them with his thumbs. Mary stood very still, her breath quick and shallow, her eyes half closed as she tried to deal with the pleasure his hands brought.

Wolf's own eyes were narrow black slits. "I wanted to do this the day I found you on the road," he murmured. "Such a pretty little body inside that ugly dress. I wanted to take it off of you and see you naked."

The heat in his eyes, in his voice, made her shiver and sway toward him. He pulled her out of the doorway and into the dark hall, then put his hands on her waist and lifted her. She remembered when he had done that before and moaned even before his mouth closed over her nipple. He sucked it so strongly that her back arched, and she cried out as her legs parted and wrapped around his hips for balance. He groaned, unable to wait a minute longer. He had to get inside her or go mad. He shifted her, guided himself and entered her.

Mary shuddered, then went very still as he slowly pushed into her. It was even better than before. Her inner muscles gently clasped and relaxed as she accommodated him, sending waves of pleasure radiating out through her body. She clung to him, gasping. Desire worked its magic on her body, tightening some muscles, loosening others, so that she was both taut and pliable as she lifted herself, then sank back down. The effect of that small movement had both of them gasping, and Wolf shifted to brace his back against the wall. She did it again, then again. He put his hands on her buttocks to take control of the motion and began driving into her. Her skin felt on fire. She radiated heat, making her skin feel tight and smooth and so extraordinarily sensitive that she could feel each of his fingers on her bottom, the rasp of his chest hair on her breasts, the tiny nubs of his nipples, the muscled wall of his belly, the coarse hair at his groin. She could feel him deep inside her.

Her back arched, and her nerves convulsed. Wolf fought his own response, not wanting it to end so quickly, and held her until she quietened. Then he carried her into the bedroom, her legs still locked around him, and eased her down on the bed.

She swallowed and relaxed her hold on him. "You haven't—?"

"Not yet," he murmured, and began moving strongly into her.

She didn't want it to end. She took his thrusts, cradled him when a harsh groan tore from his throat and the powerful shudders of completion shook him, and afterward held him as he rested on her body. She didn't want him to withdraw, to leave her empty again. She had existed in a sort of genteel limbo all her life until she had met him and begun to live. In just a few short months he had so completely taken over the focus of her life that the years before were hazy.

He gathered himself and tried to move off her. Mary tightened her legs around him, and he grunted.

"Let me up, sweetheart. I'm too heavy for you."

"No you aren't," she whispered, and kissed his throat.

"I weigh twice what you do. Do you even weigh a hundred pounds?"

"Yes," she said indignantly. She weighed a hundred and five.

"Not much more than that. I weigh two hundred, and I'm a foot taller than you. If I go to sleep on you, you'll smother."

He did sound drowsy. She ran her hand down the muscled ridges of his side. "I want to stay like this."

He thrust gently against her. "Like this?"

"Yes." She breathed the word.

He settled onto her, but shifted part of his weight to the side. "Is this okay?"

It was wonderful. She could breathe, but he was still close to her, still inside her. He quickly dozed off, as content as she with the position, and Mary smiled in the darkness as she held him.

The dark thoughts slowly intruded. Someone had deliberately tried to frame him, to put him back in prison. The thought of Wolf without his freedom was obscene and scary, because she knew enough about him to know he would never let himself be sent to prison again.

She wanted to keep him safe, to shield him in her arms, putting her own body between him and danger. Dear God, what had started it all? Things had been so quiet! What had been the trigger?

Then she knew, and horror almost stopped her breath. *She* had been the trigger.

While Wolf and Joe had been outcasts, punished for their heritage and Wolf's past, everything had been calm. Then she had come to town, an Anglo woman, but instead of aligning herself with the townspeople, she had championed the Mackenzies. With her help, Joe had achieved an honor offered to very few. Other people had begun saying what a nice thing it was that the Mackenzie boy was going to the Academy. Cathy Teele had said that Wolf was the best-looking man in the county. The boundaries between the town and the Mackenzies had begun blurring. Someone, with a maggot of hate festering deep inside, had been unable to stand it.

And she had been the cause of it all. If anything happened to Wolf, it would be her fault.

She didn't know what to do. The thought that she was the cause of all that had happened tormented her, disturbing her sleep. She moved restlessly, waking Wolf, and he sensed her distress though he attributed it to the wrong cause. He soothed her with whispers and pulled her more completely beneath him. She felt him harden inside her. His lovemaking was gentle this time, and when it was over she slept as effortlessly as a child until he awoke her again in the total darkness before dawn. She turned to him without question.

Joe drove up just as she and Wolf were preparing breakfast, and without a word Wolf broke more eggs into a bowl to be scrambled. Mary smiled at him, even though she was placing more bacon in the frying pan. "How do you know he's hungry?"

"He's awake, isn't he? My kid eats like a horse."

Joe came in the back door and headed for the coffee, which had already finished brewing. "Morning."

"Good morning. Breakfast will be ready in about ten minutes."

He grinned at her, and Mary smiled back. Wolf watched her, his gaze sharp. She looked frail this morning, her skin pale and even more translucent than usual, with faint mauve shadows under her eyes. She smiled readily, but he wondered what had made her look so delicate. Had he tired her with his lovemaking, or were memories of the attack disturbing her? He thought it must be the latter, because she had responded eagerly every time he'd reached for her. Knowing that she was still frightened made him even more determined to find whoever had attacked her. After Eli Baugh had delivered the horses and left, Wolf planned to do some tracking.

Joe was right behind Mary's car on the way to the school, and he didn't leave immediately, as she had expected. It was still too early for the students to begin arriving, so he walked with her into the empty building and even inspected the rooms. Then he leaned against the doorjamb and waited.

Mary sighed. "I'm perfectly safe here."

"I'll just wait until some other people show up."

"Did Wolf tell you to do this?"

"Nope. He knew he didn't have to."

How did they communicate? By telepathy? Each seemed to know what the other was thinking. It was disconcerting. She just hoped they couldn't read her thoughts, because she'd had some decidedly erotic ones lately.

What would everyone think of Joe's presence? He was so obviously a watchdog. She wondered if it would trigger another act of violence, and she felt sick, because she knew it might. Instinct, sharpened by her fierce protectiveness for both Mackenzies, told her that her theory was correct. Just the possibility that they could become accepted had driven someone over the edge. It revealed so much hate that she shivered.

Sharon and Dottie entered the building and halted briefly when Joe turned his head and looked at them as they passed the open door. "Mrs. Wycliffe. Mrs. Lancaster," he said in acknowledgment as he touched his fingertips to the brim of his hat in a brief salute.

"Joe," Sharon murmured. "How are you?"

Dottie gave him a brief, almost frightened look and hurried to her classroom. Joe shrugged. "I've been doing a bit of studying," he allowed.

"Just a bit?" Sharon asked wryly. She stepped past him to greet Mary, then said, "If you don't feel like working today, Dottie and I can handle your classes. I never dreamed you'd be here today, anyway."

"I was merely frightened," Mary said firmly. "Clay prevented anything else from happening. Cathy is the one who needs sympathy, not I."

"The whole town is in an uproar. Anyone who has freckles on his hands is getting the third degree."

Mary didn't want to talk about it. The image of that freckled hand made her feel nauseated, and she swallowed convulsively. Joe frowned and stepped forward. Mary put up her hand to keep him from throwing Sharon out of the classroom, but at that moment several students entered, and their chatter distracted everyone. The kids said, "Hi, Joe, howya been?" as they clustered around him. They all wanted to know about his plans for the Academy and how he'd gotten interested.

Sharon left to attend to her own classes, and Mary watched Joe with the kids. He was only sixteen, but he seemed older than even the seniors. Joe was young, but he wasn't a kid, and that was the difference. She noticed that Pam Hearst was in the group. She wasn't saying much, but she never took her eyes off Joe, looking at him with both longing and pain, though she tried to hide it. Several times Joe gave the girl a long look that made her fidget uncomfortably.

Then he checked his watch and left his former classmates to say to Mary, "Dad will be here to follow you home. Don't go anywhere alone."

She started to protest, then thought of the man out there

who hated them enough to do what he'd done. She wasn't the only one at risk. She reached out and caught his arm. "You and Wolf be careful. You could be the next targets."

He frowned, as if that hadn't occurred to him. The attacker was a rapist, so men wouldn't consider themselves in danger. She wouldn't have thought of it, either, if she hadn't been convinced that the whole thing was intended to punish the Mackenzies. What greater punishment could there be than to kill them? At some point the madman might decide to take a rifle and dispense his own twisted brand of justice.

Clay showed up at lunch with the papers for her to read and sign. Aware of the kids watching them with acute interest, she walked with him out to the car. "I'm worried," she admitted.

He propped his arm on top of the open door. "You'd be foolish if you weren't worried."

"Not for myself. I think Wolf and Joe are the real targets."

He gave her a quick, sharp look. "How do you figure that?"

Heartened that he hadn't immediately dismissed the idea, but was watching her with a troubled expression in his eyes, Mary told him her theory. "I think Cathy and I were specifically chosen as targets to punish Wolf. Don't you see the link? She said she thought Wolf was handsome, and that she'd like to date Joe. Everyone knows I've been friends with them from the first. So we were chosen."

"And you think he'll attack again?"

"I'm certain he will, but I'm afraid he'll go after one of them this time. I doubt he'd try to manhandle either of them, but what chance would they have against a bullet? How many men in this county have a rifle?"

"Every last mother's son," Clay replied grimly. "But what set this guy off?"

She paused, her face miserable. "I did."

"What?"

"I did. Before I came here, Wolf was an outcast. Everyone was comfortable with that. Then I made friends with him and worked with Joe to get him into the Academy. A lot of people were a little proud of that and were friendlier. It was a crack in the wall, and whoever is doing this just couldn't stand it."

"You're talking about a lot of hate, and it's hard for me to see. People around here don't get along with Wolf, but a lot of it is fear instead of hate. Fear and guilt. The people in this county sent him to prison for something he didn't do, and his presence constantly reminds them of it. He isn't a very forgiving person, is he?"

"Something like that would be a little hard to forgive," Mary pointed out.

He had to agree with that and sighed wearily. "Still, I can't think of anyone who seems to hate him to the point of attacking two women just because they were friendly to him. Hell, Cathy wasn't even friendly. She just made a chance remark."

"So you agree with me? That all of this is because of Wolf?"

"I don't like it, but I guess I do. Nothing else makes sense, because there may be a few coincidences in life, but none in crime. Everything has a motive."

"So what can we do?"

"*We* won't do anything," he said pointedly. "*I* will talk to the sheriff about it, but the fact is we can't arrest anyone without evidence, and all we have is a theory. We don't even have a suspect."

Her jaw set in firm lines. ''Then you're passing up a marvelous chance.''

He looked suspicious. ''To do what?''

''Set a trap, of course.''

''I don't like this. I don't know what you're thinking, but I don't like it.''

''It's common sense. He failed in his—er, objective with me. Perhaps I could—''

''No. And before you get on your high horse, just think of what Wolf would say if you told him you were setting yourself up as bait. You might—*might*—be allowed out of his house by Christmas.''

That was true enough, but she saw a way around it. ''Then I just won't tell him.''

''There's no way to keep it from him, unless it didn't work. If it did work—I sure as hell wouldn't want to be around when he found out, and something like that couldn't be kept quiet.''

Mary considered all of Wolf's possible reactions and didn't like any of them. On the other hand, she was terrified that something might happen to him. ''I'll take the chance,'' she said, making her decision.

''Not with my help, you won't.''

Her chin lifted. ''Then I'll do it without your help.''

''If you get in the way of our investigations, I'll put you in the pokey so fast your head will spin,'' he threatened. When she didn't appear impressed, he swore under his breath. ''Hell, I'll just tell Wolf and let him ride herd on you.''

She frowned and considered shaking her schoolteacher's finger in his face. ''You listen to me, Clay Armstrong. I'm the best chance you have of luring this guy out into the open. You don't have any suspects now. What are you going to do, wait until he attacks some other woman and maybe kills her? Is that how you want to work it?''

"No, that isn't how I want to work it! I want you and every other woman to stay alert and not go anywhere alone. I don't want to risk you or anyone else. Have you thought that sometimes traps don't work, that the animal gets the bait and still gets away? Do you really want to face the possibility of that?''

The thought made her sick to her stomach, and she swallowed to control the sudden rise of nausea. "No, but I'd do it anyway," she said steadily.

"For the last time, no. I understand that you want to help, but I don't like the idea. This guy is too unstable. He grabbed Cathy in her own driveway, and took you off of the town's main street. The chances he took are crazy, and *he* probably is, too.''

With a sigh, Mary decided that Clay was simply too protective for him to be able to agree to use a woman as bait; it was totally against his basic nature. That didn't mean, however, that she needed his agreement. All she needed was someone who could act as a guard. She hadn't thought of any real plan yet, but obviously there had to be two people to make even the simplest trap work: the bait, and the one who kept the bait from being harmed.

Clay got in the car and closed the door, then leaned out the open window. "I don't want to hear any more about it," he warned.

"You won't," she promised. Not talking to him about it wasn't the same as not doing it.

He gave her a suspicious look, but started the car and drove away. Mary returned to her classroom, her thoughts darting around as she tried to think of a solid plan for luring a rapist with a minimum of danger to herself.

Wolf arrived at the school ten minutes before classes

were over. He propped his shoulder against the wall just outside her classroom door and listened to her clear voice instructing her students on how geography and history had combined to produce the current state of Middle East politics. He was certain that wasn't in any of the textbooks, but Mary had a knack for giving her students a way of relating the present to their studies. It made the subjects both more interesting and more understandable. He had heard her doing the same thing with Joe, not that Joe needed encouragement to read. Her students responded easily to her; in such a small class, there was very little formality. They called her "Miss Potter," but weren't shy about asking questions, offering answers, even teasing.

Then she looked at her watch and released them, just as the doors to the other two classrooms opened. Wolf straightened from the wall and walked into her room, aware of how the kids' chatter halted abruptly when they became aware of his presence. Mary looked up and smiled, a private smile meant only for him, and it made his pulse accelerate that she was so open about how she felt.

He removed his hat and shoved his fingers through his hair. "Your escort service has arrived, ma'am," he said.

One of the girls giggled nervously, and Wolf slowly turned his head to look at the motionless teenagers. "Are you girls going home in pairs? Any of you boys making sure they get home all right?"

Christa Teele, Cathy's younger sister, murmured that she and Pam Hearst were walking together. The other four girls said nothing. Wolf looked at the seven boys. "Go with them." It was an order, one that the boys obeyed instantly. The kids left the room, automatically separating so that each girl had at least one male escort.

Mary nodded. "Very nicely done."

"You'll notice that they all had enough sense not to argue that they didn't need an escort."

She frowned at him, because she felt it hadn't been necessary for him to make that point. "Wolf, really, I'm perfectly safe on the drive from my house to here. How could anything happen to me if I don't stop?"

"What if you had a flat? What if a radiator hose blew again?"

It was obvious there was no way she could set her trap if Wolf or Joe was hovering over her every second. It was also obvious from the narrow look Wolf was giving her that he had no intention of changing his mind. Not that it mattered at the moment, as she hadn't come up with a plan yet. But when she did, she would also have to come up with some scheme for slipping away from her watchdogs.

Wolf draped her sweater over her shoulders and picked up her purse and keys, then ushered her out the door. Dottie looked up from where she was locking her own classroom door and stood transfixed while Wolf locked Mary's door, rattled the knob to make certain the lock held, then put his arm around her waist. He saw Dottie and touched the brim of his hat. "Mrs. Lancaster."

Dottie ducked her head and pretended to be having trouble with her key. Her face was flushed. It was the first time Wolf Mackenzie had ever spoken to her, and her hands shook as she dropped the key into her purse. Almost uncontrollable fear made her break out in a sweat. She didn't know what she was going to do.

Wolf's arm was solid around Mary's waist as they walked to her car. Its weight made her heartbeat quicken. All he had to do was put his hands on her and her body began to ready itself for him. An exquisite shudder began deep inside, spreading outward in a warm tide.

He felt the sudden tension in her slender body as he

opened the car door. She was breathing faster, too. He looked down at her, and his entire body tightened, because she was watching him with desire plain in her soft, slate-blue eyes. Her cheeks were flushed, her lips parted.

He stepped back. "I'll be right behind you." The words were guttural.

She drove sedately home, though her blood was thundering through her veins and pounding in her ears. Never had the isolated, bedraggled old house looked better. Woodrow was sunning on the steps, and Mary stepped over her to unlock the back door. Wolf was out of his truck and right behind her, just as he had promised, by the time she had the door open.

Without a word she took off her sweater, deposited her purse on a chair and walked up the stairs, acutely aware of the heavy tread of Wolf's boots as he followed. They stepped into her bedroom.

He had her naked before she could gather her wits, though she wouldn't have wanted to protest even if he'd given her time. He bore her down on the bed, his big body overwhelming her, his brawny arms cradling her. The hair on his chest rasped her sensitive nipples into hardened peaks, and with a low moan of excitement she rubbed her breasts against him to increase the sensation. He opened her thighs and settled himself between them. His voice was low and rough as he murmured in her ear an explicit explanation of what he was going to do.

Mary drew back a little, her blue eyes slightly shocked, feeling slightly excited, and also slightly embarrassed *because* she was excited. How was it possible to feel both scandalized and excited? "Wolf Mackenzie!" she said, her eyes going even larger. "You said…that word!"

His hard face looked both tender and amused. "So I did."

She swallowed. "I've never heard anyone say it before. I mean, not in real life. In movies—but of course that isn't real life, and in movies it almost never means what it really means. They use it as an adjective instead of a verb." She looked perplexed at such an inexplicable grammatical oversight.

He was smiling as he entered her, his black eyes shining. "This," he said, "is the verb."

He loved the way she looked when he made love to her, her eyes languorous, her cheeks flushed. She sucked in her breath and moved beneath him, taking him completely into her and enveloping him in her sweet heat. Her hands moved up to the back of his neck. "Yes," she agreed seriously. "This is the verb."

If their first lovemaking had been fierce, since then he had been teaching her how sweet it was when the pleasure was protracted, when the caresses and kisses lingered while tension slowly coiled within until it was so hot and powerful that it exploded out of control. His hunger for her was so strong that he tried to put off his climax for as long as possible, so he could stay inside her and feed that hunger. It wasn't a hunger for sex, per se, though it had a strong sexual base. He didn't simply want to make love, he wanted—*needed*—to make love to her specifically, to Mary Elizabeth Potter. He had to feel her silky, fragile skin under his hands, feel her soft body sheathing him, smell her unique scent of womanhood, forge ancient bonds with each slow thrust and acceptance of their bodies. He was a half-breed; his spirit was strong and uncomplicated, his instincts close to those of his ancestors of both races. With other women, he had had sex; with Mary, he mated.

He wrapped his arms around her and rolled onto his back. Startled, Mary sat up, accidently assuming the exact position he'd wanted her in. She gasped as the motion forced him deep inside her. "What are you doing?"

"Nothing," he murmured, reaching up to place his hands over her breasts. "I'm letting you do the doing."

He watched her face as she considered the situation and was aware of the exact second that her excitement and arousal overcame her discomfort with the unfamiliar position. Her eyelids dropped again, and she bit her lower lip as she moved gently on him. "Like this?"

He almost groaned aloud. That slow movement was exquisite torture, and she quickly got into the rhythm of it. He had thought to prolong their lovemaking by changing positions, but now he was afraid he'd outsmarted himself. As old-fashioned as she was, she was also astonishingly sensuous. After a few minutes he desperately rolled again and put her under him.

Mary linked her arms behind his neck. "I was having fun."

"So was I." He kissed her briefly, then again, their lips lingering together. "Too much."

She smiled, that secret, womanly little smile she used only with him, and the sight of it made him burn. He forgot about control, forgot about everything but the pleasure that awaited them. Afterward, sated and exhausted, they both dozed.

At the sound of a vehicle, Wolf rolled out of bed, instantly alert. Mary stirred sleepily. "What is it?"

"You have company."

"Company?" She sat up and pushed her hair out of her face. "What time is it?"

"Almost six. We must have gone to sleep."

"Six! It's time for Joe's lesson!"

Wolf swore as he began jerking on his clothes. "This

situation's getting out of hand. Damn it, every time I make love to you my own son interrupts us. Once was bad enough, but he's making a habit of it.''

Mary was scrambling into her own clothes, wishing that the circumstances weren't so embarrassing. It was hard to face Joe when it was so obvious that she and his father had just been in bed together. Aunt Ardith would have disowned her for so forgetting her morals and sense of proper behavior. Then she looked at Wolf as he stamped his feet into his boots, and her heart felt as if it had expanded until it filled her entire chest. She loved him, and there was nothing more moral than love. As for proper behavior—she shrugged, mentally kissing propriety goodbye. One couldn't have everything.

Joe had deposited his books on the table and was making a pot of coffee when they entered the kitchen. He looked up and frowned. ''Look, Dad, this situation is getting out of hand. You're cutting into my lesson time.'' Only the twinkle in his ice-blue eyes kept Wolf from getting angry; after a moment, he tousled his son's hair.

''Son, I've said it before, but you've got lousy timing.''

Joe's lesson time was even more limited because they had to take time to eat. They were all starving, so they decided on sandwiches, which were quick, and had just finished when another car drove up.

''My goodness, this house is getting popular,'' Mary muttered as she got up to open the door.

Clay took his hat off as he entered. He paused and sniffed. ''Is that coffee fresh?''

''Yep.'' Wolf stretched to reach the pot while Mary got a cup from the cabinet for Clay.

He sprawled in one of the chairs and gave a weary sigh, which turned to one of appreciation as he inhaled the fragrant steam rising from the coffee as Wolf poured it. "Thanks. I thought I'd find you two here."

"Has anything come up?" Wolf drawled.

"Nothing except a few complaints. You made some people a little nervous."

"Doing what?" Mary interjected.

"Just looking around," Wolf said in a casual tone that didn't fool her at all, nor did it fool Clay.

"Leave it alone. You're not a one-man vigilante committee. I'm warning you for the last time."

"I don't reckon I've done anything illegal, just walking around and looking. I haven't interfered with any law officers, I haven't questioned anyone, I haven't destroyed or hidden any evidence. All I've done is look." Wolf's eyes gleamed. "If you're smart, you'll use me. I'm the best tracker you're going to find."

"And if you're smart, you'll spend your time looking out after what's yours." Clay looked at Mary, and she primmed her mouth. Darn him, he was going to tell!

"That's what I'm doing."

"Maybe not as well as you think. Mary told me about a plan she's got to use herself as bait to bring this guy out in the open."

Wolf's head snapped around, and his brows lowered over narrowed black eyes as he pinned her with a gaze so furious it was all she could do to keep her own gaze steady. "I'll be damned," he said softly, and it was an expression of determination rather than surprise.

"Yeah, that's what I said. I heard you and Joe are escorting her to and from the school, but what about the time in between? And school will be out in a couple of weeks. What about then?"

Mary drew her slender shoulders up. "I won't be talked around as if I'm invisible. This is my house, and let me remind all of you that I'm well over twenty-one. I'll go where I want, when I want." Let them make of that what they would! She hadn't lived with Aunt Ardith for nothing; Aunt Ardith would have died, just on principle, before she would have let a man tell her what to do.

Wolf's eyes hadn't wavered from her. "You'll do what you're damn well told."

"If I were you," Clay suggested, "I'd take her up on the mountain and keep her there. Like I said, school will be out in a couple of weeks, and this old house is pretty isolated. No one has to know where she is. It'll be safer that way."

Enraged, Mary reached out and whisked the cup of coffee away from Clay, then dumped the contents in the sink. "You're not drinking *my* coffee, you tattletale!"

He looked astounded. "I'm just trying to protect you!"

"And I'm just trying to protect him!" she shouted.

"Protect who?" Wolf snapped.

"You!"

"Why do I need protecting?"

"Because whoever is doing this is trying to harm you! First by trying to frame you for the attacks, and second by attacking people who don't hate you as he does!"

Wolf froze. When Mary had first advanced the beginnings of her theory the night before, he and Clay hadn't believed it because it simply hadn't made sense that anyone trying to frame Wolf would try to make anyone believe he would attack Mary. But when Mary put it the way she just had, that the attacks were a sort of twisted punishment, it began to make horrible sense. A rapist was warped, so his logic would be warped.

Mary had been attacked because of him. Because he had been so attracted to her that he hadn't been able to control it, some madman had attacked her, terrified and humiliated her, tried to rape her. His lust had brought attention to her.

His expression was cold and blank as he looked at Clay, who shrugged. "I have to buy it," Clay said. "It's the only thing that even halfway makes sense. When she made friends with you and got Joe into the Academy, folks began to look at you differently. Someone couldn't stand it."

Mary twisted her hands. "Since it's my fault, the least I can do is—"

"No!" Wolf roared, surging to his feet and turning over his chair with a clatter. He lowered his voice with a visible effort. "Go upstairs and get your clothes. You're going with us."

Joe slapped his hand on the table. "About damn time." He got up and began clearing the table. "I'll do this while you pack."

Mary pursed her lips. She was torn between wanting the freedom to put her plan into action—when she thought of it—and the powerful temptation of living with Wolf. It wasn't proper. It was a terrible example to her students. The townspeople would be outraged. *He'd watch her like a hawk!* On the other hand, she loved him to distraction and wasn't the least ashamed of their relationship. Embarrassed, sometimes, because she wasn't accustomed to such intimacy and didn't know how to handle it, but never ashamed.

Also on the other hand, if she dug in her heels and remained here, Wolf would simply stay here with her, where they would be far more visible and far more likely to outrage the town's sensibilities. That was what decided her, because she didn't want even more animosity directed at Wolf because of her. That could be all that was needed to goad the rapist into attacking him directly, or going after Joe.

He put his hands on her shoulders and gave her a little push. "Go," he said gently, and she went.

When she was safely upstairs and out of hearing, Clay looked at Wolf with a troubled, angry expression. "For what it's worth, she thinks you and Joe are in danger, that this maniac may just start shooting at you. I kind of agree with her, damn it."

"Let him try," Wolf said, his face and voice expressionless. "She's most vulnerable on the way to and from school, and I don't think this guy is going to wait patiently. He hit two days in a row, but he got scared when you nearly got him. It'll take a while for him to settle down, then he'll be looking for another hit to make. In the meantime, I'll be looking for him."

Clay didn't want to ask, but the question was burning his tongue. "Did you find anything today?"

"I eliminated some people from my list."

"Scared some of them, too."

Wolf shrugged. "Folks had better get used to seeing me around. If they don't like it, tough."

"I also heard that you made the boys escort the girls home from school. The girls' parents were mighty relieved and grateful."

"They should have taken care of it themselves."

"It's a quiet little town. They aren't used to things like this."

"That's no excuse for being stupid." And it *had* been stupid to overlook their daughters' safety. If he'd been that careless in Nam, he would have been dead.

Clay grunted. "I still want to make my point. I agree with Mary that you and Joe are the primary targets. You may be good, but nobody's better than a bullet, and the same goes for Joe. You don't just have to look after Mary, you have to look after yourselves, too. I'd like it if you could keep her from even finishing out the year at school, so the three of you could stay up on your mountain until we catch this guy."

It went against Wolf's grain to hide from anyone, and that was in the look he gave Clay. Wolf had been trained to hunt; more than that, it was in his nature, in the genes passed down from Comanche and Highland warriors that had mingled in his body, in the formation of his character.

"We'll keep Mary safe," was all he said, and Clay knew he'd failed to convince Wolf to stay out of it.

Joe was leaning against the cabinets, listening. "The people in town are going to raise hell if they find out Mary's staying with us," he put in.

"Yeah, they will." Clay stood up and positioned his hat on his head.

"Let them." Wolf's voice was flat. He'd given Mary the chance to play it safe, but she hadn't taken it. She was his now, by God. Let them squawk.

Clay sauntered to the door. "If anyone asks me, I've arranged for her to live in a safer place until this is over. Don't reckon it's anyone's business where that place is, do you? Though of course, knowing Mary, she'll probably tell everyone right out, just like she did Saturday in Hearst's store."

Wolf groaned. "Hell! What did she do? I haven't heard about it."

"Didn't reckon you would have, what with all that happened that afternoon. Seems she got into it with both Dottie Lancaster and Mrs. Karr, and all but told both of them she was yours for the taking." A slow grin shaped Clay's mouth. "From what I heard, she laced into them good."

When Clay had left, Wolf and Joe looked at each other. "It could get interesting around here."

"It could," Joe agreed.

"Keep an eye out, son. If Mary and Armstrong are right, we're the ones this bastard is really after. Don't go anywhere without your rifle, and stay alert."

Joe nodded. Wolf wasn't worried about hand-to-hand fighting, not even if the other guy was armed with a knife, because he'd taught Joe how to fight the way he'd learned in the military. Not karate, kung fu, tae kwon do, or even judo, but a mixture of many, including good old street fighting. The object of a fight wasn't fairness, but winning, in any way possible, with any weapon handy. It was what had kept him alive and relatively unscathed in prison. A rifle was something else, though. They would have to be doubly alert.

Mary returned and plunked two suitcases on the floor. "I have to have my books, too," she announced. "And someone has to get Woodrow and her kittens."

M̲ary tried to tell herself that she couldn't sleep because she was in a strange bed, because she was too excited, because she was too worried, because—she ran out of excuses and couldn't think of anything else. Though she was pleasantly tired from Wolf's lovemaking, she felt too uneasy to sleep and finally knew why. She turned in his arms and put her hand on his jaw, loving the feel of his facial structure and the slight rasp of his beard beneath her fingers. "Are you awake?" she whispered.

"I wasn't," he said in a low rumble. "But I am now."

She apologized and lay very still. After a moment he squeezed her and pushed her hair away from her face. "Can't you sleep?"

"No. I just feel—strange, I think."

"In what way?"

"Your wife—Joe's mother. I was thinking of her in this bed."

His arms tightened. "She was never in this bed."

"I know. But Joe's in the other room, and I thought this was how it must have been when he was little, before she died."

"Not usually. We were apart a lot, and she died when Joe was two. That was when I got out of the military."

"Tell me about it," she invited, still in a whisper. She needed to know more about this man she loved. "You must have been very young."

"I was seventeen when I enlisted. Even though I knew I'd probably have to do a tour in Vietnam, it was my only way out. My folks were dead, and my grandfather, Mother's father, never really accepted me because I was half Anglo. All I knew was that I had to get off the reservation. It was almost as bad as prison. It *is* prison, in a different way. There was nothing to do, nothing to hope for.

"I met Billie when I was eighteen. She was a Crow half-breed, and I guess she married me because she knew I'd never go back to the reservation. She wanted more. She wanted bright lights and city life. Maybe she thought a soldier had it good, transferring from base to base, partying when he was off duty. But she didn't look down on me because I was a half-breed, and we decided to get married. A month later I was in Nam. I got her a ticket to Hawaii when I had R and R, and she went back pregnant. Joe was born when I was nineteen, but I was home from my first tour and got to see him being born. God, I was so excited. He was screaming his head off. Then they put him in my hands, and it was like taking a heart punch. I loved him so much I would have died for him."

He was silent for a moment, thinking. Then he gave a low laugh. "So there I was, with a newborn son and a wife who didn't think she'd gotten such a good deal, and my enlistment was almost up. I had no prospects of a job, no way of supporting my baby. So I re-upped, and things got so bad between Billie and me that I volunteered for another tour. She died right before my third tour ended. I got out and came home to take care of Joe."

"What did you do?"

"Worked ranches. Rodeoed. It was all I knew. Except for the time I spent in service, I can't remember not working with horses. I was horse crazy when I was a kid, and

I guess I still am. Joe and I drifted around until it was time for him to start school, and we landed in Ruth. You know the rest of it.''

She lay quietly in his arms, thinking of his life. He hadn't had it easy. But the life he'd led had shaped him into the man he was, a man of strength and iron determination. He had endured war and hell and come out even stronger than before. The thought that someone would want to harm him made her so angry she could barely contain it. Somehow she had to find some way to protect him.

He escorted her to school the next morning, and again Mary was aware of how everyone stared at him. But it wasn't fear or hatred she saw in the kids' eyes; rather, they watched him with intense curiosity, and even awe. After years of tales, he was a larger-than-life figure to them, someone glimpsed only briefly. Their fathers had dealt with him, the boys had watched him at work, and his expertise with horses only added to tales about him. It was said that he could "whisper" a horse, that even the wildest one would respond to a special crooning tone in his voice.

Now he was hunting the rapist. The story was all over the county.

Dottie wouldn't even talk to Mary that day; she walked away whenever she approached and even ate lunch by herself. Sharon sighed and shrugged. "Don't pay any attention to her. She's always had a burr under her blanket about the Mackenzies.''

Mary shrugged, too. There didn't seem to be any way she could reach Dottie.

Joe drove into town that afternoon to follow her home. As they walked out to their respective vehicles, she told him, "I need to stop at Hearst's for a few things.''

"I'll be right behind you.''

He was on her heels when she entered the store, and

everyone turned to look at them. Joe gave them a smile that could have come straight from his father, and several people hastily looked away. Sighing, Mary led her six-foot watchdog down the aisle.

Joe paused fractionally when his gaze met that of Pam Hearst. She was standing as if rooted, staring at him. He tipped his hat and followed Mary.

A moment later he felt a light touch on his arm and turned to see Pam standing behind him. "Could I talk to you?" she asked in a low voice. "I—it's important. Please?"

Mary had moved on. Joe shifted his position so he could keep her in sight and said, "Well?"

Pam drew a deep breath. "I thought…maybe…would you go with me to the town dance this Saturday night?" she finished in a rush.

Joe's head jerked. "What?"

"I said—will you go with me to the dance?"

He thumbed his hat back and gave a low whistle under his breath. "You know you're asking for trouble, don't you? Your dad just might lock you in the cellar for a year."

"We don't have a cellar." She gave him a small smile, one that had an immediate reaction on his sixteen-year-old hormones. "And I don't care, anyway. He's wrong, wrong about you and your dad. I've felt horrible about how I acted before. I—I like you, Joe, and I want to go out with you."

He was cynical enough to say, "Yeah. A lot of people started liking me when they found out I had a shot at the Academy. Sure funny how that worked out, isn't it?"

Hot spots of color appeared on her cheeks. "That's not why I'm asking you out!"

"Are you sure? It seems I wasn't good enough to be seen in public with you before. You didn't want people to say Pam Hearst was going out with a 'breed. It's different when they can say you're going out with a candidate for the Air Force Academy.''

''That's not true!'' Pam was truly angry now, and her voice rose. Several people glanced their way.

''It looks that way to me.''

''Well, you're wrong! You're just as wrong as my dad is!''

As if he'd been cued, Mr. Hearst, alerted by Pam's raised voice, started down the aisle toward them. ''What's going on back here? Pam, is this br—boy bothering you?''

Joe noticed how quickly ''breed'' had been changed to ''boy'' and lifted his eyebrows at Pam. She flushed even redder and whirled to face her father.

''No, he isn't bothering me! Wait. Yes. Yes, he is! He's bothering me because I asked him to go out with me and he refused!''

Everyone in the store heard her. Joe sighed. The fat was in the fire now.

Ralph Hearst turned purplish red, and he halted in his tracks as abruptly as if he'd hit a wall. ''What did you say?'' he gasped, evidently not believing his ears.

Pam didn't back down, even though her father looked apoplectic. ''I said he refused to go out with me! I asked him to the Saturday night dance.''

Mr. Hearst's eyes were bulging out of their sockets. ''You get on to the house. We'll talk about this later!''

''I don't want to talk about it later, I want to talk about it right now!''

''I said get on to the house!'' Hearst roared. He turned his infuriated gaze on Joe. ''And you stay away from my daughter, you—''

''He's *been* staying away from me!'' Pam yelled. ''It's the other way around! I won't stay away from him! This isn't the first time I've asked him out. You and everyone else in this town are wrong for the way you've treated the Mackenzies, and I'm tired of it. Miss Potter is the only one of us who's had the guts to stand up for what she thinks is right!''

''This is all her fault, that do-gooding—''

''Stop right there.'' Joe spoke for the first time, but there was something in his cool voice, in his pale blue eyes, that stopped the man. Joe was only sixteen, but he was tall and muscular, and there was a sudden alertness to his stance that made the older man pause.

Pam jumped in. She was bright and cheery-natured, but as headstrong as her father. ''Don't start on Miss Potter,'' she warned. ''She's the best teacher we've ever had here in Ruth, and if you do anything to get rid of her, I swear I'll drop out of school.''

''You'll do no such thing!''

''I swear I will! I love you, Dad, but you're wrong! All of us talked about it at school today, about how we'd seen the teachers treat Joe over the years, and how wrong it was, because he's obviously the smartest of us all! And we talked about how Wolf Mackenzie was the one who made sure all of us girls got home all right yesterday. No one else thought of it! Or don't you care?''

''Of course he cares,'' Mary said briskly, having walked up without anyone except Joe noticing. ''It's just that Wolf, with his military experience, knew what to do.'' She'd made that up, but it sounded good. She put her hand on Mr. Hearst's arm. ''Why don't you take care of your customers and just let them fight it out? You know how teenagers are.''

Somehow Ralph Hearst found himself at the front of the store again before he realized it. He stopped and looked down at Mary. ''I don't want my girl dating a half-breed!'' he said fiercely.

"She'll be safer with that half-breed than with any other boy around," Mary replied. "For one thing, he's steady as a rock. He won't drink or drive fast, and for another, he has no intention of getting involved with any girl around here. He'll be going away, and he knows it."

"I don't want my daughter dating an Indian!"

"Are you saying that character doesn't mean anything? That you'd rather have Pam go out with a drunk Anglo, who might get her killed in a car accident, than with a sober Indian, who would protect her with his life?"

He looked stricken and rubbed his head in agitation. "No, damn it, that isn't what I mean," he muttered.

Mary sighed. "My Aunt Ardith remembered every old chestnut she ever heard, and one of the ones she brought out most often was 'pretty is as pretty does.' You go by how people act, don't you, Mr. Hearst. You've voted according to how the candidates have stood on issues in the past, haven't you?"

"Of course." He looked uncomfortable.

"And?" she prompted.

"All right, all right! It's just—some things are hard to forget, you know? Not things that Joe has done, but just... things. And that father of his is—"

"As proud as you are," she cut in. "All he ever wanted was a place to raise his motherless son." She was laying it on so thick she expected to hear violins in the background any moment now, but it was about time these people realized some things about Wolf. Maybe he was more controlled than civilized, but his control was very good, and they would never know the difference.

Deciding it was time to give him some breathing room, she said, "Why not talk it over with your wife?"

He looked relieved at the suggestion. "I'll do that."

Joe was walking up the aisle; Pam, who had turned her

back, was busily neatening a stack of paint thinner in an obvious effort to act casual. Mary paid for the items she'd gathered, and Joe lifted the sack. Silently they walked out together.

"Well?" she asked as soon as they were outside.

"Well, what?"

"Are you taking her to the dance?"

"It looks like it. She won't take no for an answer, like someone else I know."

She gave him a prim look and didn't respond to his teasing. Then, as he opened the car door for her, a thought struck, and she looked at him in horror. "Oh, no," she said softly. "Joe, that man is attacking women who are friendly to you and Wolf."

His whole body jerked, and his mouth tightened. "Damn," he swore. He thought a minute, then shook his head. "I'll tell her tomorrow that I can't go."

"That won't do any good. How many people heard her say what she did? It will be all over the county by tomorrow, whether you take her to the dance or not."

He didn't reply, merely closed the door after she'd gotten into the car. He looked grim, far too grim for a boy his age.

Joe felt grim, too, but an idea was taking form. He'd watch out for Pam and warn her so she'd be on guard, but maybe this would draw the rapist out. He'd use Mary's plan, but with different bait: himself. He'd make certain Pam was safe, but leave himself open at times when he was alone. Maybe, when the guy realized he couldn't get at a helpless woman, he'd get so frustrated he'd go after one of his real targets. Joe knew the chance he was taking, but unless Wolf could find the track he was looking for, he didn't see any other option.

Mary looked around for Wolf when they got home, but

she couldn't find him. She changed into jeans and walked outside. She found Joe in the barn, grooming a horse. "Is Wolf out here?"

He shook his head and continued brushing the horse's gleaming hide. "His horse is gone. He's probably checking fences." Or hunting for a certain track, but he didn't say that to Mary.

She got him to show her how to brush the horse and took over for him until her arm began to hurt. The horse snorted when she stopped, so she went back to brushing. "This is harder than it looks," she panted.

Joe grinned at her over the back of another horse. "It'll give you a few muscles. But you've finished with him, so don't spoil him. He'll stand there all day if someone will keep brushing him."

She stopped and stepped back. "Well, why didn't you say so?" He put the horse in his stall, and Mary walked back to the house. She had almost reached the porch when she heard the rhythmic thudding of a horse's hooves and turned to see Wolf riding up. She caught her breath. Even though she was ignorant about horses, she knew that not many people looked the way he did on a horse. There was no bouncing or jiggling; he sat so easily in the saddle, and moved so fluidly with the animal, that he looked motionless. The Comanche had arguably been the world's best horsemen, better even than the Berber or Bedouin, and Wolf had learned well from his mother's people. His powerful legs controlled the big bay stallion he was riding, so that the reins were lightly held and no harm done to the horse's tender mouth.

He slowed the horse to a walk as he approached her. "Any trouble today?"

She decided not to tell him about Pam Hearst. That was Joe's business, if he wanted it known. She knew he'd tell

Wolf, but in his own time. "No. We didn't see anyone suspicious, and no one followed us."

He reined in and leaned down to brace his forearm on the saddle horn. His dark eyes drifted over her slim figure. "Do you know how to ride?"

"No. I've never been on a horse."

"Well, that situation is about to be remedied." He kicked his boot free of the stirrup and held his hand out to her. "Put your left foot in the stirrup and lift yourself as I swing you up."

She was willing. She tried. But the horse was too tall, and she couldn't reach the stirrup with her foot. She was staring at the bay with an aggravated expression when Wolf laughed and shifted back in the saddle. "Here, I'll pick you up."

He leaned out of the saddle and caught her under the arms. Mary gasped and grabbed at his biceps as she felt her feet leave the ground; then he straightened and set her firmly on the saddle in front of him. She grabbed the saddle horn as he lifted the reins, and the horse moved forward.

"This is a long way up," she said, bouncing so hard her teeth rattled.

He chuckled and wrapped his left arm around her, pulling her back against him. "Relax and let yourself go with the horse's rhythm. Feel how I'm moving and move with me."

She did as he said and felt the rhythm as soon as she relaxed. Her body automatically seemed to sink deeper into the saddle, and her torso moved with Wolf's. The bouncing stopped. Unfortunately by that time they had reached the barn and her first ride was over. Wolf lifted her down and dismounted.

"I liked that," she announced.

"You did? Good. We'll start you on riding lessons to-morrow."

Joe's voice came to them from a stall farther down. "I started her on grooming lessons today."

"You'll be as comfortable with horses as if you'd been around them all of your life," Wolf said, and leaned down to kiss her. She went on tiptoe, her lips parting. It was a long moment before he lifted his head, and when he did, his breathing was faster. His eyes were hooded and narrow. Damn, she got to him so fast he reacted like a teenager when he was around her.

When Mary had gone back to the house, Joe came out of the stall and looked at his father. "Find anything to-day?"

Wolf began unsaddling the bay. "No. I've had a good look around the ranches, but none of the prints match. It has to be someone from town."

Joe frowned. "That makes sense. Both of the attacks were in town. But I can't think of anyone it could be. I guess I've never noticed before if someone has freckled hands."

"I'm not looking for freckles, I'm looking for that print. I know how he walks, toeing in a little and putting his weight on the outside of his feet."

"What if you find him? Do you think the sheriff will arrest him just because he has freckles on his hands and walks a certain way?"

Wolf smiled, a movement of his lips that was totally without mirth. His eyes were cold. "When I find him," he said softly, "if he's smart, he'll confess. I'll give the law a chance, but there's no way he'll walk free. He'll be a lot safer in jail than out on the streets, and I'll make certain he knows it."

It was an hour before they finished with the horses. Joe

lingered to look over his tack, and Wolf walked up to the house alone. Mary was absorbed in cooking, humming as she stirred the big pot of beef stew, and she didn't hear him come in the back door. He walked up behind her and put his hand on her shoulder.

Blind terror shot through her. She screamed and threw herself sideways, to press her back against the wall. She held the dripping spoon in her hand like a knife. Her face was utterly white as she stared at him.

His face was hard. In silence they stared at each other, time stretching out between them. Then she dropped the spoon on the floor with a clatter. "Oh God, I'm sorry," she said in a thin voice, and covered her face with her hands.

He drew her to him, his hand in her hair, holding her head to his chest. "You thought it was him again, didn't you?"

She clung to him, trying to drive away the terror. It had come out of nowhere, taking her by surprise and shattering the control she'd managed to gain over her memory and emotions. When Wolf's hand had touched her shoulder, for a brief, horrifying moment it had been happening all over again. She felt cold; she wanted to sink into his warmth, to let the reality of his touch overcome the hideous memory of another touch.

"You don't have to be afraid," he murmured into her hair. "You're safe here." But he knew her memory was still there, that a touch from behind meant a nightmare to her. Somehow he had to take away that fear, so she could be free of it.

She regained control and eased herself away from him, and he let her, because he knew it was important to her. She appeared almost normal through dinner and Joe's lesson; the only sign of strain was an occasional haunted expression in her eyes, as if she hadn't completely succeeded in pushing the memory away.

But when they went to bed and her silky body was under his hands, she turned to him as eagerly as ever. Wolf's lovemaking left her no room for anything else, no lingering memories or vestiges of terror. Her entire body and mind were occupied with him. Afterward she curled against him and slept undisturbed, at least until the graying dawn, when he woke her and pulled her beneath him again.

Mary was fully aware of the tenuousness of both her relationship with Wolf and her presence in his house. He often told her explicitly how much he wanted her, but in terms of lust, not love. He never spoke a word about loving, not even during lovemaking, when she was unable to keep from telling him over and over that she loved him. When the fever of lust passed, he might well cut her out of his life, and she tried to prepare herself for that possibility even while she absorbed the maximum pleasure from the present situation.

She knew that living with him was for her protection, and only temporary. She also knew that it was nothing short of scandalous for a small-town schoolteacher to shack up with the local black sheep, and that was exactly how the townspeople would view the situation if they knew about it. She knew the risk she was taking with her career, and decided that the days and nights with Wolf were worth it. If she lost her job, there were other jobs, but she knew there would be no other loves for her. She was twenty-nine and had never even felt a twinge of interest or excitement over any other man. Some people loved only once, and it appeared she was one of them.

The only time she allowed herself to worry over the future was on the drives to and from school, when she was alone in the car. When she was with Wolf she didn't want to waste even a single second on regrets. With him, she was totally alive, totally female.

She worried about Wolf and Joe, too. She knew Wolf was actively hunting the man who had attacked her, and she was terrified he would be hurt. She couldn't let herself even think that he might be killed. And Joe was up to something; she knew it. He was too much like Wolf for her not to recognize the signs. He was preoccupied, and far too sober, as if faced with making a choice when neither of the alternatives was very attractive. But she couldn't get him to open up to her, and that alone frightened her, for Joe had talked to her from the beginning.

Joe was on edge. He'd told Pam to be more cautious than usual, and he tried to make certain she never walked home alone, but there was always a chance she'd be careless. He'd also made a point of letting himself be seen alone, and evidently unaware of the need for caution, but nothing happened. The town was quiet, if edgy. He was forced to the same awareness that Wolf already had, that with so few clues, all they could do was stay alert and wait until the man made a mistake.

When Joe told his father that he was going to the dance with Pam, Wolf looked piercingly at the boy. "Do you know what you're doing?"

"I hope so."

"Watch your back."

The terse advice brought a thin smile to Joe's mouth. He knew he could be making a big mistake by going to that dance, that the scene could turn ugly, but he'd told Pam he'd take her, and that was that. He'd have to be doubly alert, but damn, he wanted to hold her in his arms while they shuffled slowly across the sawdust floor. Even though he knew he was going away and they'd never have anything permanent between them, he was strongly attracted to her. He couldn't explain it and knew it wouldn't last, but he felt it *now*, and it was now that he had to deal with it.

Pam was edgy, too, when he picked her up. She tried to hide it by talking too fast and too brightly, until he put his hand over her mouth. "I know," he muttered. "It worries me, too."

She tossed her head, freeing her mouth. "I'm not worried. It'll be all right, you'll see. I told you, all of us have talked about it."

"Then why are you so nervous?"

She looked away from him and cleared her throat. "Well, this *is* the first time I've been out with you. I just felt—I don't know—nervous and scared and excited all at once."

He thought about that for a few minutes, and silence filled the cab of the truck. Then he said, "I guess I can understand being nervous and excited, but why scared?"

Now it was Pam's turn to be silent, and she flushed a little when she finally said, "Because you're not like the rest of us."

That grim look settled around Joe's mouth. "Yeah, I know. I'm a 'breed."

"It isn't that," she snapped. "It's—you're *older* than the rest of us, somehow. I know we're the same age, but inside you're all grown up. We're ordinary people. We'll stay right here and ranch the way our folks have. We'll marry people from the same background and stay in the county, or move to another county just like it, and have kids and be content. But you're not like that. You're going to the Academy, and you won't be back, at least not to stay. You may come back for a visit, but that's all it'll be."

It surprised him that she had it so neatly pegged. He did feel old inside, and always had, especially in comparison to other kids his age. And he knew he wouldn't be back here to ranch. He belonged in the sky doing Mach 2, marking his place in the universe with a vapor trail.

They were quiet the rest of the way to the dance. When Joe parked his truck with the collection of other trucks and a few cars, he braced himself for whatever could happen.

He was prepared for almost anything, but not for what actually took place. When he and Pam walked into the run-down old building used for the dances, for a moment there was a certain stillness, a strange silence; then in the next heartbeat the noise picked back up and everyone returned to his own conversation. Pam put her hand in his and squeezed it.

A few minutes later the live band started up, and couples drifted onto the sawdust-covered planks of the dance floor. Pam led him to the middle of the floor and smiled at him.

He smiled back, wryly admitting and admiring her courage. Then he took her in his arms to enter the slow rhythm of the dance.

They didn't talk. After wanting for so long just to touch her, he was content to hold her and move with her. He could smell her perfume, feel the softness of her hair, the resilient mounds of her breasts, the movement of her legs against his. As young people have done from the beginning of time, they swayed together in their own private world, reality suspended.

Reality intruded, however, when he heard an angry mutter of ''dirty Indian'' and automatically stiffened as he looked around for the speaker.

Pam said, ''Please,'' and drew him back into the dance.

When the song ended, a boy stood on his chair and yelled, ''Hey, Joe! Pam! Over here!''

They looked in the direction of the yell, and Joe couldn't help grinning. Every student in the three classes Mary taught was grouped at the table, with two empty chairs waiting for him and Pam. They were waving and calling.

The kids saved the evening. They enveloped him and Pam in a circle of laughter and dancing. Joe danced with every girl in the group; the boys talked horses, cattle, ranching and rodeoing, and between them made certain none of the girls had a chance to sit down much. The kids also talked to the other people at the dance, and soon everyone knew that the half-breed was going to the Air Force Academy. Ranchers are generally hard-working, conservative and firmly patriotic, and before too long, anyone who had a hard word to say about the half-breed found himself hushed and told to mind his manners.

Joe and Pam left before the dance was over, because he didn't want to keep her out too late. As they walked to his truck, he shook his head. "I never would have believed it," he said softly. "Did you know they would all be here?"

Pam denied it. "But they knew I'd asked you. I guess the whole town knew I'd asked you. It was fun, wasn't it?"

"It was fun," he agreed. "But it could have gotten rough. You know that, don't you? If it hadn't been for the guys—"

"And girls!" she interrupted.

"Them, too. If it hadn't been for them, I'd have been thrown out."

"It didn't happen. And next time it will be even better."

"Is there going to be a next time?"

She looked suddenly unsure of herself. "You—you can still come to the dances, even if you don't want to come with me."

Joe laughed as he opened the truck door. He turned and put his hands on her waist, then lifted her onto the seat. "I like being with you."

About halfway back to Ruth, Pam put her hand on his arm. "Joe?"

"Yeah?"

"Do you want to—uh, that is, do you know any place to stop?" She faltered on the words.

He knew he should resist the temptation, but he couldn't. He turned off on the next side road they came to, then left the road to bounce across a meadow for about a mile before he parked beneath a stand of trees.

The mild May night wrapped around them. The moonlight couldn't penetrate the shelter of the trees, and the dark cab of the truck was a warm, safe cave. Pam was a pale, indistinct figure as he reached for her.

She was pliant and eager, yielding to his hands, pressing against him to take more of his kisses. Her firm young body made him feel as if he would explode. Barely aware of what he was doing, Joe shifted and twisted until they were lying on the seat with Pam half beneath him. Soon her breasts were bare, and he heard her strangled intake of breath as he took a nipple into his mouth. Then her nails were digging into his shoulders, and her hips arched.

It was quickly getting out of control. Clothing was opened and pushed aside. Bare skin touched bare skin. Somehow, Pam's jeans were off. But when he slid his hands inside her panties, she whispered, "I've never done this before. Will it hurt?"

Joe groaned aloud, but forced himself to stillness. It took every ounce of willpower he possessed, but he stopped his hands. His body throbbed painfully, and he savagely controlled it. After a long minute he sat up and pulled Pam to a sitting position astride his lap.

"Joe?"

He leaned his forehead against hers. "We can't do it," he murmured regretfully.

"But why?" She moved against him, her body still empty and aching with a need she didn't understand.

"*Because* it would be your first time."

"But I want you!"

"I want you, too." He managed a wry grin. "I guess it's pretty obvious. But your first time—baby, it should be with someone you love. And you don't love me."

"I could," she whispered. "Oh, Joe, I truly could."

He was so frustrated that he could barely control his voice enough to speak, but he managed. "I hope you don't. I'm leaving. I have a chance waiting for me that I'd die before I'd give up."

"And no girl is going to change your mind?"

Joe knew the truth inside him, and he knew Pam wouldn't like it, but he had to be honest with her. "No girl *could* change my mind. I want to go to the Academy so much that nothing can keep me here."

She caught his hands and shyly brought them up to her breasts. "We could still, you know, do it. No one would know."

"You'd know. And when you fall in love with some guy, you'd regret that your first time wasn't with him. God, Pam, don't make this so hard for me! Slap my face or something." The way her firm young breasts filled his hands made him wonder if he wasn't crazy for passing this up.

She leaned forward and rested her head on his shoulder. He felt the way her body shook as she began to cry, and he folded his arms around her.

"You've always been special to me," she said in a stifled tone. "Do you have to be so darn conscientious?"

"Do you want to take a chance on getting pregnant at sixteen?"

That stopped her tears. She sat up. "Oh. I thought you'd have a—don't all boys carry them?"

"I guess not. And it wouldn't matter if I did have one. I don't want to get involved—not this kind of involved—with you or anyone else, because no matter what, I'm going to the Academy. Besides, you're too young."

She couldn't stop the giggle that burst out. "I'm as old as you are."

"Then *we're* too young."

"You're not." She sobered and cupped his face in her hands. "You're not young at all, and I guess that's why you stopped. Every other boy I know would have had his jeans off so fast he'd have fabric burns on his legs. But let's make a bargain, okay?"

"What kind of bargain?"

"We'll still be friends, won't we?"

"You know it."

"Then we'll go around together and keep things light. No more messing around like this, because it hurts too much when you stop. You go away to Colorado like you've planned, and I'll take things as they come. I may get married. But if I don't, you come on back here one summer and we'll *both* be old enough then. Will you be my first lover?"

"It won't keep me in Ruth," he said steadily.

"I don't expect it to. But is it a bargain?"

He accepted that the years could make a difference, and he knew she'd most likely be married. If not—maybe.

"If you still want to then, yeah, it's a bargain."

She held out her hand, and they solemnly shook to seal the deal. Then she kissed him and began putting on her clothes.

Mary was waiting up for him when he got home, an anxious look in her eyes. She got to her feet and tightened the belt of her robe. "Are you okay?" she asked. "Did anything happen?"

"I'm fine. Everything went okay."

Then he saw that the anxious look was really fear. She touched his arm. "You didn't see anyone who—" She stopped, then started again. "No one shot at your truck, or tried to run you off the road?"

"No, it was quiet." They looked at each other for a moment, and Joe realized that Mary had feared the same thing that had occurred to him. More than that, she knew he had decided to take the chance in an effort to draw the rapist out.

He cleared his throat. "Is Dad in bed?"

"No," Wolf said quietly from the doorway. He wore only a pair of jeans. His black eyes were steady. "I wanted to make certain you were okay. This was like watching Daniel walk into the lion's den."

"Well, Daniel made it out okay, didn't he? So did I. It was even fun. The whole class was there."

Mary smiled, the dread lifting from her mind. She knew now what had happened. Knowing that the situation could get ugly if Joe had gone to the dance without backup, the kids had taken it on themselves to make him a part of their group and let everyone at the dance know he was accepted.

Wolf held out his hand, and Mary went to him. She could sleep now. They were safe for another night, these two men whom she loved.

Chapter Eleven

School was out. Mary was intensely proud of her students. The seniors had all graduated, and all of the undergraduates had passed. All of them intended to finish high school, and a couple of them wanted to go to college. It was a record to thrill any teacher's heart.

Joe didn't get a respite. Mary decided he needed more advanced classes in math than she was qualified to teach and began a search for a teacher who was qualified. She found one in a town seventy miles distant, and three times a week Joe made the trip for a two-hour accelerated course. She continued to teach him at night.

The days passed in a haze of happiness for Mary. She seldom left the mountain, seldom saw anyone except Wolf and Joe. Even when they were both gone, she felt safe. It had been only a little over two weeks since the attack, but it seemed as if it had happened a long time ago. Whenever a sliver of memory surfaced to unsettle her emotions, she scolded herself for letting it bother her. Nothing had happened, except she had been terrified. If anyone needed care and consideration, it was Cathy Teele. So Mary pushed the memories away and concentrated on the present. The present, inevitably, was Wolf.

He dominated her life, waking and sleeping. He began teaching her how to ride and how to help him with the horses, and she suspected he used the same method with her that he used with the young colts and fillies that were brought to him. He was firm and demanding, but utterly clear in his instructions and what he wanted out of both her and the horses. When they obeyed, he rewarded them with approval and affection. In fact, Mary mused, he was easier on the horses than he was on her! When *they* disobeyed, he was unfailingly patient. When *she* didn't do something exactly as he'd told her, he let her know about it in unmistakable terms.

But he was always affectionate. Actually, she decided "lusty" was a better description. He made love to her every night, sometimes twice. He made love to her in the empty stall where Joe had interrupted them. He made love to her in the shower. She knew she wasn't even close to voluptuous, but he seemed enthralled with her body. When they lay in bed at night he would turn on the lamp and lean on his elbow, watching as he stroked his hand over her from shoulders to knees, seemingly fascinated by the difference between her pale, delicate skin and his dark, powerful work-callused hand.

Wyoming weather in the summer was generally cool and dry, at least compared to Savannah, but the summer vacation from school had scarcely begun when a heat wave sent the temperatures into the nineties, even edging into the low hundreds by late afternoon. For the first time in her life Mary wished she had some shorts to wear, but Aunt Ardith had never allowed them. She did find, however, that her plain cotton skirts were cooler than the new jeans she was so proud of, allowing for the circulation of whatever breeze happened to wander by. Not that Aunt Ardith would have approved of Mary's attire even then, for Mary declined to wear a slip or hosiery. Aunt Ardith had donned both articles of clothing every day of her life and would have considered anyone who dared to go without a slip an out-and-out hussy.

One morning just after Joe had left to drive to his class, Mary walked out to the barn and reflected on her state of hussiness. All in all, she was satisfied with it. Being a hussy had its advantages.

She could hear some horses snorting and stamping around in the small corral behind the barn, though Wolf usually used the larger one adjacent to the stables for training. The sound of activity, however, told her where she could find him, and that was all she wanted to know.

But when she rounded the corner of the barn, she stopped in her tracks. Wolf's big bay stallion was mounting the mare she had been riding during her lessons. The mare's front hooves were hobbled, and protective boots covered her rear hooves. The stallion was snorting and grunting, and the mare squealed as he entered her. Wolf moved to her head to steady her, and then she stood quietly. "There, sweetheart," he crooned. "You can handle this big old guy, can't you?"

The mare shivered under the impact of the stallion's thrusts, but she stood still for the service and it was over in only a couple of minutes. The stallion snorted and dropped off her, his head down low as he snuffled and blew.

Wolf continued talking in that low, soothing voice to the mare as he bent down to remove the hobble. As he started to remove the boots, Mary stepped forward and caught his attention. "You—you *tied* her!" she said accusingly.

He grinned as he finished unbuckling the protective boots. Miss Mary Elizabeth Potter stood before him in full form, her back ramrod-straight, chin lifted. "I didn't tie her," he said with amused patience. "I hobbled her."

"So she couldn't get away from him!"

"She didn't want to get away from him."

"How do you know?"

"Because she would have kicked him if she hadn't been ready for him to cover her," he explained as he led the mare back into the barn. Mary followed, her face still filled with indignation.

"A lot of good it would have done if she'd kicked him—you put those boots on her so she wouldn't hurt him!"

"Well, I didn't want my stallion damaged. On the other hand, if she had resisted service, I would have gotten her out of there. When a mare resists, it means I've misjudged the time, or something is wrong with her. But she took him nicely, didn't you girl?" he finished, patting the mare's neck.

Mary watched, fidgeting, as he washed the mare. She still didn't like the idea of the mare being unable to run away from the stallion, even though this particular mare was now standing as placidly as if nothing had happened a few minutes ago. It disturbed her on a deep emotional level that didn't respond to logic, and she felt uneasy.

Wolf led the mare to her stall, fed her and gave her fresh water. Then he squatted in front of the faucet to wash his hands and arms. When he looked up, Mary was still standing there, a troubled, almost frightened look in her eyes. He straightened. "What's wrong?"

Desperately she tried to shrug her uneasiness aside, but it didn't work. It was plain in her face and voice. "It looked—it looked...." Her voice trailed off, but suddenly he understood.

He moved slowly toward her and wasn't surprised when she backed up a step. "Horses aren't people," he said gently. "They're big, and they snort and squeal. It looks rough, but that's just how horses mate. It would be even rougher if they were allowed to run free, because they kick and bite."

She looked at the mare. "I know. It's just—" Sh

stopped, because she really couldn't say what was bothering her.

Wolf reached her and put his hands on her waist, holding her lightly so she wouldn't be alarmed and wouldn't know that she couldn't break free unless he let her. "It's just that the roughness reminded you of being attacked?" he finished for her.

She gave him a quick, disturbed look, then just as quickly looked away.

"I know the memory is still there, baby." He slowly tightened his hands, bringing her close against him and just holding her. After a moment she began to relax, and her silky head rested against his chest. Only then did he put his arms around her, because he didn't want her to feel restrained.

"I want to kiss you," he murmured.

She lifted her head and smiled at him. "That's why I came out here: to tempt you into a kiss. I've become a shameless hussy. Aunt Ardith would have disowned me."

"Aunt Ardith sounds like a pain in the—"

"She was wonderful," Mary said firmly. "It's just that she was very old-fashioned and had strict notions of what was proper and what wasn't. For instance, only shameless hussies would wear a skirt without a proper petticoat underneath." She lifted her skirt a little to show him.

"Then let's hear it for shameless hussies." He bent his head and kissed her, and felt the familiar hot excitement begin building in his body. Ruthlessly he controlled it, because control was critical right now. He had to show Mary something, and he couldn't do it if his libido overcame his common sense. He had to do something to banish that ever-present fear from the back of her mind.

He raised his head and hugged her for a minute before letting his arms drop. Instead he took her hands and held them, and the expression on his face made the smile leave her eyes. He said slowly, "Are you willing to try something that might get you over being frightened?"

She looked cautious. "Such as?"

"We could reenact parts of the attack."

Mary stared at him. She was curious, but also wary. Par of her didn't want to do anything that would remind her o. that day, but on the other hand, she didn't like being afraid She said, "Which parts?"

"I could chase you."

"He didn't chase me. He grabbed me from behind."

"So will I, when I catch you."

She considered it. "It won't work. I'll know it's you."

"We could try."

She stared at him for a long time, then stiffened as thought came to her. "He threw me facedown on th ground," she whispered. "He was on top of me, rubbin himself against me."

Wolf's face was strained. "Do you want me to do tha too?"

She shuddered. "Want you to? No. But I think you'r going to have to. I don't want to be afraid any longer. Mak love to me like that—please."

"What if you get really scared?"

"Don't—" She swallowed. "Don't stop."

He looked at her for a long minute, as if measuring h resolve; then his mouth began to quirk up on one side. "A right. Run."

She didn't. She stared at him. "What?"

"Run. I can't chase you if you don't run."

All of a sudden she felt silly at the thought of runni about the yard like a child. "Just like that?"

"Yeah, just like that. Think of it this way: when I cat

you, I'm going to pull your clothes off and make love to you, so why are you waiting?''

He removed his hat to hook it on a post. Mary took a step backward, then, despite her dignity, whirled and ran. She heard the thudding of his boots as he came after her, and laughed with excitement despite herself. She knew she didn't have a prayer of reaching the house; his legs were much longer than hers. Instead she relied on agility and dodged around his truck, then a tree.

"I'm going to get you," he growled, his voice right behind her, and his hand closed briefly on her shoulder before she sprinted away from him.

She sought refuge behind his truck again, with him on the other side. They feinted, but neither gained an advantage. Panting, her face alight with both excitement and triumph, Mary taunted him, "Can't catch me, can't catch me."

A slow, unholy smile touched his mouth as he looked at her. She was almost glowing with her success, her silky brown hair tumbling around her face, and he wanted her so much it hurt. He wanted to take her in his arms and make love to her, and he swore to himself because he couldn't, not right now. First he had to play this through, and, despite her brave words, he hoped she could bear it.

They had been staring at each other, and suddenly it struck her how savage he looked. He was aroused. She knew that look on his face as well as she knew her own, and her breath caught. He wasn't playing; he was deadly earnest. For the first time, fear began to creep in on her. She tried to tamp it down, because she knew Wolf would never hurt her. It was just—oh, damn, something about it did remind her of the attack, no matter how she tried to push the thought away. The playfulness drained out of her, and an unreasonable panic took its place. "Wolf? Let's stop now."

His chest rose and fell with his breathing, and a bleak look entered his eyes, but his voice was guttural. "No. I'm going to catch you."

She ran blindly, leaving the dubious safety of the truck. His running steps behind her sounded like thunder, obscuring every other sound, even that of her rasping breath. It was like being in that alley again, even though a part of her clung to the knowledge that this was Wolf, and she wanted him to do this. She hadn't had a chance to run from her attacker, but he had been behind her; she had heard his breathing just as she now heard Wolf's. She screamed, a high, terrified sound, just before Wolf caught her and bore her down, on her stomach, to the ground, his heavy weight coming down on top of her.

He supported himself on his arms to keep from crushing her, and nuzzled her ear. "Ha, I caught you." He forced himself to say the words lightly, but his chest was tight with pain at what she was going through. He could feel the terror that held her in its grip, and he began trying to loosen its bonds, speaking softly to her, reminding her of the heated, sensuous pleasures they had shared. Tears stung his eyes at the sounds she made, those of a trapped and terrified animal. God, he didn't know if he could do it. The lust had died in him at her first scream.

At first she struggled like a wild thing, kicking and bucking, trying to free her arms, but he held them clamped down. She was maddened with fear, so much so that despite the difference in their sizes and strength, she might have hurt him if not for his training. As it was, all he could do was hold her and try to break through the black mist of fear that enveloped her.

"Calm down, sweetheart, calm down. You know I won

hurt you, and I won't let anyone else hurt you. You know who I am." He repeated it over and over, until exhaustion claimed her, and her struggles became weak and aimless. Only then could she begin to listen; only then could his crooning words penetrate the barrier of fear. Suddenly she collapsed on the ground with her face buried in the hot, sweet grass and began to cry.

Wolf lay on top of her with his arms still locked securely around her and soothed her while she cried. He petted her and kissed her hair, her shoulder, her delicate nape, until at last she lay limply on the grass, both tears and energy exhausted. The endless caresses affected him, too, now that she was calmer; he felt a return of the desire that was never far away from him since he'd met her.

He nuzzled her neck again. "Are you still frightened?" he murmured.

Bruised, swollen eyelids were closed over her eyes. "No," she whispered. "I'm sorry I keep putting you through this. I love you."

"I know, sweetheart. Hold on to that thought." Then he lifted himself back on his knees and pushed her skirt to her waist.

Mary's eyes flared open when she felt him pulling down her underpants, and her voice was sharp. "Wolf! No!"

He stripped the garment down her legs, and Mary trembled in reaction. It was so much like before, in the alley. She was on her stomach on the ground, with a man's weight on top of her, and she couldn't bear it. She tried to scramble forward, but he locked one arm around her waist and held her while he unfastened his jeans with the other hand. He kneed her thighs farther apart and eased himself against her, then let his weight down on her again.

"This reminds you of it, doesn't it?" he asked in a low, gentle voice. "Being on the ground, on your stomach, with me behind you. But you know I won't hurt you, that you don't have to be afraid, don't you?''

"I don't care. I don't like this! Let me up, I want up!''

"I know, baby. Come on now, relax. Think of how many times I've made love to you and how much you've enjoyed it. Trust me.''

The smell of the hot earth was in her nostrils. "I don't want you to make love to me now,'' she managed to say, albeit raggedly. "Not like this.''

"Then I won't. Don't be afraid, baby. I won't go any further unless you want me to. Just relax, and let's feel each other. I don't want you to be afraid when I come up behind you. I admit, your pretty little rear end turns me on. I like to look at it and touch it, and when you cuddle it against me in bed it drives me crazy. I guess you've noticed, though, haven't you?''

Dazedly, she tried to gather her scattered senses. He'd never hurt her before, and now that the haze of fear was fading, she knew he never would. This was Wolf, the man she loved, not her attacker. She was in his strong arms, where she was safe.

She relaxed, her tired muscles going limp. Yes, he was definitely aroused. She could feel him, nestled between her spread legs, but true to his word he was making no move to enter her.

He stroked her sides and kissed her neck. "Are you all right now?''

She sighed, a barely audible release of breath. "Yes,'' she whispered.

He shifted to his knees again and sat back on his heels. Before she could guess what he was about, his steely hands lifted her up and back, so she was sitting astride his thighs, but facing away from him. Their naked loins were pressed together, but still he didn't enter her.

The first twinge of excitement sang along her nerves. The moment was doubly erotic because they were out in the open, crouched on the grass with the hot, bright sun blazing down on them. If anyone happened to drive up, they would be caught. The sudden sense of danger sharply heightened her arousal. Actually, from the front they were covered, because her skirt was draped over his thighs.

Then that protective cover was whisked away as he pulled her skirt up and to the side. He held her to him with one hand on her stomach, and the other hand slid down between her legs. The intimate contact brought a sharp little cry to her lips.

"Do you like that?" he murmured against her ear and gently nipped the lobe.

Mary made some incoherent answer. His rough fingertips were rasping over her most sensitive flesh, creating and building such pleasure that she could barely speak. He knew exactly how to touch her, how to build her to readiness and take her to ecstasy. Mindlessly she arched back against him; the movement brought his manhood more solidly against her, and she groaned aloud.

"Wolf—please!"

He groaned, too, from between clenched teeth. "I'll please you any way you want, baby. Just tell me how."

She could barely speak for the powerful coil of sensation tightening inside her. "I want you."

"Now?"

"Yes."

"Like this?"

She moved against him and this time had to choke back a cry. "Yes!"

He eased her forward until she was on her stomach again and covered her. His entry was slow and gentle, and fever enveloped her. Eagerly she met the impact of his thrusts, her body on fire, all thoughts suspended before such all-consuming need. This wasn't a nightmare; this was another part of the sensual delights he'd been teaching her. She writhed against him and felt the coil tighten unbearably. Then it sprang free, and she convulsed in his arms. He clamped his hands on her hips and loosed his own responses, driving into her hard and fast until his pulsing release freed him.

They lay together on the grass for a long time, half-dozing, too exhausted to move. Only when Mary felt her legs begin to tingle from too much sun did she find the strength to push her skirt down. Wolf murmured a protest and slid his hand up her thigh.

She opened her eyes. The sky was bright blue, cloudless, and the sweet scent of fresh grass filled her lungs, radiated through her body. The earth was hot beneath her, the man she loved dozed beside her, and every inch of her still held the remnants of sensation from their lovemaking. The memory of it, so fresh and powerful, began to warm her body to desire again, and suddenly she realized that his plan had worked. He had recreated the scenario that had so terrified her, but substituted himself for the attacker. Instead of fear, pain and humiliation, he had given her desire and, ultimately, an ecstasy so strong it had taken her out of herself. He had replaced a terrible memory with a wonderful one.

His hand was lying low on her abdomen now, and the simple intimacy of his touch stunned her. She could be carrying his child. She had been aware of the probable consequences of making love without protection, but it was what she wanted, and he had made no mention of birth control. Even if their relationship didn't last, she wanted his baby, a child with his strength and fire. If it could be a duplicate of him, nothing would make her happier.

She stirred, and the pressure of his hand on her abdomen

increased. "The sun is too hot," she murmured. "I'm getting burned."

He groaned, but fastened his jeans and sat up. Then he picked up her underpants, put them in his pocket and lifted her in his arms in the same motion he used to get to his feet.

"I can walk," she informed him, though she wound her arms around his neck.

"I know." He grinned down at her. "It's just that it's more romantic to carry you into the house to make love."

"But we just made love."

There was fire in his black eyes. "So?"

Wolf was just about to enter the feed store when a tingle touched the back of his neck like a cool wind. He didn't stop, which would have signaled an alarm to anyone watching, but, using his peripheral vision, he took a quick look around. The sense of danger was like a touch. Someone was watching him. His sixth sense was highly developed from hard training and years of application, and further enhanced by the strong mysticism of his heritage.

It wasn't just that he was being watched; he could feel the hatred directed toward him. He strode into the feed store and immediately stepped to the side, flattening himself against the wall as he looked out the door. Conversation in the store halted as if the words had hit a stone wall, but he ignored the thick silence. Adrenaline pumped through his body; he didn't notice that his gloved hand automatically slid over his chest to touch the knife that had been securely attached to the webbing he'd worn sixteen years before, in a steamy, hauntingly beautiful little country that reeked of blood and death. Only when his hand encountered nothing but his shirt did he realize that old habits had come to the fore.

Suddenly he realized that it was the man he'd been hunting, standing somewhere out there and staring at him with hatred, and rage surged through him. He didn't need a knife. Without a word he removed his hat and boots, the hat because it increased his silhouette, the boots because they were too noisy. In his sock feet he ran lightly past the stunned and silent little knot of men who had been standing around chewing the fat. Only one voiced a hesitant, "What's going on?"

Wolf didn't take time to answer, but slipped out the back door of the feed store. His movements were silent, deliberate, as he used every available bit of cover while moving from building to building, working his way around so he would come out behind where he had estimated the man to be. It was hard to pinpoint his position, but Wolf had automatically picked out the best locations for concealment. If he kept looking long enough, he'd find another of the tracks he'd been searching for; the guy would get careless, and Wolf would get him.

He slid around the back of the drugstore, feeling the heat of the sun-warmed boards against his back. He was more cautious than before, not wanting the wood to rasp against his shirt. It was gravelly here, too, and he placed his feet with care to keep the little rocks from making a telltale grinding.

He heard the heavy, thudding sound of someone running, as if he had bolted in panic. Wolf ran around the front of the building and knelt briefly to inspect a faint print in the dust, only a part of a print, but his blood surged. It was the same print, same shoe, same toeing-in stride. He sprinted like the big timber wolf he'd been named for, no longer caring about noise, racing up the street, looking left and right for anyone in the street.

Nothing. No one. The street was empty. He stopped to

listen. He heard birds, the rustle of a fitful breeze in the trees, the far-off sound of an engine climbing the slight rise on the north side of the town. Nothing else. No fast breathing, no running footsteps.

Wolf swore to himself. The guy was worse than an amateur, he was clumsy and made stupid moves, as well as being out of shape. If he'd been anywhere close by, Wolf would have been able to hear his labored breathing. Damn it, somehow his quarry had slipped away.

Wolf looked at the quiet houses nestled under the trees. Ruth didn't have residential and commercial zoning; it was too small. The result was that the houses and few businesses were mixed together without order. The man could have gone into any of the houses; the way he'd disappeared so suddenly left no other possibility. It verified Wolf's conviction that the rapist lived in Ruth; after all, both attacks had happened right in town.

He noted who lived in the houses on the street and tried to think of who inside them matched Mary's description of a heavily freckled man. No one came to mind. But someone would. By God, Wolf vowed, someone would. He was slowly eliminating men from his mental list. Eventually, there would be only one left.

From inside a house, a curtain moved fractionally. The sound of his own raspy breathing as he sucked air into his laboring lungs filled the man's ears. Through the tiny crack he'd made, he could see the Indian still standing in the street, staring at first one house, then another. Murderous black eyes moved across the window where the man stood, and he automatically stepped back out of sight.

His own fear sickened and enraged him. He didn't want to be afraid of the Indian, but he was.

"Damn filthy Indian!" He whispered the words, then

echoed them in his head. He liked doing that, saying things out loud the first time, then saying them to himself for his private understanding and enjoyment.

The Indian was a murderer. They said he knew more ways of killing people than normal folks could even imagine. The man believed it, because he knew firsthand how Indians could kill.

He'd like to kill the Indian, *and* that boy of his with the strange, pale eyes that looked through him. But he was afraid, because he didn't know how to kill, and he knew he'd wind up getting killed himself. He was too afraid of getting that close to the Indian to even try it.

He'd thought about it, but he couldn't come up with a plan. He'd like to shoot the Indian, because he wouldn't have to get close to do that, but he didn't have a gun, and he didn't want to draw attention to himself by buying one.

But he liked what he'd done to get back at the Indian. It gave him savage satisfaction to know he was punishing the Indian by hurting those stupid women who had taken up for him. Why couldn't they see him for the filthy, murdering trash he was? That stupid Cathy had said the Indian was good-looking! She'd even said she'd go out with the boy, and he knew that meant she'd let the boy touch her, and kiss her. She'd been willing to let the filthy Mackenzies kiss her, but she'd fought and screamed and gagged when *he'd* touched her.

It didn't make sense, but he didn't care. He'd wanted to punish her and punish the Indian for—for being there, for letting stupid Cathy look at him and think he was good-looking.

And the schoolteacher. He hated her almost as much as he hated the Mackenzies, maybe more. She was so goody-goody, making people think the boy was something special, trying to talk people around so they'd be friendly to the half-breeds. Preaching in the general store!

He'd wanted to spit on her. He'd wanted to hurt her, bad. He'd been so excited he almost hadn't been able to stand it when he'd dragged her down that alley and felt her squirming beneath him. If that stupid deputy hadn't shown up, he'd have done to her what he'd done to Cathy, and he knew he'd have liked it more. He'd wanted to hit her with his fists while he did it to her. That would have shown her. She would never have stuck up for the half-breeds again.

He still wanted to get her, to teach her a lesson, but school was out now, and he'd heard people say that the deputy had made her move to some safe place, and no one knew where she was. He didn't want to wait until school started again, but he thought he might have to.

And that stupid Pam Hearst. She needed a lesson, too. He'd heard that she had gone to a dance with the half-breed boy. He knew what that meant. He'd had his hands on her, and she'd probably let him kiss her and maybe do a lot more, because everyone knew what the Mackenzies were like. As far as he was concerned, that made Pam a slut. She deserved to be taught a lesson just like Cathy, and just like the lesson the schoolteacher still had coming.

He peeked outside again. The Indian was gone. He immediately felt safe, and he began to plan.

When Wolf walked back into the feed store, the same group of men were still there. "We don't much like you tracking folks around like we're criminals," one man snapped.

Wolf grunted and sat down to pull on his boots. He didn't care if they liked it or not.

"Did you hear what I said?"

He looked up. "I heard."

"And?"

"And nothing."

"Now look here, damn it!"

"I'm looking."

The men fidgeted under his cold black stare. Another spoke up. "You're making the women nervous."

"They should be nervous. It might keep them on guard, keep them from getting raped."

"It was some drifter trash who blew in and blew out! Likely the sheriff won't ever find who did it."

"It's trash, all right, but he's still here. I just found his track."

The men fell silent and looked at each other. Stu Kilgore, the foreman on Eli Baugh's spread, cleared his throat. "We're supposed to believe you can tell it was made by the same man?"

"I can tell." Wolf gave them a smile that was closer to a snarl. "Uncle Sam made sure I got the best training available. It's the same man. He lives here. He slipped into one of the houses."

"That's hard to believe. We've lived here all our lives. The only stranger around is the schoolteacher. Why would someone just up and start attacking women?"

"Someone did. That's all I care about, that and catching him."

He left the men murmuring among themselves while he loaded his feed.

Pam was bored. Since the two attacks, she hadn't even stepped outside the house by herself; she'd been pretty scared at first, but the days had passed without any more attacks, and the shock had worn off. Women were beginning to venture out again, even by themselves.

She was going to another dance with Joe, and she wanted a new dress. She knew he was going away, knew sh couldn't hold him, but there was still something about him that made her heart race. She refused to let herself love him, even though she knew any other boyfriend would have a hard time replacing Joe. Hard, but not impossible. She wasn't going to mope after he'd left; she'd get on with her life—but right now he was still *here*, and she savored every moment with him.

She really wanted a new dress, but she'd promised Joe she wouldn't go anywhere alone, and she didn't intend to break her promise. When her mother returned from shopping with a neighbor, she'd ask her about going with her to get a new dress. Not in Ruth, of course; she wanted to go to a real town, with a real dress shop.

Finally she picked up a book and walked out onto the back porch, away from the sun. There were neighbors on both sides, and she felt safe. She read for a while, then became sleepy and lay down on the porch swing, arranging her long legs over the back of the swing. She dozed immediately.

The abrupt jolting of the swing awakened her some time later. She opened her eyes and stared at a ski mask, with narrowed, hate-filled eyes glittering through the slits. He was already on her when she screamed.

He hit her with his fist, but she jerked her head back so that the blow landed on her shoulder. She screamed again and tried to kick him, and the unsteady swing toppled them to the porch. She kicked again, catching him in the stomach, and he grunted, sounding oddly surprised.

She couldn't stop screaming, even as she scrabbled away from him. She was more terrified than she'd ever been before in her life, but also oddly detached, watching the scene from some safe distance. The wooden slats of the porch scraped her hands and arms, but she kept moving backward. He suddenly sprang, and she kicked at him again, but he caught her ankle. She didn't stop. She just kicked, using both legs, trying to catch him in the head or the groin, and she screamed.

Someone next door yelled. The man jerked his head up and dropped her ankle. Blood had seeped through the multicolored ski mask; she'd managed to kick him in the mouth. He said "Indian's dirty whore" in a hate-thickened voice, and jumped from the porch, already running.

Pam lay on the porch, sobbing in dry, painful gasps. The neighbor yelled again, and somehow she garnered enough strength to scream "Help me!" before the terror made her curl into a ball and whimper like a child.

Wolf wasn't surprised when the deputy's car pulled up and Clay got out. He'd had a tight feeling in his gut since he'd found that footprint in town. Clay's tired face told the story.

Mary saw who their visitor was and automatically got a cup for coffee; Clay always wanted coffee. He took off his hat and sat down, heaving a sigh as he did so.

"Who was it this time?" Wolf asked, his deep voice so rough it was almost a growl.

"Pam Hearst."

Joe's head jerked up, and all the color washed out of his face. He was on his feet before Clay's next words came.

"She fought him off. She isn't hurt, but she's scared. He jumped her on the Hearsts' back porch, for God's sake. Mrs. Winston heard her screaming, and the guy ran. Pam said she kicked him in the mouth. She saw blood on the ski mask he was wearing."

"He lives in town," Wolf said. "I found another print, but it's hard to track in town, with people walking around destroying what few prints there are. I think he ducked into one of the houses along Bay Road, but he might not live here."

"Bay Road." Clay frowned as he mentally reviewed the people living on Bay Road; most of the townspeople lived along it, in close little clusters. There was also another cluster of houses on Broad Street, where the Hearsts lived. "We might have him this time. Any man who has a swollen lip will have to have an airtight alibi.''

"If it just split his lip, you won't be able to tell. The swelling will be minimal. She would have to have really done some damage for it to be visible more than a day or so." Wolf had had more than his share of split lips, and delivered his share, too. The mouth healed swiftly. Now if Pam had knocked some teeth out, that would be a different story.

"Any blood on the porch?"

"No."

"Then she didn't do any real damage." There would have been blood sprayed all over the porch if she'd kicked out his teeth.

Clay shoved his hand through his hair. "I don't like to think of the uproar it would cause, but I'm going to talk to the sheriff about making a house-to-house search along Bay Road. Damn it, I just can't think of anyone it could be."

Joe abruptly left the room, and Wolf stared after his son. He knew Joe wanted to go to Pam, and knew that he wouldn't. Some of the barriers had come down, but most of them were still intact.

Clay had watched Joe leave, and he sighed again. "The bastard called Pam an 'Indian's dirty whore.'" His gaze shifted to Mary, who had stood silently the whole time. "You were right."

She didn't reply, because she'd known all along that she was right. It made her sick to hear the name Pam had been called, because it so starkly revealed the hatred behind the attack.

"I suppose all the tracks at Pam's house have been ruined." Wolf said it as a statement, not a question.

"Afraid so." Clay was regretful, but practically everyone in town had been at the Hearsts' house before he' gotten there, standing around the back porch and tromping around the area.

Wolf muttered something uncomplimentary under his breath about damn idiots. "Do you think the sheriff will go along with a house-to-house search?"

"Depends. You know some folks are going to kick up about it no matter what the reason. They'll take it personally. This is an election year," he said, and they took his point.

Mary listened to them talking, but she didn't join in. Now Pam had been hurt; who was next? Would the man work up enough courage to attack Wolf or Joe? That was her real terror, because she didn't know if she could bear it. She loved them with all the fierceness of her soul. She would gladly put herself between them and danger.

Which was exactly what she would have to do.

It made her sick to even think of that man's hands on her again, but she knew in that moment that she was going to give him the opportunity. Somehow, she was going to lure him out. She wouldn't allow herself the luxury of hiding out on Mackenzie's Mountain any longer.

She would begin driving into town by herself. The only problem would be in getting away from Wolf; she knew he'd never agree if he had any idea what she was doing. Not only that, he was capable of preventing her from leaving at all, either by disabling her car or even locking her in the bedroom. She didn't underestimate him.

Since he had moved her up on the mountain with him, he'd been delivering and picking up horses, rather than letting the owners come up to the ranch, where they might see her. Her whereabouts were a well-kept secret, known only to Wolf, Joe and Clay. But that meant she was left alone several times a week while Wolf and Joe ran errands and delivered horses. Joe also left for his math lessons, and they had to ride fences and work the small herd of cattle, just as every rancher did. She really had a lot of opportunities for slipping away, at least the first time. It would be infinitely more difficult to get away after that, because Wolf would be on his guard.

She quietly excused herself and went in search of Joe. She peeked into his bedroom, but he wasn't there, so she went out on the front porch. He was leaning against one of the posts, his thumbs hooked in his front pockets.

"It isn't your fault."

He didn't move. "I knew it could happen."

"You aren't responsible for someone else's hate."

"No, but I am responsible for Pam. I knew it could happen, and I should have stayed away from her."

Mary made an unladylike sound. "I seem to remember it was the other way around. Pam made her choice when she made that scene in her father's store."

"All she wanted was to go to a dance. She didn't ask for this."

"Of course not, but it still isn't your fault, any more than it would have been your fault if she'd been in a car accident. You can say you could have delayed her so she'd have been a minute later getting to that particular section of road, or hurried her up so she'd have been earlier, but that's ridiculous, and you know it."

He couldn't prevent a faint smile at the starchiness of her tone. She should be in Congress, cracking her whip and haranguing those senators and representatives into some sort of fiscal responsibility. Instead she'd taken on Ruth, Wyoming, and none of them had been the same since she'd set foot in town.

"All right, so I'm taking too much on myself," he finally said. "But I knew it wasn't smart to go out with her in the first place. It isn't fair. I'll be leaving here when I finish school, and I won't be back. Pam should be dating someone who's going to be around when she needs him."

"You're still taking too much on yourself. Let Pam make her own decisions about who she wants to date. Do you plan to isolate yourself from women forever?"

"I wouldn't go that far," he drawled, and in that moment he sounded so much like his father that it startled her. "But I don't intend to get involved with anyone."

"It doesn't always work out the way you want. You were involved with Pam even before I came here."

That was true, as far as it went. He sighed and leaned his head against the post. "I don't love her."

"Of course not. I never thought you did."

"I like her; I care for her. But not enough to stay, not enough to give up the Academy." He looked at the Wyoming night, the almost painful clarity of the sky, the brightly winking stars, and thought of jockeying an F-15 over these mountains, with the dark earth below and the glittering stars above. No, he couldn't give that up.

"Did you tell her that?"

"Yes."

"Then it was her decision."

They stood in silence, watching the stars. A few minutes later Clay left, and neither of them thought it strange that he hadn't said goodbye. Wolf came out on the porch and automatically slid his arm around Mary's waist, hugging her to his side even as he put his hand on his son's shoulder. "You okay?"

"Okay enough, I suppose." But he understood now the total rage he'd seen in Wolf's eyes when Mary had been attacked, the same rage that still burned in a rigidly controlled fire inside his father. God help the man if Wolf Mackenzie ever got his hands on him.

Wolf tightened his arm around Mary and led her inside,

knowing it was best to leave Joe alone now. His son was tough; he'd handle it.

The next morning Mary listened as they discussed their day. There were no horses to deliver or pick up, but Joe had a math lesson that afternoon, and they intended to use the morning inoculating cattle. She had no idea how long it would take to treat the whole herd, but imagined they would both be tied up the entire morning. They would be riding a couple of the young quarter horses, to teach them how to cut cattle.

Joe had changed overnight; it was a subtle change, but one that made Mary ache inside. In repose, his young face held a grimness that saddened her, as if the last faint vestiges of boyhood had been driven from his soul. He'd always looked older than his age, but now, despite the smoothness of his skin, he no longer looked young.

She was a grown woman, almost thirty years old, and the attack had left scars she hadn't been able to handle alone. Cathy and Pam were just kids, and Cathy had to handle a nightmare that was far worse than what Mary and Pam had undergone. Joe had lost his youth. No matter what, that man had to be stopped before he damaged anyone else.

When Wolf and Joe left the house, Mary gave them plenty of time to get far enough away so they wouldn't hear her car start, then hurried out of the house. She didn't know what she was going to do, other than parade through Ruth on the off chance that her presence might trigger another attack. And then what? She didn't know. Somehow she had to be prepared; she had to get someone to keep watch so the man could be caught. It should have been easy to catch him; he'd been so careless, attacking out in the open and in broad daylight, making stupid moves, as if he attacked on impulse and without a plan. He hadn't ever taken the simplest precautions against getting caught. The whole thing was strange. It didn't make sense.

Her hands were shaking as she drove into town; she was acutely aware that this was the first time since the day she'd been attacked that she was without protection. She felt exposed, as if her clothing had been stripped away.

She had to get someone to watch her, someone she trusted. Who? Sharon? The young teacher was her friend, but Sharon wasn't aggressive, and she thought the situation called for aggressiveness. Francie Beecham was too old; Cicely Karr would be too cautious. She discounted the men, because they would get all protective and refuse to help. Men were such victims to their own hormones. Machismo had killed a lot more people than PMS.

Pam Hearst sprang to mind. Pam would be extremely interested in catching the man, and she'd been aggressive enough to kick him in the mouth, to fight him off. She was young, but she had courage. She'd had the courage to go against her father and date a half-breed.

Conversation ceased when she walked into Hearst's store; it was the first time she'd been seen since the end of school. She ignored the thick silence, for she had what she suspected was a highly accurate guess as to the subject of the conversation she'd interrupted, and approached the checkout counter where Mr. Hearst stood.

''Is Pam at home?'' she asked quietly, not wanting her question to be heard by the entire store.

He looked as if he'd aged ten years overnight, but there was no animosity in his face.

He nodded. The same thing had happened to Miss Potter, he thought. If she could talk to Pam, maybe she could take that haunted look out of his baby girl's eyes. Miss Potter had a lot of backbone for such a little thing; maybe he didn't always agree with her, but he'd damn sure learned to respect her. And Pam thought the world of her.

"I'd appreciate it if you'd talk to her," he said.

There was an odd, almost militant expression in her soft bluish eyes. "I'll do that," she promised, and turned to leave. She almost bumped into Dottie and was startled into a gasp; the woman had been right behind her.

"Good morning," Mary said pleasantly. Aunt Ardith had drilled the importance of good manners into her.

Strangely, Dottie seemed to have aged, too. Her face was haggard. "How are you doing, Mary?"

Mary hesitated, but she could detect none of the hostility she was accustomed to from Dottie. Had the entire town changed? Had this nightmare brought them to their senses about the Mackenzies? "I'm fine. Are you enjoying the vacation?"

Dottie smiled, but it was merely a movement of her facial muscles, not a response of pleasure. "It's been a relief."

She certainly didn't look relieved; she looked worried to a frazzle. Of course, everyone *should* be worried.

"How is your son?" Mary couldn't remember the boy's name, and she felt faintly embarrassed. It wasn't like her to forget names.

To her surprise, Dottie went white. Even her lips were bloodless. "W—why do you ask?" she stammered.

"He seemed upset the last time I saw him," Mary replied. She could hardly say that only good manners had prompted the question. Southerners always asked after family.

"Oh. He—he's all right. He hardly ever leaves the house. He doesn't like going out." Dottie looked around, then blurted "Excuse me," and left the store before Mary could say anything else.

She looked at Mr. Hearst, and he shrugged. He thought Dottie had acted a bit strange, too.

"I'll go see Pam now," she said.

She started to walk to the Hearst house, but the memory of what had happened the last time she'd walked through town made chills run up her spine, and she went to her car. She checked the back seat and floorboard before opening the door. As she started the engine, she saw Dottie walking swiftly up the street, her head down as if she didn't want anyone to speak to her. She hadn't bought anything, Mary realized. Why had she been in Hearst's store, if not to make a purchase? It couldn't be browsing, because everyone knew what every store in town carried. Why had she left so suddenly?

Dottie turned left down the small street where she lived, and abruptly Mary wondered what Dottie was doing walking around alone. Every woman in town should know better. Surely she had enough sense to be cautious.

Mary drove slowly up the street. She craned her neck when she reached the street where Dottie had turned and saw the woman hurrying up the steps of her house. Her eyes fell on the faded sign: Bay Road.

Bay Road was where Wolf thought the rapist had dodged into a house. It made sense that he wouldn't have entered a house that wasn't his home, unless he was a close friend who came and went just like a family member. That was possible, but even a very close friend would give a yell before just walking into someone else's house, and Wolf would have heard that.

Dottie was certainly acting odd. She'd looked as if she'd been stung by a bee when Mary had asked about her son.... Bobby, that was his name. Mary was pleased that she'd remembered.

Bobby. Bobby wasn't "right." He did things in a skewed

way. He was unable to apply logic to the simplest of chores, unable to plan a practical course of action.

Mary broke out in a sweat and had to stop the car. She'd only seen him once, but she could picture him in her mind: big, a little soft-looking, with sandy hair and a fair complexion. A fair, freckled complexion.

Was it *Bobby*? The one person in town who wasn't totally responsible for himself? The one person no one would ever suspect?

Except his mother.

She had to tell Wolf.

As soon as the thought formed, she dismissed it. She couldn't tell Wolf, not yet, because she didn't want to put that burden on him. His instincts would tell him to go after Bobby; his conscience would argue that Bobby wasn't a responsible person. Mary knew him well enough to know that, no matter which decision he made, he would always have regrets. Better for the responsibility to be hers than to push Wolf into such a position.

She'd call Clay. It was his job, after all. He'd be better able to deal with the situation.

Only a few seconds passed as her thoughts rushed through her mind. She was still sitting there staring at Dottie's house when Bobby came out on the porch. It took him a moment, but suddenly he noticed her car and looked straight at her. A distance of less than seventy-five yards separated them, still too far for her to read his expression, but she didn't need a close-up for sheer terror to spurt through her. She stomped on the gas pedal and the car shot forward, slinging gravel, the tires squealing.

It was only a short distance to the Hearst house. Mary ran to the front door and banged her fist on it. Her heart felt as if it would explode. That brief moment when she had been face-to-face with him was almost more than she could stand. God, she had to call Clay.

Mrs. Hearst opened the door a crack, then recognized Mary and swung it all the way open. "Miss Potter! Is something wrong?"

Mary realized that she must look wild. "Could I use your phone? It's an emergency."

"Why—of course." She stepped back, allowing Mary inside.

Pam appeared in the hallway. "Miss Potter?" She looked young and scared.

"The phone's in the kitchen."

Mary followed Mrs. Hearst and grabbed the receiver. "What's the number of the sheriff's department?"

Pam got a small telephone book from the countertop and began flipping through the pages. Too agitated to wait, Mary dialed the number for Information.

"Sheriff's department, please."

"What city?" the disembodied voice asked.

She drew a blank. For the life of her, she couldn't remember the name of the town.

"Here it is," Pam said.

Mary disconnected the call to Information, then dialed as Pam recited the number. The various computer clicks as the connection was made seemed to take forever.

"Sheriff's office."

"Deputy Armstrong, please. Clay Armstrong."

"One moment."

It was longer than one moment. Pam and her mother stood tensely, not knowing what was going on but reacting to her urgency. Both of them had dark circles under their eyes. It had been a bad night for the Hearst family.

"Sheriff's office," a different voice said.

"Clay?"

"You looking for Armstrong?"

"Yes. It's an emergency!" she insisted.

"Well, I don't know where he is right now. You want to tell me what the trouble is—hey, Armstrong! Some lady wants you in a hurry." To Mary, he said, "He'll be right here."

A few seconds later Clay's voice said, "Armstrong."

"It's Mary. I'm in town."

"What the hell are you doing there?"

Her teeth were chattering. "It's Bobby. Bobby Lancaster. I saw him—"

"Hang up the phone!"

It was a scream, and she jumped, dropping the receiver, which dangled from the end of its cord. She flattened against the wall, for Bobby stood there, inside the kitchen, with a huge butcher knife in his hand. His face was twisted with both hate and fear.

"You told!" He sounded like an outraged child.

"Told—told what?"

"You told him! I heard you!"

Mrs. Hearst had shrunk back against the cabinets, her hand at her throat. Pam stood as if rooted in the middle of the floor, her face colorless, her eyes locked on the young man she'd known all her life. She could see the slight swelling of his lower lip.

Bobby shifted his weight from one foot to the other, as if he didn't know what to do next. His face was red, and he looked almost tearful.

Mary strove to steady her voice. "That's right, I told him. He's on his way now. You'd better run." Maybe that wasn't the best suggestion in the world, but more than anything she wanted to get him out of the Hearsts' house before he hurt someone. She desperately wanted him to run.

"It's all your fault!" He looked hunted, as if he didn't

know what to do except cast blame. "You—you came here and changed things. Mama said you're a dirty Indian-lover."

"I beg your pardon. I prefer clean people."

He blinked, confused. Then he shook his head and said again, "It's your fault."

"Clay will be here in a few minutes. You'd better go."

His hand tightened on the knife, and suddenly he reached out and grabbed her arm. He was big and soft, but he was faster than he looked. Mary cried out as he twisted her arm up behind her back, nearly wrenching her shoulder joint loose.

"You'll be my hostage, just like on television," he said and pushed her out the back door.

Mrs. Hearst was motionless, frozen in shock. Pam leaped for the phone, heard the buzzing that signaled a broken connection and held the button down for a new line. When she got a dial tone, she dialed the Mackenzies' number. It rang endlessly, and she cursed, using words her mother had no idea she knew. All the while she leaned to the side, trying to see where Bobby was taking Mary.

She was just about to hang up when the receiver was picked up and a deep, angry voice roared, "Mary?"

She was so startled that she almost dropped the phone. "No," she choked. "It's Pam. He has Mary. It's Bobby Lancaster, and he just dragged her out of the house—"

"I'll be right there."

Pam shivered at the deadly intent in Wolf Mackenzie's voice.

Mary stumbled over a large rock hidden by the tall grass and gagged as the sudden intense pain made nausea twist her stomach.

"Stand up!" Bobby yelled, jerking at her.

"I twisted my ankle!" It was a lie, but it would give he an excuse to slow him down.

He'd dragged her across the small meadow behind the Hearsts', through a thick line of trees, over a stream, and now they were climbing a small rise. At least it had looked small, but now she knew it was deceptively large. It was a big open area, not the smartest place for Bobby to head but he didn't plan well. That was what had thrown everyone off from the beginning, what had never seemed quite *right*. There had been no logic to his actions; Bobby reacted rather than planned.

He didn't know what to do for a twisted ankle, so he didn't worry about it, just pushed her along at the same speed. She stumbled again, but somehow managed to retain her balance. She wouldn't be able to bear it if she fell on her stomach and he came down on top of her again.

"Why did you have to tell?" he groaned.

"You hurt Cathy."

"She deserved it!"

"How? How did she deserve it?"

"She liked him—the Indian."

Mary was panting. She estimated they'd gone over mile. Not a great distance, but the gradual uphill climb w telling on her. It didn't help that her arm was twisted between her shoulder blades. How long had it been? When could she expect Clay to arrive? It had been at least twenty minutes.

Wolf made it off his mountain in record time. His eyes were like flint as he leaped from the truck before it had rocked to a complete stop. He and Joe both carried rifle but Wolf's was a sniper rifle, a Remington with a powerful scope. He'd never had occasion to try a thousand-yard shot with it, but he'd never missed his target at closer range.

People milled around the back of the house. He and Joe shouldered their way through the crowd. "Everybody freeze, before you destroy any more tracks!" Wolf roared, and everyone stopped dead.

Pam darted to them. Her face was streaked with tears. "He took her into the trees. There," she said and pointed.

A siren announced Clay's arrival, but Wolf didn't wait for him. The trail across the meadow was as plain to him as a neon sign would have been, and he set off at a lope, with Joe on his heels.

Dottie Lancaster was terrified, and nearly hysterical. Bobby was her son, and she loved him desperately no matter what he'd done. She'd been sick when she'd realized he was the one who had attacked Cathy Teele and Mary; she'd almost worried herself into an early grave as she wrestled with her conscience and the sure knowledge that she'd lose her son if she turned him in. But that was nothing compared to the horror she'd felt when she discovered he'd slipped from the house. She'd followed the sounds of a disturbance and found all of her nightmares coming true: he'd taken Mary, and he had a knife. Now the Mackenzies were after him, and she knew they would kill him.

She grabbed Clay's arm as he surged past her. "Stop them," she sobbed. "Don't let them kill my boy."

Clay barely glanced at her. He shook her loose and ran after them. Distraught, Dottie ran, too.

By then some of the other men had gotten their rifles and were joining the hunt. They'd always felt sorry for Bobby Lancaster, but he'd hurt their women, and there was no excuse for it.

Wolf's heartbeat settled down, and he pushed the panic away. His senses heightened, as they always did when he was on the hunt. Every sound was magnified in his ears, instantly recognizable. He saw every blade of grass, every broken twig and overturned rock. He could smell ever⟩ scent nature had left, and the faint acrid, coppery tang o⟩ fear. His body was a machine, moving smoothly, silently

He could read every sign. Here Mary had stumbled, an⟩ his muscles tightened. She had to be terrified. If he hu⟩ her—she was so slight, no match at all for a man. Th⟩ bastard had a knife. Wolf thought of a blade touching he⟩ delicate, translucent skin, and rage consumed him. He ha⟩ to push it away because he couldn't afford the mistake⟩ rage could cause.

He broke out of the tree line and suddenly saw them⟩ high on the side of the rise. Bobby was dragging Mar⟩ along, but at least she was still alive.

Wolf examined the terrain. He didn't have a good angl⟩ He moved east, along the base of the rise.

"Stop!"

It was Bobby's voice, only faintly heard at that distanc⟩ They had halted, and Bobby was holding Mary in front ⟨ him. "Stop or I'll kill her!"

Slowly, Wolf went down on one knee and raised the ri⟩ to his shoulder. He sighted through the scope, not for⟩ shot, but to see how he should set it up. The powerful sco⟩ plainly revealed the desperation on Bobby's face and t⟨ knife at Mary's throat.

"Bobbeee!" Dottie had reached them, and she scream⟩ his name.

"Mama?"

"Bobby, let her go!"

"I can't! She told!"

The men had clustered around. Several of them measur⟩ the distance by eye and shook their heads. They could⟩ make the shot, not at that range. They were as likely to⟩ Mary as Bobby, if they hit anything at all.

Clay looked down at Wolf. "Can you make the shot⟩

Wolf smiled, and Clay felt that chill run up his spine again at the look in Wolf's eyes. They were cold and murderous. "Yeah."

"No!" Dottie sobbed the word. "Bobby!" she screamed. "Please, come down!"

"I can't! I've got to kill her! She likes him, and he's a dirty Indian! He killed my father!"

Dottie gasped and covered her mouth with her hands. "No," she moaned, then screamed again. "No! He didn't!" Pure hell was living in her eyes.

"He did! You said—an Indian—" Bobby broke off and began dragging Mary backward.

"Do it," Clay said quietly.

Wolf braced the barrel of the rifle in the notch of a sapling. It was small but sturdy enough to be steady. Without a word he sighted in the cross hairs of the scope.

"Wait," Dottie cried, anguish in her voice.

Wolf looked at her.

"Please," she whispered. "Don't kill him. He's all I have."

His black eyes were flat. "I'll try."

He concentrated on the shot, shutting everything out as he always had. It was maybe three hundred yards, but the air was still. The image in the scope was huge and clear and flattened, the depth perception distorted. Mary's face was plain. She looked angry, and she was tugging at the arm around her shoulder, the one that held the knife to her throat.

God, when he got her back safe and sound, he was going to throttle her.

Because she was so small, he had a larger target than would normally have been presented. His instincts were to go for a head shot, to take Bobby Lancaster completely out of life, but he'd promised. Damn, it was going to be a bitch of a shot. They were moving, and he'd limited his own target area by promising not to go for a kill.

The cross hairs settled, and his hands became rock steady. He drew in a breath, let out half of it and gently squeezed the trigger. Almost simultaneously with the sharp thunder in his ear he saw the red stain blossom on Bobby' shoulder and the knife drop from his suddenly useless hand even as he was thrown back by the bullet's impact. Mar staggered to the side and fell, but was instantly on her fee again.

Dottie sagged to her knees, sobbing, her hands over he face.

The men surged up the hill. Mary ran down it and me Wolf halfway. He still had the rifle in his hand, but h caught her up in his arms and held her locked to him, h eyes closed as he absorbed the miracle of her, warm an alive against him, her silky hair against his face, her swe scent in his lungs. He didn't care who saw them, or wh anyone thought. She was his, and he'd just lived throug the worst half hour of his existence knowing that at ar moment her life could be ended.

Now that it was over, she was crying.

She'd been dragged up the hill, and now Wolf dragge her down it. He was swearing steadily under his breat ignoring her gasping protests until she stumbled. Then snatched her up under his arm like a sack and continu down. People stared after them in astonishment, but no o moved to stop him. After today, they all viewed Wolf Ma kenzie differently.

Wolf ignored her car and thrust her into his truck. Ma pushed her hair out of her face and decided not to menti the car; they would pick it up later. Wolf was in a ra; his face set and hard.

They had almost reached the road that wound up

mountain before he spoke. "What in hell were you doing in town?" The even tone didn't fool her. The wolf was dangerously angered.

Perhaps she wasn't as cautious as she should have been, but she still wasn't afraid of him, not of the man she loved. She respected his temper, but she didn't fear him. So she said, just as calmly, "I thought seeing me might trigger him into doing something stupid, so we could identify him."

"You *triggered* him, all right. What he did wasn't nearly as stupid as what you did. What did you do, parade up and down the streets until he grabbed you?"

She let the insult pass. "Actually it never came to that. I intended to talk to Pam first. I stopped at the store to ask Mr. Hearst if she was home and bumped into Dottie. She acted so strange and looked so worried that it made me wonder. She almost ran out of the store. Then, when I saw her turn onto Bay Road, I remembered Bobby, what he looked like. He came out on the porch and looked at me, and I knew he was the one."

"So you made a citizen's arrest?" he asked sarcastically.

Mary got huffy. "No. I'm not stupid, and you'd better not make another smart remark, Wolf Mackenzie. I did what I thought I had to do. I'm sorry if you don't like it, but there it is. Enough was enough. I couldn't take the chance someone else could be hurt, or that he might start taking shots at you or Joe.

"I drove to Pam's house and called Clay. I had no intention of confronting Bobby, but it didn't work out that way. He followed me to Pam's and heard me talking on the phone. So he grabbed me. You know what happened then."

She was so matter-of-fact about it that he tightened his hands on the steering wheel to keep from shaking her. If she hadn't been crying just a few minutes ago, he might have lost his tenuous control on his temper.

"Do you know what might have happened if I hadn't come back to the barn for something and noticed your car was missing? It was just chance I was there when Pam called to tell me Bobby had grabbed you!"

"Yes," she said patiently. "I know what could have happened."

"It doesn't bother you that he came close to cutting your throat?"

"Close doesn't count except in horseshoes and hand grenades."

He slammed on the brakes, so enraged he could barely see. He wasn't aware of shutting off the motor, only of closing his hands on her slender shoulders. He was so close to pulling her across his knees that he was shaking, but she didn't seem to realize that she should be frightened. With a faint sound she dived into his arms, clinging to him with surprising strength.

Wolf held her and felt her trembling. The red haze left his vision, and he realized that she *was* frightened, but not of him. With her normal damn-the-torpedoes attitude, she'd done what she'd thought was right and was probably trying to put up a calm front so he wouldn't be alarmed.

As if anything could ever alarm him more than seeing an unbalanced rapist hold a knife to her throat.

Frantically he started the truck. It wasn't far to his house, but he didn't know if he could make it. He had to make love to her, soon, even if it was in the middle of the road. Only then would the fear of losing her begin to fade, when he felt her beneath him once more and she welcomed him into her delicate body.

Mary brooded. It had been four days since Wolf had shot Bobby; the first two days had been filled with statements and police procedures, as well as newspaper interviews and even a request from a television station, which Wolf had refused. The sheriff, not being a fool, had hailed Wolf as a hero and praised the shot he'd made. Wolf's military service record was dug up, and a lot was written about the "much-decorated Vietnam veteran" who had saved a schoolteacher and captured a rapist.

Bobby was recuperating in a hospital in Casper; the bullet had punctured his right lung, but he was lucky to be alive under the circumstances. He was bewildered by everything that had happened and kept asking to go home. Dottie had resigned. She'd have to live the rest of her life knowing that her hatred had taken seed in her son's mind and caused the entire nightmare. She knew Bobby would be taken away from her, at least for a time, and that they would never be able to live in Ruth again, even if he was ever a free man. But wherever Bobby was sent, she intended to be close by. As she'd told Wolf, he was all she had.

It was over, and Mary knew that Wolf would never be treated as an outcast again. The threat was past, and the town was safe. Just knowing who it was and that he'd been caught made a lot of difference in Cathy Teele's recovery, though what had happened would always mark her life.

So there was no reason why Mary couldn't return to her own house.

That was why she was brooding. In those four days, Wolf hadn't said a word about her remaining with him. He'd never said a word of love, not even during their wild lovemaking after he'd snatched her to safety. He hadn't said anything at all about their personal situation.

It was time to go home. She couldn't stay with him forever, not when there was no fear for her safety now. She knew their affair would probably continue, at least for a while, but still the thought of leaving his house depressed her. She'd loved every minute of her time on Mackenzie's Mountain, loved sharing the little commonplace things with him. Life consisted of the small things, with only scattered moments of intensity.

She calmly packed and refused to let herself cry. She was going to be under control and not make a scene. She loaded her suitcases into her car, then waited for Wolf to return to the house. It would be childish to sneak off, and she wouldn't do it; she'd tell him she was returning to her home, thank him for his protection and leave. It would be immensely civilized.

As it happened, it was late afternoon when Wolf got back. He was sweaty and coated with dust, and limping a little, because a cow had stepped on his foot. He wasn't in a good mood.

Mary smiled at him. "I've decided to get out of your hair, since there's no reason to be afraid of staying by myself now. I've already packed and loaded everything in the car, but I wanted to stay until you got home to thank you for everything you've done."

Wolf paused in the act of gulping cool, fresh water down his parched throat. Joe froze on the step, not wanting them to see him. He couldn't believe Wolf would let her leave.

Slowly, Wolf turned his head to look at her. There was a savage expression in his eyes, but she was concentrating too hard on maintaining control to see it. She gave him another smile, but this one was harder, because he hadn't said a word, not even, "I'll call you."

"Well," she said brightly, "I'll see you around. Tell Joe not to forget his lessons."

She marched out the front door and down the steps.

She'd gotten halfway to her car when a hard hand clamped down on her shoulder and spun her around.

"I'll be damned if you're setting foot off this mountain," he said in a harsh tone.

He towered over her. For the first time Mary felt it was a disadvantage that she only reached his shoulder. She had to tilt her head back to talk to him, he was so close. The heat from his body enveloped her like steam. "I can't stay here forever," she replied reasonably, but now she could see the look in his eyes and she shivered. "I'm a small-town schoolteacher. I can't just cohabit with you—"

"Shut up," he said.

"Now see here—"

"I said shut up. You aren't going anywhere, and you're damn well going to cohabit with me for the rest of your life. It's too late today, but first thing in the morning we're going into town for our blood tests and license. We're going to be married within a week, so get your little butt back in that house and stay there. I'll bring your suitcases in."

His expression would have made most men back up a few steps, but Mary crossed her arms. "I'm not marrying someone who doesn't love me."

"Hellfire!" he roared and jerked her up against him. "Not love you? Damn, woman, you've been wrapping me around your little finger since the first time I set eyes on you! I'd have killed Bobby Lancaster in a heartbeat for you, so don't you ever say I don't love you!"

As a declaration of love cum marriage proposal, it wasn't exactly romantic, but it was certainly exciting. Mary smiled up at him and went on tiptoe to loop her arms around his neck. "I love you, too."

He glared down at her, but noticed how pretty she looked with her soft pink sweater bringing out the delicate roses in her cheeks, and her slate-blue eyes twinkling at him. A breeze flirted with her silky, silvery-brown hair, and suddenly he buried his face in the baby-fine strands at her temple.

"God, I love you," he whispered. He'd never thought he would love any woman, least of all an Anglo, but that was before this slight, delicate creature had bulldozed her way into his life and completely changed it. He could no more live without her now than he could live without air.

"I want children," she stated.

He smiled against her temple. "I'm willing."

She thought about it some more. "I think I'd like four."

A slight frown creased his brow as he held her tighter. "We'll see." She was too small and delicate for that many pregnancies; two would be better. He lifted her in his arms and started for the house, where she belonged.

Joe watched from the window and turned away with a grin as his father lifted Mary against his chest.

Air Force Academy, Colorado Springs, Colorado

Joe opened the letter from Mary and began grinning as he read. His roommate looked at him with interest. "Good news from home?"

"Yeah," Joe said without looking up. "My stepmother is pregnant again."

"I thought she just had a baby."

"Two years ago. This is their third."

His roommate, Bill Stolsky, watched Joe finish the letter. Privately he was a little awed by the calm, remote half-breed. Even when they'd been doolies, first-year cadets, and normally regarded as lower than the low, there had been something about Joe Mackenzie that had kept the upper-classmen from dealing him too much misery. He'd been at the top of his class from the beginning, and it was already known that he was moving on to flight training after graduation. Mackenzie was on the fast track to the top, and even his instructors knew it.

"How old is your stepmother?" Stolsky asked in curiosity. He knew Mackenzie was twenty-one, a year younger than himself, though they were both seniors in the Academy.

Joe shrugged and reached for a picture he kept in his

locker. "Young enough. My dad's pretty young, too. He was just a kid when I was born."

Stolsky took the picture and looked at the four people in it. It wasn't a posed photograph, which made it more intimate. Three adults were playing with a baby. The woman was small and delicate, and was looking up from the baby in her lap to smile at a big, dark, eagle-featured man. The man was one tough-looking dude. Stolsky wouldn't want to meet him in an alley, dark or otherwise. He glanced quickly at Joe and saw the strong resemblance.

But the baby was clinging to the big man's finger with a dimpled fist and laughing while Joe tickled his neck. It was a revealing and strangely disturbing look into Mackenzie's private life, into his tightly knit family.

Stolsky cleared his throat. "Is that the newest baby?"

"No, that picture was made when I was a senior in high school. That's Michael. He's four years old now, and Joshua is two." Joe couldn't help grinning and feeling worried at the same time when he thought of Mary's letter. Both his little brothers had been delivered by cesarean, because Mary was simply too slender to have them. After Joshua's birth, Wolf had said there would be no more babies, because Mary had had such a hard time carrying Josh. But Mary had won, as usual. He'd have to make a point of getting off on leave when this baby was due.

"Your stepmother isn't—uh—"

"Indian? No."

"Do you like her?"

Joe smiled. "I love her. I wouldn't be here without her." He stood and walked to the window. Six years of hard work, and he was on the verge of getting what he'd lived for: fighter jets. First there was flight training, then Fighter Training School. More years of hard work loomed before him, but he was eager for them. Only a small percentage made it to fighters, but he was going to be one of them.

The cadets in his class who were going on to flight training had already been thinking of fighter call signs, picking theirs out even though they knew some of them would wash out of flight training, and an even greater number would never make it to fighters. But they never thought it would be them; it was always the other guy who washed out, the other guy who didn't have the stuff.

They'd had a lot of fun thinking up those signs, and Joe had sat quietly, a little apart as he always was. Then Richards had pointed at him and said, "You'll be Chief."

Joe had looked up, his face calm and remote. "I'm not a chief." His tone had been even, but Richards had felt a chill.

"All right," he'd agreed. "What do you want to be called?"

Joe had shrugged. "Call me 'Breed.' It's what I am."

Already, though they hadn't even graduated yet, people were calling him Breed Mackenzie. The name would be painted on his helmet, and a lot of people would forget his real name.

Mary had given him this. She'd pushed and prodded, fought for him, taught him. She'd given him his life, up in the blue.

Mary turned into Wolf's arms. She was nude, and his big hand kept stroking down her pale body as if searching out signs of her as-yet-invisible pregnancy. She knew he was worried, but she felt wonderful and tried to reassure him. "I've never felt better. Face it, pregnancy agrees with me."

He chuckled and stroked her breasts, lifting each one in turn in his palm. They were fuller now, and more sensitive.

He could almost bring her to satisfaction just with his mouth on her nipples.

"But this is the last one," he said.

"What if it's another boy? Wouldn't you like to try for a girl just once more?"

He groaned, because that was the argument she'd used to talk him into getting her pregnant this time. She was determined to have her four children.

"Let's make a deal. If this one is a girl, there won't be any more. If it's a boy, we'll have one more baby, but that's the limit, regardless of its sex."

"It's a deal," she agreed. She paused. "Have you thought that it's possible you could father a hundred children and they'd all be boys? You may not have any female sperm. Look at your track record, three boys in a row—"

He put his hand on her mouth. "No more. Four is the absolute limit."

She laughed at him and arched her slender body against him. His response was immediate, even after five years of marriage. Later, when he slept, Mary smiled into the darkness and stroked his strong back. This baby was a boy, too, she felt. But the next one—ah, the next one would be the daughter he craved. She was certain of it.

INTERNATIONAL BESTSELLING AUTHOR

DIANA PALMER

FIT FOR A King

They were friends, neighbors and occasional confidants. But now Kingston Roper needs a favor from Elissa Dean—he needs her to get caught in his bed. Elissa's glad to play the temptress in order to help King out of an awkward situation—just to be neighborly, of course. But she's not supposed to want the make-believe to become a reality. And he's not supposed to find such passion. Could they go from neighbors to lovers without destroying their friendship...or their hearts?

"The dialogue is charming, the characters likeable and the sex is sizzling..."
—*Publishers Weekly* on *Once in Paris*

Available mid-March 2000 wherever paperbacks are sold!

BARBARA

DELINSKY

When Leah Gates arrives at a remote cabin in the woods, all she is seeking is refuge from a vicious storm. But instead she finds Garrick Rodenheiser, a man wary of strangers and hiding from his past. He can't refuse Leah shelter, but he's determined to protect his isolated life. But somehow Leah and Garrick can't seem to resist each other. Because sometimes love finds you, no matter how well you hide....

Twelve Across

"Ms. Delinsky is a joy to read."
—*Romantic Times Magazine*

Available mid-April 2000 wherever paperbacks are sold!

LINDA HOWARD

66549	COME LIE WITH ME	___ $5.99 U.S.	___ $6.99 CAN.
66457	LOVING EVANGELINE	___ $5.50 U.S.	___ $6.50 CAN.
66480	DIAMOND BAY	___ $5.99 U.S.	___ $6.99 CAN.
66432	ALL THAT GLITTERS	___ $5.50 U.S.	___ $6.50 CAN.
66479	DUNCAN'S BRIDE	___ $5.99 U.S.	___ $6.99 CAN.
66153	MIDNIGHT RAINBOW	___ $5.50 U.S.	___ $6.50 CAN.
66478	THE CUTTING EDGE	___ $5.99 U.S.	___ $6.99 CAN.
66274	WHITE LIES	___ $5.50 U.S.	___ $6.50 CAN.

(limited quantities available)

TOTAL AMOUNT	$_____
POSTAGE & HANDLING	$_____
($1.00 for one book; 50¢ for each additional)	
APPLICABLE TAXES*	$_____
TOTAL PAYABLE	$_____

(check or money order—please do not send cash)

To order, complete this form and send it, along with a check or money order for the total above, payable to MIRA Books®, to: **In the U.S.:** 3010 Walden Avenue, P.O. Box 9077, Buffalo, NY 14269-9077; **In Canada:** P.O. Box 636, Fort Erie, Ontario, L2A 5X3.

Name:_____

Address:_____ City:_____

State/Prov.:_____ Zip/Postal Code:_____

Account Number (if applicable):_____

075 CSAS

*New York residents remit applicable sales taxes.
Canadian residents remit applicable GST and provincial taxes.

MIRA®

Visit us at www.mirabooks.com

MLH0400BL